How to Charm a Duke

HONEYFIELD HEARTS
BOOK 1

ARDEN CONROY

Dragonblade Publishing, Inc. is an imprint of Kathryn Le Veque Novels, Inc.
P.O. Box 23
Moreno Valley, CA 92556
ceo@dragonbladepublishing.com

Produced in the United States of America

First Edition February 2026
Trade Paperback Edition

ARE YOU SIGNED UP FOR DRAGONBLADE'S BLOG?

You'll get the latest news and information on exclusive giveaways, exclusive excerpts, coming releases, sales, free books, cover reveals and more.

Check out our complete list of authors, too!

No spam, no junk. That's a promise!

Sign Up Here

www.dragonbladepublishing.com

Dearest Reader;

Thank you for your support of a small press. At Dragonblade Publishing, we strive to bring you the highest quality Historical Romance from some of the best authors in the business. Without your support, there is no 'us', so we sincerely hope you adore these stories and find some new favorite authors along the way.

Happy Reading!

CEO, Dragonblade Publishing

For all of us with our own brand of charm.

Author Foreword

Dear Reader,

I am so pleased to bring you a new Victorian series! This time, we are heading to the 1870s, a few decades before The Harp & Thistle series. This was an interesting time in history. Titled families, as many historical romance readers know, were losing money partly because their tenants were abandoning farm work in the country for factory work in the cities. This would ultimately lead to the influx of Dollar Princesses (American heiresses marrying English nobility) in the coming decades.

Of interest during the 1870s is the rise of the labor union in England. While they had been formed before that decade, they didn't hold significant power. However, the Trade Union Act of 1871 amplified unions' rights and gave workers the legal right to go on strike. Previously, it was criminal for workers to do so and could land them in prison. To me, this made the 1870s an ideal decade in which to set a series with a factory at its heart. But make no mistake, there are still balls and glamorous dinners, with the prettiest glittering dresses you can imagine.

I do want to take this opportunity to call attention to something. Like many of you, I read (and write) historical romance to escape to another time where cellphones and laptops don't exist. Child labor did exist during this time, but it will not be present in my books. There are no child workers at the mill in this story, even though historically there would have been, but frankly, I did not want to write or read that. In my fictional Victorian era, children run amok with their friends to explore and create mischief. They did not risk life and limb at factories. You will, however, see in this series a group of hard-working women who deserve more.

Always,
Arden

Chapter One

London
June 1875

WHEN JULIA HONEYFIELD heard the word *fate*, what came to mind was the ageless, epic fairy tale of a brave knight slaying a terrifying dragon who just so happened to have a beautiful princess imprisoned in its dungeon lair. The knight, not expecting to cross the path of the surly beast on his noble travels, proceeds to rescue the princess, the pair falls hopelessly in love, and they live happily ever after.

It was perfect.

Neat.

Precisely the way a love story should be.

Thus, Julia never would have expected her version of *fate* to begin with a haphazardly tossed blueberry.

As it was, there wasn't a dragon to slay, a happily ever after or a handsome, brave knight in her life. Merely Julia and her sister, Helen, polishing off their third glass of champagne. They were at yet another Mayfair ball, not that she was complaining. Balls and parties were what the Honeyfield family thrived off of. After all, everyone had only one life. Why not spend it having as much fun as possible?

The pretty brunettes walked arm-in-arm as they slid through the crowd of the *ton* in sparkling evening gowns, no particular destination in mind. A footman passed by with an empty silver tray. The sisters quickly downed the remainder of their champagne glasses and set them atop his tray in order to free their hands for any fresh refills they may come across.

The orchestra began a fast-paced number and Julia let out a squeal. "Let us dance together, Helen," Julia said, "since no men have been brave enough to ask!" Rarely being asked to dance was an unfortunate part of being a Honeyfield, but one Julia tried not to bother herself over.

Their heads swimming, the sisters took each other's hands and began to frolic around the dance floor.

Ladies made noises of surprise.

Gentlemen gasped and shouted, "My word!"

But Julia and Helen hardly noticed, as they were Honeyfields, and the Honeyfield family was the biggest laughingstock of the *ton*. To the sisters, this was simply another evening.

After a few moments, the women fell into each other's arms with laughter as they received scornful looks from everyone around them. But when they noticed, their laughter only strengthened.

"Miss Honeyfield," a woman's haughty voice said, interrupting the reverie, "and Miss Julia. No surprise you're here making a spectacle of yourselves."

Julia choked off her laughter as she noted three blonde women with coiffures of various sizes fanning themselves daintily with pale-pink, feathered fans. Though none of them were related, all three were the picture of beauty with their fair hair and blemish-free skin. Never had Julia spotted a raging red spot upon their foreheads or freckles across their noses from the sun.

Julia and Helen used to be great friends with these women. Lady Georgette Pelham was and remained the ringleader. And at her side stood Miss Sophie Grey and Lady Cressida Ridley, wearing matching expressions of boredom. As children, they had all been inseparable, but the blonde trio had, at some point, decided climbing trees was too common and stopped associating with the Honeyfield sisters.

Julia would never admit it aloud, but sometimes she still missed them.

"Why, Lady Georgette." Julia hiccupped, causing her body to jolt. A tuft of brown hair dropped over her eye. She swept it to the side. "What a sight for foxed eyes you are."

Lady Georgette evidently knew better than to react, though she did give Julia a skeptical look over. "I don't suppose it would be too much to ask you two to behave tonight. This is, after all, my family's home. And you are guests."

Julia closed her eyes and lifted her chin. Somewhere in the background, her mother's loud cackle rang clear above all other noise. Technically her chaperone, Mama was often remiss in that responsibility. "So?"

"So, the Duke of Rivenhall is here tonight and my mother is working on garnering his favor. I know he states he is not looking for a duchess, but he was in America too long and doesn't realize yet what he truly wants, which is, of course, me. Mama is set on convincing him tonight that marrying me would be in his best interest."

Julia accidentally let out a squeak of laughter and Lady Georgette crossed her arms. "Don't tell me you think *you* have a chance."

"Don't be daft, Georgette. I have no interest in the man." The blasted tuft of hair fell over her face again. Julia felt nervous talking to her old friends knowing she didn't hold up compared to them. For one, the lack of a chaperone reflected quite poorly on Julia, though it gave her more freedom than most other women and girls in the *ton*. This pretty much took her off the marriage mart, though she wasn't sure how upset she truly was over this. And sometimes when she was nervous, her mouth spewed the most ridiculous nonsense to cover up said nerves. Occasionally, these facts collided. "Would I accept an offer of a brief liaison? Perhaps. After all, he is the most handsome man in the *ton*. But he's so *unlikable*."

Lady Georgette's mouth dropped open while her friends gasped along with her.

Helen made a choking sound.

"I suppose such behavior is to be expected from a spinster," Lady Georgette indicated to Helen, whose wild reputation was well known, "and her oft unchaperoned younger sister. Is your mother even here?" The blonde made a show of looking everywhere she could.

Julia ignored these reactions and swept the errant tuft of hair to the side again, a bit more forcefully this time. "We both know you would win any contest for his affections, anyway. You're the one with the ample—"

Helen interrupted with a snort. *"Julia!"*

"Well, she is!" Julia indicated Lady Georgette's ampleness as proof.

Helen burst out laughing, and even Miss Grey cracked a smile. Lady Georgette shot her friend a severe look, wiping it away.

"There's His Grace now!" Helen quite obviously pointed at the Duke of Rivenhall through the crowd as Lady Georgette slapped her hand down with her pink fan.

Julia looked in the direction Helen had pointed. There he had emerged in all his black-haired, black tail-coated, ill-humored glory. "Sir Crabby," she whispered.

"What did you say?" Lady Georgette whipped her head around.

Julia felt her cheeks flush from being overheard. "I call him 'Sir Crabby.' Because he's quite crabby. He never cracks a smile, never laughs even if the whole room is laughing. Since his return, I've never seen him with any expression on his face other than disdain."

"Maybe he's like that when *you're* around," Lady Georgette replied with a smirk.

Julia lifted one shoulder, but she knew that wasn't true. The Duke of Rivenhall had captured her curiosity when he had returned months ago, after his father had passed and the title transferred. Ever since, every party Julia attended, she secretly hoped to see him.

Oh, he was a gorgeous man. But that was the only positive quality about him. He was rather nice to observe, but otherwise, he had airs.

And Julia couldn't stand airs. People usually directed them at her, after all.

All five women watched the tall, attractive duke move through the crowd, acknowledging people with a head nod or a brief verbal greeting as he passed. Lady Georgette, Miss Grey, and Lady Cressida sighed in unison.

"I would pay good money to learn anything about him." Lady Georgette's eyes were locked on to the dark-haired man.

"*I* heard he was a cowboy in America's Wild West," Lady Cressida replied quickly, her feathered fanning increasing in speed.

Julia wondered if that were true. One aspect about the duke that was impossible to overlook was how large his form was. No other men in the *ton* looked that way. The duke, however, had the build of a laborer but the elegant posture and movement of an aristocrat.

How he had come to be that way, no one seemed to know, but theories and rumors were always circulating.

Lady Georgette turned to Lady Cressida. "Where did you hear that?"

Lady Cressida stammered. "I-I—"

"You're lying." Lady Georgette immediately waved off her friend's claim. "Either that, or the information is incorrect. No one has been able to find anything out regarding where he was all those years, other than in America. I can't imagine you, of all people, would be the first to learn anything."

This year's gossip seemed to solely revolve around the Duke of Rivenhall. For the past twenty or so years, the duke—before being a duke, of course—had been living in America. That much was known. But no one knew why, when he'd been a twelve-year-old boy, his mother had swept him away in the middle of the night and disappeared, leaving the former Duke of Rivenhall behind. Alone.

No one had known why the former duke had let it happen or if he'd attempted to retrieve his son. No one had even known the current duke had been in America. Many had supposed he'd been dead. All had been shocked beyond belief when he announced his return. Julia supposed the former duke must have searched for his son but either hadn't found him or for whatever reason had not wanted him back while he'd remained alive. Usually, children stayed with their fathers and not their mothers in such situations, rare as they might have been.

Julia's father, Baron Odstone, had tried his best to trick the duke into offering up information. But the man never bit, unfortunately.

Everything about the Duke of Rivenhall's past was an enormous question mark. And the fact that he clearly didn't want to offer up information only made everyone hungrier for it.

As the women watched, the duke was almost forcibly stopped for a deep discussion with Mr. and Mrs. Sunbury, relations of Viscount Beckwith. The gray-haired couple spoke animatedly, with chuckles and expressive hand movements, but the duke merely nodded every so often, occasionally offering up a few words. Not a single smile or even a hint of a smirk crossed his face in their interaction. And then, in the midst of the couple talking, he seemed to excuse himself with a hasty, apologetic bow and promptly departed.

He often suddenly ended conversations that way, Julia had noticed.

"There's my chance." Lady Georgette was trying to follow his movement through the crowd. She shot a narrow-eyed look to Julia and Helen before tugging the low neckline of her dress even lower. "Go ahead and judge, but there's a reason evening gowns have low necklines. Now, don't ruin this for me," she warned.

"I would *never*." Julia dramatically placed a hand over her heart as her old group of friends scurried away, the bustles of their dresses swaying with their movements.

Helen spun around, her brown eyes glittering with mischief. "Let's have some fun."

"What do you have in mind?" Julia replied. Helen was by and far the biggest troublemaker of their family of troublemakers, and Julia was quite interested in what her sister was up to.

Helen twisted her mouth and began looking around the room. Her eyes stopped upon a footman walking with a tray of glasses containing what appeared to be blueberry lemonade. Helen dragged Julia in the direction of the man.

"Excuse me, sir." Helen eyed the refreshing drink, her hand still clamped around Julia's arm. "Could I have a bowl of blueberries?"

He stopped and frowned. "What for?"

"For eating, of course. Why else would someone want a bowl of blueberries?"

The footman blinked a few times before excusing himself. Moments later, he returned with the requested bowl of blueberries.

Helen thanked him and turned her attention up toward the ceiling as she popped a blueberry into her mouth.

"It's rather early for blueberry season, don't you think?" Julia followed her sister's gaze and helped herself to a berry as well.

"I overheard Lady Georgette call them '*imported Spanish blueberries*,' like they're some exceptional wine vintage," Helen replied absently. She was not watching the ceiling, Julia noted after a moment. She was watching the second floor.

The ballroom loomed two stories high, and the second floor had balustrades around the ballroom for those upstairs to watch the festivities below.

If Julia remembered correctly, upstairs held the library and the room Lady Georgette's father would use for entertaining his male guests. Smoking, drinking, and whatever else it was men did when women weren't around. Frankly, Julia didn't care to know what that entailed.

Julia realized her sister had left her side and, for a moment, felt panic at losing Helen. With haste, she searched the area and found her sister not too far away. Breathing out a sigh of relief, Julia hurried forward. She didn't like being without her family, particularly at social events.

"What idea is forming in that head of yours?" Julia asked as she retook Helen's side.

Helen grinned widely, showing off perfect, white teeth, one blessing of the Honeyfield family. "I'll show you. Follow me."

They passed a table with chilled bottles of champagne for the footmen to use to refill glasses. At Helen's request, Julia grabbed one that had just been opened, to the apparent notice of no one.

Once upstairs, Julia stood with her sister at the balustrade. She took a deep drink from the champagne bottle.

"Watch." Helen shot Julia an impish grin, plucked a blueberry from the bowl she had set atop the balustrade, and flicked it off her palm. Julia tried to watch the berry arch down, but it disappeared somewhere in the ballroom crowd. "What are you trying to do, exactly?"

Helen laughed as she picked another blueberry. "Look, there's Viscountess Montgomery. She once called me an *'insufferable chit.'* I believe a *'trollop'* once or twice as well."

As she took another mouthful of champagne, Julia looked to where Helen's attention had landed, nearly directly below. From here, they could see down the viscountess's dress.

"Helen!" Julia hissed the name out through a laugh, understanding what her sister was trying to do.

Helen tossed the blueberry but missed her target. She grinned and handed another berry to Julia. Julia gave the champagne bottle to her sister, did her best to aim for the viscountess, and threw the berry. It landed perfectly in the target.

The viscountess stiffened. Looked around with haste. Adjusted her dress.

The sisters fell in a fit of hysterical laughter.

As Helen took a gulp of champagne, Julia decided whom her next target would be.

It only took a moment to find Lady Georgette, Miss Grey, and Lady Cressida. They had, apparently, caught up with the Duke of Rivenhall and surrounded him like a pack of wolves around a bunny. A crabby bunny.

In a way, she felt a bit bad for him. But not really.

Julia threw the blueberry, but it fell in a gap between people and landed on the floor.

"Oh, excellent target! Do try again," Helen said encouragingly.

Julia threw another one. And as it arched down, she realized that not only was she going to miss her target, but it—

—landed squarely in the Duke of Rivenhall's drink. With a visible splash.

Immediately, the black-haired man looked down at his drink with a deep frown before lifting it up to observe the blueberry that had sunken to the bottom. The trio of women surrounding him looked around, their mouths twisted with confusion.

The duke, however, didn't search. Instead, he looked directly up at Julia and made eye contact. And he gave her a deadly glare.

Immediately, Julia and Helen dropped to the ground, grabbing the bowl of blueberries on the way, and crawled off to get out of sight with bottle and bowl in hand. But they couldn't get too far, as their body-shaking laughter was too inhibiting to movement.

They did, however, make it to a wall and leaned against it to share the berries and champagne.

But then two large, polished black shoes appeared, halting at Julia's side.

Julia gulped.

"Pardon me," a deep male voice dripping with pure scorn said. "But I believe this belongs to you."

Julia looked up, her heart racing, and now felt rather sheepish. Perhaps the sisters' game wasn't the most appropriate one. The Duke of Rivenhall's huge, white-gloved hand held his drink low enough so she could see the blueberry at the bottom of the clear glass. He gently swirled the amber liquid and the berry rolled around with it.

Helen started laughing but slapped her hand over her mouth.

"Apologies, Your Grace." Julia took in a deep breath. "I had wondered where that had gone."

"Naturally," he replied, again with that scornful voice. "And you are who, exactly?"

Smartly, Helen rose up to her feet and pulled Julia along.

"This is my elder sister, Miss Helen Honeyfield," Julia spoke up when Helen remained mute.

Helen hurried a curtsy and finally said, "Hello, Your Grace."

"And, I am Miss Julia Honeyfield." Julia gave her own nervous curtsy.

The duke barely glanced at Helen upon her introduction but took his time looking Julia over with a snarl and furrowed black brow. The prolonged attention was clearly meant to be interpreted as judgment, but it still sent a ridiculous, secret thrill through her that he'd looked at her for more than a fraction of a second.

"Your father is Baron Odstone," the duke finally replied.

She hiccupped and cleared her throat again, hoping to cover it up. "Yes, that's correct."

"Rather unfortunate how his lack of charm and wit extends so glaringly to his progeny." The duke's voice may have been flat, his shoulders loose, but the obvious insult cut through so deeply Julia nearly felt real pain.

In return, she tamped down the ire that rose. If she had been clearheaded, she knew she wouldn't have said something back to a complete stranger. A complete stranger duke, on top of it. As tempting as it was, it was best to bite her tongue in the moment. Especially as any retort would only prove him right.

But she hardly even had a chance to decide that because, as was his habit, the duke suddenly turned around and left without any warning.

"What a strange man," Helen said as they watched him skulk down the hallway behind them.

"Calling him '*a strange man*' is being kind. I despise him." Julia turned to her sister, taking the bowl of blueberries. "Let's not let him ruin our fun. He's gone, thankfully. Even better, I'll never speak to him again."

Chapter Two

NATHANIEL BLACKWELL—THE NEW Duke of Rivenhall—had only been back in England for six months. Usually happy his former life remained behind him, this evening was truly testing his patience, and the urge to go back to America increased by the minute.

Baron Odstone—father to the two silly women with whom he had unfortunately just crossed paths—was a complete buffoon. His booming, foxed voice filled the billiards room with crass jokes about priests and courtesans, a far-too detailed story about a rendezvous with a stage actress at a masquerade, and endless liquid sloshing over his glass as he humiliated himself in a room full of the most respectable men in the country.

His gray-streaked brown hair was messy with his inebriation, and his white necktie loose and crooked.

The baron had no idea what an absolute laughingstock he was.

The Earl of Fenwick, who had just appeared with a crystal carafe for refills, took to Nathaniel's side.

"Does that man possess a modicum of shame?" Nathaniel asked in a low voice as Fenwick poured whiskey into his glass. The pair stood at the back of the room. Nathaniel may have possessed the title of duke, may have been easing well enough into his new responsibilities, but he still had not quite nailed everything down and felt most comfortable observing when in a crowd.

Fenwick let out a chuckle as he refilled his own glass, then set the crystal carafe to the side. "Odstone has been a horrific joke for as long as I can remember. Do you not remember him from when you were a boy?"

Nathaniel shook his head as he sipped his drink. He did recall Fenwick as a young boy, with flame-red hair, twigs for arms and legs, and teeth too big for his scrawny frame. The earl's hair had darkened over the years and was now auburn, and that skinny, string-bean child had shot up and filled out, which gave him the extra benefit of growing into his grin. Nathaniel had been surprised when he'd learned his old friend had not yet married but supposed it shouldn't have been so unexpected. Fenwick had been teased endlessly, particularly by girls, for his appearance when he'd been younger. Those girls were now the women he was supposed to be charming but likely still saw him as the awkward, shy, gangly child he once had been.

It seemed strange, though, how time could affect someone so greatly. Nathaniel never in a million years would have guessed the modern Earl of Fenwick and the past Viscount Draycott were the same person.

While the pair had been friends as children, alas, they had not kept in touch when Nathaniel had left England. Though it was nice to have someone with whom he felt relatively comfortable in situations such as this one.

"I suppose you wouldn't remember," Fenwick said. "That was a time ago."

A loud guffaw caused the two gentlemen to look in the baron's direction again. He had snagged the attention of the whole room, but by the way everyone shifted or hid behind their cigars and glasses of spirits, Nathaniel could tell they were only humoring him by pretending to listen.

"And what about you, young man?" a slurring voice called

out. The way the room went completely still caught Nathaniel's attention. Fenwick's awkward shifting told Nathaniel what he dreaded—the baron had his sights on Nathaniel and was addressing him directly.

The entire room waited to see how the duke would react.

He swallowed. Getting used to his new life had not been easy, but somehow, Nathaniel managed. There was that one issue of business his father had, for some godforsaken reason, stuck him with. But aside from that, learning how to address others was probably the most difficult part. Whom to address as "Lord," whom to address as "Lady" versus "Miss." But he *did* know that a baron calling a duke "young man" was quite the offense. And the baron, of course, knew this.

Lord Odstone, who neared the bottom of the *ton*'s social chain, whereas Nathaniel was only below the Royal Family, was being rude to the Duke of Rivenhall. It seemed steeped in some form of dislike. Possibly a leftover feeling from the baron's attitude toward the former duke—Nathaniel didn't know for certain. But it was an insult of the highest order.

And while Nathaniel may have been out of his element, may have felt like the oddity in the room, he still had his pride.

He shot Fenwick a look and could feel the fire sparking in his eyes. Fenwick took Nathaniel's glass and raised his eyebrows, but the corners of his mouth twitched with amusement.

For a short moment, it felt like they were back to being children about to cause mischief.

Nathaniel made his way across the room, the throng of men parting for him. He forced an easy, cocky smile on his face as he came face-to-face with the instigator.

"'Young man'?" Nathaniel said to the baron with a chuckle. "I do believe you mean to insult me."

The baron let out another guffaw and stood from his chair to clap Nathaniel on the shoulder. Then swayed a bit. His eyes and nose were red, thanks to the alcohol.

"Nonsense!" the baron boomed. "Now what say you? Care to

indulge us in any of your escapades in America?"

"'Escapades'? I'm not sure what you mean."

The baron gestured to the room. "Every man here has some sordid story to share. I just shared mine. Here's one from another fellow: waking up ill in Lady Fox's rose garden. After jumping out her window the night before."

The crowd mumbled and the small Duke of Chalworth raised his glass with a grin and said, "Guilty! That one was me. I still have scars from the thorns." The white-haired man stared off at nothing with a veil of a smile on his face. His eyes widened. "That was, of course, before I knew my late wife. May she continue to rest in peace." He added, almost too quiet, "Oh, I hope that doesn't get back to Vivian and Bernard."

Murmurs of respectful words scattered through the room.

"We all have stories like that." The baron gave Nathaniel a narrow-eyed, studious grin. "What are yours? We'd all like to get to know the new Duke of Rivenhall better."

Nathaniel pushed back the rising irritation. Outwardly, he remained cool and controlled, his shoulders slack, a lazy grin on his face. "A gentleman doesn't share his secrets," he finally offered.

Something flashed in the baron's eyes. Interest? What it meant, Nathaniel couldn't say. But it made him uneasy. So as the men around him became animated at his response, a sudden ingenious idea struck Nathaniel like a bolt of lightning.

That hair-tearing stressor his father had left with him? He could get rid of it. Easily. So easily. And also create a diversion with it.

Nathaniel glanced around the smoky room. There were varying levels of clear-headedness in here, but not one man was fully in his right mind, including himself.

As the seconds ticked by, the room became silent once more, the men waiting to see what Nathaniel would do next.

"How about a wager, my lord?" Nathaniel said suddenly, and by the way a few of the men straightened, it was evident he'd caught them all off guard. "You do like a good wager, do you not?"

The baron watched Nathaniel, and there was a sharpness behind his gaze Nathaniel hadn't been expecting. "A wager? You mean like a card game?"

"No. We can get a bit more creative than that." Nathaniel rubbed his chin in a show, then began to glance around the room. "Can someone bring two bottles of liquor? It must be the same type and amount."

Twin bottles of spirits appeared in seconds flat. He handed one to the blasted baron. "Lord Odstone, we're going to partake in a favorite American pastime: a drinking contest." He tapped his bottle. "We drink this down in one fell swoop, and the first man on his arse loses the wager. No limit on what the wager may be. What say you?"

The room became animated by this, with loud conversation buzzing in the air, while the baron studied him quite deeply. The older man rubbed his chin in thought as a gentleman came to his side and whispered in his ear. The baron nodded slow and commented that he was "thinking along the same lines."

Doubt curled in Nathaniel's stomach, but he pushed it away. He knew the baron wasn't to be trusted. He also knew he wouldn't lose the wager, either.

A figure appeared at Nathaniel's side. Fenwick. The earl talked low into his ear. "What are you up to, Your Grace?"

"You'll see."

"I'm looking forward to it."

Nathaniel shot his friend a wisp of a grin before turning back to the baron. "What is your wager, Lord Odstone?"

The baron chewed on his bottom lip in thought—a hesitation, Nathaniel privately noted. Likely, he was going to wager a large sum of cash. Perhaps a favorite horse, or a priceless painting.

Nathaniel was not at *all* expecting what did come out of the baron's mouth.

The baron took a step forward. "I have one son, whom we

don't speak of, and two daughters. My daughters are not married and are well into their twenties. If you fall on your arse first, you must marry one of them. I'll give you the good grace of at least being able to choose which one."

The room gasped in unison.

Nathaniel was stunned and sickness swirled in his stomach. What kind of progeny would he and one of those hellion Honeyfields create? They were the most detestable family in the *ton*. Every time he'd ever seen the baron, the man had been foxed and creating a scene of some sort. To be married into a family like that? Create a child with that family?

Good lord.

Nathaniel looked over to Fenwick to see his reaction. The grimace on his face told Nathaniel everything.

But he wasn't going to lose, he reassured himself.

"Very well, I accept your wager." Nathaniel lifted his bottle in acknowledgment. Off to the side, someone was recording this all in a book, making it official. "And my wager is that if you fall on your arse first, you take over my ownership of the Brumstock Mill."

The baron frowned amongst low background chatter. "The Brumstock Mill? What is that?"

"It's a textile mill my father bought before his death. I don't want it. It's as simple as that."

"Why don't you just sell it then?"

"*Lord Odstone.*" Nathaniel added a bite to his words to distract him. "May I remind you that I'm not some fellow with whom you might toss back drinks at the gentleman's club. I may be a younger man than you, but I am also the Duke of Rivenhall. So far this evening, you seem to be forgetting that key fact."

The baron's thin face flushed, and he nodded. "I accept your wager."

Someone began a countdown and together, the men lifted the bottles to their lips. As soon as *zero* was called out, they began chugging down their liquor.

Only, Nathaniel had a trick up his sleeve. Without anyone being able to see, he covered the opening with his thumb, slowing down the flow. Exactly one minute later, both men pulled the bottles down from their mouths to take a quick, gasping breath for air.

And the baron fell on his arse.

For the few seconds that the room was entirely distracted by this, Nathaniel poured liquor into a nearby potted plant to make it seem he had drunk more than he truly did. No one saw this maneuver, and he knew that because he had mastered this trick years ago thanks to his old friends in America. They were far bigger drinkers than he was, and he would often have to fake inebriation; otherwise, they would become quite persistent about him catching up with them.

As the baron was dragged limp out of the room, Nathaniel went over to the record keeper and set his bottle down. "Note that my solicitor will be visiting Lord Odstone tomorrow afternoon. Ensure a note is sent to the baron informing him of this. I'll give him enough time to be able to think relatively clearly."

The gentleman nodded as Fenwick appeared.

"Good thing you escaped that," the auburn-haired man said.

"Those sisters are attractive enough, I suppose, but I would be signing up for a nightmare if I'd had to choose one."

Fenwick's shoulders tensed despite the genial grin on his face. "Whom would you have chosen? Definitely not the elder Miss Honeyfield, correct? She is considered the true beauty of the two, but…"

Nathaniel's eyebrows furrowed deep at this comment, but Fenwick didn't finish his thought. "Fortunately, I don't have to decide, nor do I wish to even as conjecture." He then shook his friend's hand goodbye, but got the strangest feeling that his response did not satisfy the earl.

Nathaniel left the smoky room to return home. It wasn't long before he'd settled into bed with a satisfied sigh. There was no shred of his father left in the bedroom, and it was now completely to his liking. Masculine, with dark wood furniture, forest-green walls, and the dark-brown leather furniture he had swapped from the library.

With his mother not here, there was no one with whom to share his space, no one to add floral pillows or vases of ghastly roses, no one who would toss and turn in her sleep and interrupt his. He was wonderfully alone and would remain that way. Perfectly alone, with one epically failing mill soon to be off his plate.

He drifted off to sleep with a smile. It all had gone exactly as planned. An unexpected outcome to the evening, yes, but he would take it. Perhaps being back in England would be better than expected.

Chapter Three

WHEN A FOOTMAN spooned scrambled eggs onto her plate with a plop and a jiggle, Julia Honeyfield placed a hand over her mouth, sure she was going to hurl.

But the headache that throbbed from her own sudden movement distracted her from her stomach, and no hurling followed.

"Hello, my darling," Mama sang out as if it were the line of an opera.

Julia had just joined her family at the table, the last one to arrive. Mama's greeting, usually exuberant, appeared to suffer from the same post-party heaviness everyone else appeared to feel at the moment.

"I can't eat." Julia looked past Helen to her mother, who didn't appear any better than she probably did, at the end of the long table. The bags under her mother's eyes were swollen and her skin sallow. Her almost-fully-gray hair was a messy nest after not letting her lady's maid take her hair down before bed the night before. Collapsing into bed immediately after parties is always a priority for the entire family. And breakfast immediately upon waking. "I'm sorry. I don't think I'll keep anything down," Julia added.

"Bacon," was all Mama responded with, and she gave a weak

wave to the stoic footman to serve Julia.

"Me, too." Helen's eyes were half-closed, her brown hair suffering a similar fate as Mama's. And as bacon was placed on her plate, Helen declared, "I'm never drinking again."

Father chuckled from the other end of the table before placing a closed fist at his mouth, presumably suffering his own battle against his roiling stomach. After a moment, he recovered back to a more leveled misery. "You always say that, Helen. And then there's always another silly ball to attend and you end up going and having a good time."

Helen merely groaned in response.

The four Honeyfields slowly poked and ate through their breakfast—at two o'clock in the afternoon—each one battling an earth-shattering illness.

"Did you end up dancing with anyone last night, Helen? I don't recall." Julia couldn't handle another bite of food. She rested her head back against the chair and, remembering her mother's and sister's coiffures, patted the nest upon her own head. A few tufts of hair had fully fallen out and dangled at strange intervals.

Helen had to take a moment to search her memory. "I did, actually, once they were all properly foxed as usual. No one of note, though. You?"

"No one of note, either."

The sisters sighed in unison.

Julia had just passed her twenty-third birthday, and Helen approached twenty-six. Both were painfully unwed—that was, the only male attention received was from drunkards at balls and always past midnight. Helen seemed to have better adapted to this than Julia, however, and never appeared too bothered by her spinsterhood.

Helen had once been betrothed but had never again expressed a desire to marry after that had been broken off. All Julia knew was something had happened between Helen and the Earl of Fenwick—before he'd been the earl, that was—and that had caused the end of Helen's betrothal to the man. The *ton* didn't even speak of it, which was quite unusual and meant something truly scandalous had happened. But what exactly had occurred, to this day, Julia still did not fully know. She had once tried to ask Helen about it and nearly gotten her head bitten off. That mistake was not made twice.

But in the end, Helen didn't seem to mind being unmarried, so it all worked out in her favor. Julia knew her sister and brother were especially close, and Helen likely had been told by Evander that he would take care of her if she never married. Of course, she knew he would take care of her as well, though the family spoke of her marrying on occasion and clearly thought that would be how she'd be cared for. But this also meant either Helen was in denial about their brother's disappearance or genuinely believed him to be hale and hearty, just out of contact for an extended time. Or assumed she could live with Julia and whomever Julia married.

Which of course Julia would be quite fine with.

Although while Helen didn't mind being a spinster, Julia wasn't quite sure how she felt about that possibility for herself.

Perhaps being unmarried wouldn't bother Julia, either, if she had the beauty and self-assurance Helen had. At least she would know that she could marry if she truly wished to. Alas, she did not possess those attributes. Plus, she didn't want them to be destitute, either, which meant *one* of them would have to marry. Especially if Evander never returned.

Upon this thought, Julia observed her parents. Her father slowly sipped coffee. Hearing a sigh from her mother, he looked across the table to his wife and his face softened. He rose up, walked to the other end of the table with his plate, and placed the rest of his bacon on hers. Neither of them reacted to this gesture, as it was just the type of couple they were. But little moments like this always stood out to Julia.

She would love to have a marriage like theirs, a marriage with love as its foundation. Of course, that was impossible for most. Especially for someone like her, when there weren't even any suitors in the first place. And there weren't many mamas who wanted their sons to marry a silly young woman like her with a bad familial reputation and a smaller dowry than most of the other ladies who were out.

Julia took a sip of coffee, knowing it would help her head. The dining room was rather quiet, with the clinking of silverware and dishware the only sound. Her father kept making a funny face, though, as he ate. *There he is, doing it again*, she noted. His coffee cup was suspended in midair and his eyes squinted while he tilted his head, as if mentally searching for something. Then he shook it off and took the sip.

A few minutes later, he did all of that again.

"Papa." Julia settled her hands into her lap, but worry twisted in her stomach. "Are you well?"

Mama immediately jumped out of her seat and hurried over to him to place the back of her hand over his forehead.

"I'm fine." He gently waved his wife off. "I'm feeling fine at least—well, as fine as I can from last night." He let out a long breath. "But I keep getting the strangest feeling."

"Oh, do you need to use the privy?" Mama tried to ask quietly. But being quiet was an impossible feat for the woman.

"Mama, *please!*" Helen replied. Mama only tut-tutted back.

"That's not what I meant," Papa hurried the words out. "It's more of a sensation. Almost… Almost of doom." He twisted his mouth. "But that doesn't make sense, does it? Why would I feel doom?"

"Did something happen last night?" Julia asked.

But he only shook his head. "No. Not that I can recall. It seemed to be a good night. I remember telling jokes and stories with the men. I was in good form." He puffed his chest.

"Of course you were, dear." Mama patted his hand.

Papa rubbed a palm over his stubble. "And then…oh! I remember a bit more now. The Duke of Rivenhall was there. Strange fellow, he is. Don't like him much, to be honest."

This caught Julia's attention. The duke had been on her mind since they'd crossed paths the previous evening. He was curious, and though he was unlikable, she couldn't help but wonder about him. The first time she'd seen him after his return had been at a dinner party during a snowstorm. Even though a frightening blizzard had roared outside, everyone had been watching *him*. A brand-new duke, a relatively young one at that, captured attention. And then, she'd seen him a month later at a ball. Each time she saw him somewhere, whisperings about him increased, especially once it had been confirmed he did not return to England with a wife in tow.

Once that bit of gossip had reached the duke's ears, he'd wisely informed the loosest lips of the *ton* that taking over the responsibilities of his new title would make it impossible to consider marriage for the foreseeable future. This had staved off most of the eager mamas, but not all. At the ball the night before, Julia had noted three mamas approaching him with their unmarried daughters, including the mama of Lady Georgette. The duke would spend one entire minute talking to them, not a second more, and would excuse himself with haste.

A strange fellow, indeed.

"What is he like?" Julia tried not to sound too curious. Aside from the previous evening, she had never dared speak to the duke at any of the events they had both attended despite the fact that they had already been formally introduced months ago. He never seemed to notice her existence. However, her experience with him last night, and the strange way he had paid more attention to her than Helen when men never noticed her over Helen, had admittedly made her a bit curious about him. Which was only natural, of course.

Father looked at her for a long moment, then patted at his mouth with his white cloth napkin. "He is a man of contrasts."

"What does that mean?"

"I can't quite figure that out just yet, though I aim to. But, for example, when he's around us men, he's always off to the side alone or with the Earl of Fenwick. They were close friends as children, apparently."

Helen snorted. Julia looked over to her sister, raising her eyebrow in a question. But Helen ignored her.

"But then he'll come forward without an ounce of hesitation and demand the attention of the room. It's rather strange, don't you think?"

Julia had to agree, thus she nodded.

That odd look came over his face again, where he seemed to stare off at nothing. He tapped at the table. "I swear something happened with him last night, though." Papa squinted and looked up at the ceiling. "I shared with everyone the story of meeting your mother at the masquerade, but then the rest of the night gets hazy, so it's merely a feeling I have that I'm forgetting something."

Mama handed the morning newspaper over to him. "Why don't you try focusing on something else? You'll never remember it if you think about it too deeply."

Papa smiled warmly and accepted the paper, then placed a kiss on the top of Mama's hand, causing her to giggle like a young girl as she returned to her chair.

Julia watched her parents with a smile and as Papa unfolded the newspaper, she turned to Helen. "What do *you* think about the new duke?"

Helen, apparently feeling a bit better now, was now sitting up straighter and slathered strawberry jam on her toast. "He's all right," she said with a shrug.

Julia's eyebrows lifted high.

Helen looked over, caught the expression, and rolled her eyes. "I've had better."

Mama's responding gasp was sharp. *"Helen!"*

"On the ballroom floor!" Helen huffed. "I meant dance partners, Mama. I've danced with more handsome men than him. Goodness. Whatever did you think I meant?"

Mama, of course, merely frowned, knowing well enough that Helen would do as she pleased and there was nothing anyone could do to stop her.

"If he were to ask you to dance, would you accept?" Julia smoothed the napkin on her lap. Technically, social rules would require them to accept, but the Honeyfields weren't known for their etiquette.

Helen watched her do this just as she lifted a slice of toast halfway to her mouth. However, she paused before taking a bite. "Why do you keep talking about him?"

Julia shifted and swallowed. Did she? "Surely, I don't know what you mean."

But Helen squealed. "You have your sights on him! Oh, Mama, Julia has a thing for the Duke of Rivenhall!"

Julia gasped, indignant. "I do not! I'm simply curious is all. How can you not be? He disappeared to America!"

"Who *cares*? He's a stuffy old duke now. Snore! But you think he's dashing, don't you? I bet you want to pinch his bottom. Not that I would blame you, as it is pinchable."

Julia saw their footman shift and immediately covered her mouth with her hand, trying to hold back the laughter. "Absolutely not."

"*Ladies!*" Mama tried her best to bring some semblance of respect to the conversation but likely knew it was an impossible feat.

"I will admit." Julia paused. "That I do think he is handsome. But so does everyone else. You saw the way our old friends surrounded him."

"She does have a point," Papa said as he flipped the newspaper to the next page.

"See?" Julia then stuck her tongue out to Helen.

Helen returned the gesture.

"Wait," Papa said. And something in his voice caused everyone to pause. He then looked straight at Julia over the top of the newspaper, his eyes boring into her.

"Well, what is it?" Mama asked when he didn't continue.

Papa didn't look away from Julia as he took in a deep inhale.

But the concentration faded from his eyes. "Never mind. I thought I was remembering something." He returned his attention to the newspaper while Julia and Helen exchanged a prolonged glance.

"Oh, well, that's a bad bit of business," Papa said, his eyes on the page under his nose. He had already moved on from that odd moment. Perhaps it had truly been nothing.

Like Helen, Julia was starting to feel much better and decided the scrambled eggs didn't look so bad, after all. She lifted her fork and shoveled into the eggs. "What bad bit of business is that?" Julia asked before taking a giant bite.

Papa folded back the paper and turned it to face it to her. The headline read: "Iron Workers Threaten Strike."

Julia squinted to read the headline. "What about it?" she asked, not understanding what he meant by *bad business*. Bad business for the factory owner? Or for the workers? Perhaps both.

Father cleared his throat and studied the article. "Looks like our biggest mill for steel and iron production is having problems with the workers." He paused to read further. "The workers unionized a few years ago and now they're threatening to picket. Even though they can't."

Julia didn't know much about factory work, but she knew unions were an organized group of workers, giving them more power against employers—power in numbers. She also knew picketing was one of the favorite tools of labor unions. "What is picketing. Isn't it just a protest?"

Papa shook his head. "As I understand it, yes, but it's a type of strike. The workers, outside of their workplace, attempt to persuade others to support them. Suppliers, for example. Or perhaps their colleagues who aren't yet striking. Anyone who has a contract with the employer, they want them to break it in support of the workers."

"Oh." Julia mulled this over. "Why can't they picket?"

"Because it's been illegal since '71."

Julia finished chewing another bite of food and swallowed.

"That doesn't make sense. How can unions be legal, but picketing cannot? How else are workers supposed to stand up for themselves?" Maybe unions were weaker than she had thought. But even she could see that must have been by design. Was having miserable workers really so important to employers? She frowned to herself. Likely, she was missing something.

Papa folded the paper back up and set it to the side. "Frankly, I don't know much about any of that. Perhaps they find other forms of protest, though I don't know how effective those are. All I know about all of this business is picketing leads to arrests. Truthfully, I haven't had a reason to think about it much. We are fortunate to have the life that we have. Don't worry yourself over such matters, Julia."

Julia looked around the room. It was a plain room, and their townhome was quite small compared to the others. Her father was only a baron, amongst the lower ranks of the nobility. Mama was a commoner, a former singer and actress at that, so they didn't have any titled family on her side. The Honeyfield family didn't have tons of money, either, but they did have enough to live comfortably with a few servants as well as the ability to spoil their fashion-loving hearts. So long as Papa was alive, at least.

Though they were wealthy enough to not have to worry, unlike many of the nobility, they didn't have farm tenants to help with income. The small bit of land they lived upon out in the country, this small townhome in Mayfair, and their annual income was granted to them from the monarchy thanks to her father's ancestor who had been gifted the title of baron after heroic service in the Napoleonic wars.

The Honeyfield family was in a strange spot. Julia was well aware they lived a privileged life, but to the rest of the nobility, they may as well have been middle class.

To the middle class, they were a bunch of nobs.

But, once Papa passed on which, God willing was a long time from now, the Honeyfield women would be out of the house and without a penny, as the title would pass on to some distant relative, assuming her brother really had departed from this world.

Julia had tried not to think of it too much, but what would happen to them? To her? Helen may not have worried about it, but Julia certainly did.

"Should I get a job?" Julia suddenly asked without thinking.

The table went silent as everyone exchanged looks.

But then Helen laughed. "You're very funny, Julia. Imagine you sauntering into a bakery asking if they need help kneading dough. They would kick you out."

"I'm serious, though. We've never really talked in depth about this, but what if something happens to Papa? What would we do? Even if it's years from now and you and I are in our sixties, Helen. Oh, gosh, especially then. What happens?"

Helen held her gaze and Julia sensed that perhaps her older sister had thought about this more than Julia had given her credit for. Anxious, Julia ferociously spread more strawberry jam on a piece of toast.

"We have enough money for you not to worry about it right now," Papa said, though his voice sounded less certain. "Evander will surely take care of you when the time comes." So Papa was in denial as well. "Or you could go with the apparently illogical choice of getting married."

"No one wants us. You already know that," Julia said matter-of-factly.

Papa didn't respond. As Julia took a bite of her toast, she noted he had gone alarmingly pale. His eyes slowly widened, as if something had just dawned on him. "Oh," he finally said. "Oh, no."

Julia swallowed hard, alarm thrumming within her. But before anyone could ask what the matter was, their butler, Tomlins, entered the room. Their previous butler, who had been with the family since before even her brother had been born, had retired a year prior. Unlike him, Tomlins was quite young. Too young, Mama had thought at the time. According to her, butlers should be tall with long faces and gray hair and an air of distinction. Tomlins was hardly any older than Julia and often fumbled in speech and step. He wasn't tall, and he had light-brown hair instead of gray. However, his salary was much less than that of the previous fellow, and one could hardly argue against that.

"My lord." Tomlins gave a quick bow to the baron, the tails of his necktie hanging at different lengths. "There's a gentleman here to see you."

Papa jumped to his feet and began to smooth out his hair and morning jacket. "Is it a solicitor?"

Tomlins pulled back. "Yes. He claimed he was expected, but I didn't know what to say. Solicitors simply don't show up unexpectedly. But you hadn't mentioned anything about it."

Papa rubbed his hands over his face. "Blast. Oh, blast. And look at me!" He looked down at himself. "This is quite bad."

Mama rushed to his side, frowning deeply. "What's going on? Why is a solicitor here to see you?"

"The wager." Papa's eyes went vacant as he stared out into the room. "I forgot all about the wager."

"'*Wager*'!" Mama shrieked. "What in the devil are you talking about? What did you do?"

Papa looked around the room at the three bedraggled Honeyfield women. And then he suddenly said, "Excuse me," and rushed out of the room.

Naturally, the ladies ran after him.

With their townhouse being so small, the foyer was just a few steps outside the dining room. A middle-aged man in a crisp, navy suit holding a brown, leather satchel blinked several times at the emergence of the bedraggled Honeyfields. "Erm, is this a bad time?" He directed the question to Papa.

"No, let's just get this over with." Papa started to direct him over to the library.

"Just a moment." The solicitor turned around and looked back toward the front door, as if expecting someone else to appear.

Julia and Helen stood beside Mama as they waited for some kind of explanation. Nervous curiosity roiled in Julia's stomach. With whom had Papa made a wager?

That question, however, was answered immediately in the most unfortunate way when *he* walked through the door.

The Duke of Rivenhall in all his black-haired, black-suited, Sir Crabby glory.

Julia let out an audible, "Eep." This was quite literally the last person she would *ever* want to see walk through her door right now.

Naturally, the duke looked directly at her upon her noise and he froze, eyes widening as he seemed to take in her horrific appearance. Normally, the Honeyfields dressed after breakfast the morning after a party. Their lady's maid would otherwise get too frustrated with their post-party groaning. Now, she regretted this habit. Hoping to expire on the spot from a heart racing far too quickly, Julia immediately tried to smooth out her hair. As if that would do anything.

The duke cleared his throat and hurried past the women, greeting them as quickly as possible and with hardly a glance.

Mama took this most inopportune time to suggest their welcome song. Whenever they had important guests, they sang a song Mama had written years ago. "Helen, Julia, the welcome song? One, two, three." Mama shook her finger at them in time with her counting.

Julia and Helen exchanged a glance, as this didn't seem a good time to be singing, but they went with it, anyway, as their visitor did happen to be an important duke.

Julia took a deep breath.

"Welcome to our home,
We're glad to have you here.
Life wouldn't be as fun,
If we didn't hold you dear!"

Mama and Helen's voices were beautiful, of course, while, as usual, Julia's voice cracked and screeched like a screaming cat.

Why Mama insisted she sing this blasted song, she still didn't understand. *"We do everything together,"* Mama always explained. But, still, Julia didn't wish to cause their guest's ears to bleed.

Aside from her horrific voice, Julia could only imagine how messy they looked. And how they smelled. Oh, blast, *did* she smell? As the duke, baron, and solicitor came out of their frozen stupor from the welcome song and cautiously greeted each other, she took a quick sniff under her arm. At that exact moment, Papa said, "And these are my daughters, Miss Helen Honeyfield and Miss Julia Honeyfield."

She was caught in the act. By everyone.

Helen made a choking sound, as if trying not to laugh. The duke, however, stared at Julia with raised eyebrows.

Julia stood up to her full height and lifted her chin. Who cared? Was this the most humiliating moment of her life? Yes, it was. But why should she let it be? Who cared if the Duke of Rivenhall was exceedingly handsome, who cared if she secretly looked for him at every event she attended and now he stood here in her house while she sniffed her underarm, her hair still in its style from the previous evening?

Who cared?

Unfortunately, *she* did. Greatly.

Julia tried mustering up fake courage and curtsied in her nightgown. "Good morning, Your Grace."

He continued his stare, clearly unsure what to do in this awkward situation, and then nodded at her while avoiding her eye before turning back to her father.

"Strangle me," Julia whispered to Helen.

"No," Helen replied in her own whisper. "This is far too entertaining for me to help you escape it."

Papa cleared his throat to get the duke's full attention back. "As I now quite hazily recall, a note sent to me at the most inopportune time last night, Your Grace, indicated you would be here in the afternoon."

"It's after three o'clock. I had even meant to be here earlier," the duke said, his deep voice dripping with disdain. "What does your family consider afternoon, Lord Odstone? The dinner hour?"

Papa stammered, but there wasn't really a way to come back from that, as the duke was right. "P-Please, this way." Papa directed the duke and solicitor toward the library, then turned his attention to the footman. "Paul, please take their jackets."

"I prefer to keep my suit jacket on, thank you," the duke replied as Paul approached.

Papa's face reddened. "We're an easygoing family, Your Grace. And if you came here to ruin me, the least you can do is take off your jacket while you do it."

Julia grabbed Helen's arm as Helen let out a squeak. Shock couldn't begin to describe how Julia felt in the moment. She could not *believe* how her father was speaking to a duke! What in the blazes had happened last night?

But after a considering pause, the duke removed his jacket and handed it to the stoic footman, keeping any emotion off of his face. He was freshly shaved, and Julia wondered what his soap would smell like on his skin if she were able to get close enough to find out.

Oh, the Duke of Rivenhall was so nice to look at even when morose. If only his dark eyes weren't always full of irritation, and his perfect, pretty, sharp jaw always so tight. And how hard would she find those shoulders, if she were able to feel them?

Helen nudged Julia in the side and made a show of pinching her fingers together while wiggling her eyebrows up and down. Julia accidentally let out a loud laugh as she took a quick glance at the duke's bottom, mentally agreeing with Helen's earlier admiring assessment of it.

She giggled again. Arse-essment.

But as luck would have it, as if the blasted man could read her mind, the Duke of Rivenhall turned around the exact moment she admired him, catching her in the act yet again.

Chapter Four

THEY WERE LAUGHING at him.

Nathaniel had heard yet another obnoxiously loud giggle—the Honeyfield women were a ridiculous lot, and quite the next-morning mess as well, where were their blasted ladies' maids—and looked back over his shoulder as he handed his suit jacket to Paul. Miss Julia stood rigid, digging her fingers into her sister's arm. Though the ladies were rather obnoxious last night while in their cups, he had to admit that Miss Julia mussed from sleep while in her rumpled nightgown (did this family possess any shame?) wasn't too terrible to look at. He might even consider her somewhat pretty if her spirit wasn't too bold for his liking. He did not care for loud or forward people. Or especially, thinking back on the berry throwing, childish.

But she did have large, attractive, brown eyes framed by dark lashes, and full lips a perfect, soft pink. And he found he couldn't help but study her features, overtaken by them. The previous evening, Fenwick had told Nathaniel that Miss Honeyfield was considered the beauty of the two sisters. Nathaniel had to disagree.

As he stared too long, he came to realize Miss Julia was looking down at something on his person. Humiliation swept over him with a force. Had he sat in something without knowing it?

Blood rushed to his face as he swept his hand over the seat of his trousers a few times and frowned when she met his gaze with widened eyes. She at least had the grace to turn as red as he surely was in the moment.

"Ignore them. Please," Lord Odstone said, pulling Nathaniel away from his family and toward the library, the solicitor following.

"Is there something on me?" Nathaniel asked the solicitor in a low voice, but the man turned up his hands after checking.

The baron released an exasperated sigh as they entered the library and angled toward his desk.

The room was nice enough, small but comfortable. The back of the library, where a desk sat, had a fireplace and windows that looked out over a small, lush garden. The rest of the room consisted of books, from floor to ceiling. He wouldn't dare go look at the titles but couldn't help but wonder what books the Honeyfield family had in their possession.

Just as the men made to sit at the desk, however, all three Honeyfield women burst into the room.

"What is going on?" the baroness asked, her voice shrill with worry. Somehow, her gray-and-brown nest of hair had become even bigger in the few minutes the men had stepped into this room.

Your husband is a drunken idiot, Nathaniel wanted to say, but he kept his mouth sealed shut. Clearly, he was not the only one with this thought, though, based on the baron's inability to look his wife in the eye.

Lord Odstone tried to dismiss the women with hand waves and weak words, but they refused to budge, nearly shouting over each other trying to get information. Nathaniel had the urge to cover his ears and focused on the moment he could leave this ridiculous house with a promise to never return to it.

To help his mood, he put his mind on the relaxing evening he had planned. After this business was taken care of, he had numerous letters to write, invoices to review, visitors to tend to for business matters masked as social calls.

But then his comfy chair awaited him after all of that. The silence of his home, the crackling fireplace, pajamas, smoking jacket, and a drink or two to imbibe uninterrupted. Perhaps it would rain, the gentle tapping against the windows adding to the peaceful atmosphere. And there would, of course, be a book in his lap.

Those quiet evenings alone were what got him through the hectic days. And he was especially looking forward to it this evening.

Impatience got the best of Lord Odstone, and he rose to his feet and slammed his palms onto the table, immediately causing the women's overlapping chatter to cease. "Ladies, this is not something I need or want you involved in. I beg of you to *please* take leave so I can get this over with!"

Nathaniel's gaze went to Miss Julia, and he was surprised to find her watching him. She shifted and lifted her chin, clearly unhappy with his presence, and put her attention squarely on her father.

Well, then. The dislike was mutual.

Lady Odstone let out a harumph. "If you want me to leave, then I require payment."

Nathaniel frowned and watched to see what the baron would do next. Would the man really give in to such a demand? Payment to leave a room? Was that what kind of family they were, where everything was a transaction?

Nathaniel tried not to imagine what would have happened to his mother had she ever demanded payment from his father to comply with a request. Nay, from him, it would have been an order.

All Nathaniel knew was that it wouldn't have been pretty.

The baron let out a dramatic sigh as he stood from the desk. As he approached his wife, who was as bedraggled as their daughters except more ample in every way, the baron mumbled, "Are you *trying* to embarrass me?" But then he leaned down and placed a kiss upon his wife's cheek.

Lady Odstone gave him a smug smile, like she had won a game, before turning around and walking back through the door, Miss Julia and Miss Honeyfield following obediently behind.

The door clicked closed.

Lord Odstone looked between Nathaniel and the solicitor Mr. Frankfurt—the same Mr. Frankfurt the former duke had used for many decades—and slowly took his seat behind the desk, studying his foe with a furrowed, gray brow.

Mr. Frankfurt took that as his cue and opened his leather satchel, removed papers, and placed them upon the desk. "His Grace and I have already gone through the minutiae, but, to get us all on the same page, the two of you placed a wager last night and you lost, Lord Odstone. This means you are now the proud owner of the Brumstock Textile Mill in Hamwich."

"Hamwich?" The baron frowned. "I've never heard of it."

"There are thousands of towns and villages in England, most of which you wouldn't know about." Nathaniel leaned back in his chair, forcing a bored look on his face.

"Where exactly is this Hamwich?"

"Up north. It borders the city of Manchester."

"Manchester! Why, that's over two hundred miles away, even more from my house in the country! What would I want with a silly factory I know nothing about and can't easily visit?" The baron leaned forward to look at the papers—ownership transfer of the textile factory building and business—then fell back into his chair and crossed his arms. "This is ridiculous. I refuse."

Nathaniel had been afraid this would happen. A drunken wager wasn't exactly legally binding, but he *had* to get rid of it. Desperately. His tenants had approached him several times with lists of repairs needed for their homes. For updates to their farming equipment. And some farmers were finding that work in cities was more lucrative than farming (except in the case of his own factory, naturally). He was fortunate to still have more than enough farm tenants to be financially secure—not just for himself, but for everyone he was responsible for—but the blasted mill his father had bought was bleeding the estate dry. Every month, he'd had to pay hundreds of pounds to cover expenses and taxes and Lord-knew-what-else, while getting nothing in return to replenish what had been spent.

And still, the tenants needed his help. He has been doing what he could to keep people safe and their farms still running. But he was slapping a bandage on a major issue. One that could be solved right this moment.

In doing this, was he ruining the Honeyfields like the baron claimed? He absolutely was. He wouldn't deny it. But his tenants and estate came first above all else, and he didn't care what it took to get rid of the blasted leech of a mill.

He met the baron's eye and they stared each other down. Nathaniel resisted the urge to scratch his face, twitch his eye, fidget in his chair. If he played his hand correctly, not only would the issue of the factory be solved, he could finally leave this blasted city, go back to the country, where it was nice and quiet, and destress.

"You can't go back on your word," Nathaniel said. Wagers were important to the men of the aristocracy. A currency of clout, in a way. The bigger the wager, the more impressive. And there were few things more shameful to a gentleman than reneging on a wager. Nathaniel made a point to remind the baron of this. "What would everyone think of you if you did?"

As if the man cared at all about appearances.

To Nathaniel's surprise, though, the baron weaved his fingers together in consideration. Then said, "I won't pay you for this."

Nathaniel ignored the leap of hope. The man was ready to talk. Could it really have been this easy? "I don't want you to pay me for it. I merely want to sign over ownership to you."

The baron nodded slightly, then reached out to grab the papers. He rose to his feet and began to slowly walk around the room, reading through. "By the way, I'm sorry for the loss of your father," the baron said, not looking up from the papers.

Nathaniel blinked. "Thank you."

"Do you know why he got involved with this textile mill in the first place?"

Nathaniel hesitated. But the baron seemed to be coming around to the idea. "No, but I hadn't once talked to him since my mother and I"—he paused and cleared his throat—"left."

Lord Odstone glanced up from the papers, as if hoping to hear more. But Nathaniel wasn't going to oblige the man's curiosity.

"I don't know anyone who has dipped their toe into industry." The baron returned his attention to the papers and began pacing again. "It seems rather risky."

That was why he presumed his father had bought it in the first place. To be the first one. Unfortunately, it had been a stupid decision. "It *is* risky. But you lost the wager."

And then, the baron surprised him. He let out a loud sigh of defeat and said, "Very well. Let me get my pen."

While Nathaniel exchanged a glance with Mr. Frankfurt, the baron went back to his seat behind the desk and lifted his inkwell pen. The pen hovered over the signature line for several moments. Nathaniel had to do everything he could to keep from gripping the arm of the chair or leaning forward with eagerness.

But the pen continued to torturously hover. Nathaniel had spent the entire morning reading through the few pieces of paper. There was nothing questionable in them; it was all quite clear. Nathaniel swallowed, his throat suddenly dry. Was it getting warmer in the room?

The baron looked dour as he slowly set the pen down, leaving the papers unsigned.

Nathaniel took in a sharp inhale but kept his face level.

"What would you have done if you had lost the wager?" Lord Odstone asked. There was a veil of smugness on his face, the way the corners of his mouth just barely curled up, a sparkle of mischief in his eyes.

Nathaniel resisted the urge to swear. "Clarify."

"Would you have chosen one of my daughters to marry?"

He scratched the side of his nose. And blatantly lied. "Yes, of course. That's the point of a wager, isn't it?"

"Which one?"

A long pause. "Sorry?"

"You know who my daughters are. And you saw them this morning in all their post-ball morning glory. My wife and daughters cannot function at all the mornings after parties, even for dressing, until they have food in their stomachs. Knowing that, which one would you have chosen? Helen? Or Julia?"

Nathaniel stammered. "I-I—"

"I will sign this." The baron tapped at the papers. "If you answer that question. And answer honestly. Don't just throw a name out. I will be able to tell if your answer is genuine."

Nathaniel shifted in his seat, looking over to Mr. Frankfurt, who shrugged. The baron never ceased to irritate him, but this was really testing it.

The duke quickly thought back over the previous evening, where he had seen the two women dancing together and then laughing in each other's arms like madwomen while people around them stared and whispered. What they'd been laughing about, he could only imagine. Then he thought back over the morning. Over Miss Julia and her bed-mussed hair, her large, brown eyes wide with shock when he'd stepped into their home. How she'd done her best to smooth out her appearance.

Miss Julia was far too loud and energetic at all hours of the day—except true morning, apparently—but then again, so was Miss Honeyfield.

Oh, blast it all, why was he thinking this deeply about it?

"Miss Julia," he simply stated, hoping his voice sounded as bland as he meant it to.

The baron was taken aback. "Julia? Really? That surprises me."

Nathaniel frowned deeply at this. "Why?"

The baron clasped his hands together, taking a moment to

think before responding. He was choosing his words carefully. "Helen is generally the one who captures the male eye."

Fenwick had made a similar comment. "I answered your question. Now may we continue?" Nathaniel used his all-important duke voice.

The baron's smile fell away. "Yes. Of course." Lord Odstone reached for the pen and looked up at the solicitor. "Just to clarify, this is for the factory building and business? Nothing else?"

The solicitor opened his mouth to speak, but Nathaniel spoke first, hoping to hurry this along. "'Nothing else'? What else would there be? It's the building, the business, and everything that runs it. There's already a foreman there, if that's what you're wondering about. All you're doing is becoming the owner of the building and the business. Other people manage the day-to-day. Of course you'll still have to make major decisions, but your involvement will be quite passive."

Mr. Frankfurt was quickly rifling through the documents, as if searching for something. "Yes, that's correct," he said with haste.

"Very well." The baron's voice sounded heavy while he watched the pen spin between his fingers, and then he finally signed the paper.

The duke stretched his legs out with a sigh of satisfaction. "I think we're both glad for this bit of business to be over, that any paths crossed in the future will be minimal."

"I will agree that we don't much care for each other, Your Grace," the baron said with a grin, folding his hands over his stomach.

The duke nodded. But there was another strange glimmer in the baron's eye that caused him pause.

But surely, it was nothing.

Chapter Five

THE SECOND THE door to the library opened, Julia and Helen rushed down the stairs, trailing their mother. While they had waited for the men to wrap up their meeting, their lady's maid had attempted to fix their appearances by throwing on housecoats, washing their faces, brushing their teeth, and fixing their hair as best as she could in such short time. The Honeyfield women, and the lady's maid as well, were too afraid a full bathing and dressing would cause them to miss seeing the duke out.

Thankfully, they were at least somewhat presentable now, and Julia was feeling a little bit better about her appearance.

The first person to emerge from the library was the duke. Julia tensed upon seeing him step through first. He was so different from the others, with his dark suits, dark hair, and equally dark expression. He was an elegant man, make no mistake, but there was something very different about him, almost a perpetual heaviness about him. She wondered if it had to do with his time in America.

But, oddly, his usual dourness was nowhere to be seen in the moment. Wearing a triumphant grin, the duke actually looked rather pleased with himself. Papa's claim that the man had been there to ruin him appeared to be an accurate one.

As she watched the duke, curious as to what had gone on

behind closed doors, his eyes found hers, causing a feeling inside of her that felt like a frog hopping. Was that leap in her stomach, or in her heart?

No, it had to have been her intestines.

Stepping out into the hall while the other men followed, the duke lifted his gaze from her eyes to study her hair but then quickly looked away.

"Will you tell me *now* what is going on?" Mama was frantic, rushing up to Papa and searching his thin face.

"Just a second," he replied, evidently trying to tamper her nerves while still not telling her anything. He turned back to the solicitor and said something in a low voice. The solicitor left after retrieving his hat and coat from the footman Paul, and then Papa shook the duke's hand. Both men forced a small, tight smile that looked more like a grimace than anything.

The front door opened again, and the solicitor and one other gentleman—the duke's coachman, based on his uniform—reappeared each carrying a large box. Papa gestured toward the library and Julia watched as they entered and set the boxes on the desk, brushed their hands together, then walked back out of the front door.

"Well, that's that, then," the duke said as Paul helped him with his jacket. It was a strangely common turn of phrase for a duke.

And with the quickest and most unenthusiastic goodbye a person could muster, the Duke of Rivenhall left their home for good, the door shutting hard behind him.

Good riddance, Julia thought. He was best enjoyed visually. *Not* through genuine interaction.

Mama immediately started into Papa. "You were in there for nearly an hour, torturing us! Simply *torturing* us!"

"I'm, sorry, my dear. Torturing you was not my intention." Papa let out a sigh and then returned to the library, angling toward the drink cabinet. With a clink of crystal, he poured a finger's worth of cognac. With his back still toward the Honeyfield women, he took his first sip, let out a sound of satisfaction, and then turned to face them.

"Last night, the duke and I made a wager. I lost." Papa took another sip and walked back to his desk, set the glass down, and studied the two boxes sitting neat atop the surface. "And because of that wager, we are now the proud owners of a textile mill."

For the first time since Julia could remember, all Honeyfield women were rendered silent.

Papa looked up with raised eyebrows, as if he thought they had left the room and was surprised to see them still there. "That's what that was all about. These two boxes contain business records, payroll, and who-knows-what-else. I have absolutely no interest in going through it. In fact, I have no interest in this business at all. The duke said it's already up and running and my role as owner is rather passive."

"Usually, men wager a horse. Or money," Helen said, a slight downward pull on her face.

Mama tilted her head. "Where is it?"

"Manchester."

Julia's eyes went large. "That's quite far. I would think it would be here in London!"

Papa shook his head. "That is why I want nothing to do with it. Perhaps I'll try to find a buyer. Regardless, I'm not going to think about it right now." He finished off the rest of his drink and then regarded the empty glass. "Don't we have a dinner party tonight?"

Normally, the mention of a dinner party would get Julia excited. But something about this mill business didn't sit right with her. "Papa, don't you have a million questions about this? Like, why did he want to get rid of it?"

He shrugged. "Said he didn't want it. His father had bought it, and now he wants nothing to do with it."

"All right. Then what sum did you have pay him for it?" Julia asked.

Mama gasped, likely considering the high sum a mill would cost.

"I didn't pay a sum," the baron responded.

That was good news, then. But Julia still had other questions, as it was more than a bit odd that the duke had given away a business so freely. "Do factories have loans or rent or mortgage payments?"

Papa hesitated. Clearly, he had not thought about that. He set his glass down and walked past the women. "I am going to go wash up and then take a nap. Tonight, we will leave around, say, nine this evening?"

Julia's family then began to discuss plans for the evening, with Helen and Mama debating which dresses to wear. It was as if this mill business had not happened! How could they be so unconcerned? The Duke of Rivenhall despised her father; it seemed obvious there was some bad business with this mill if he wanted to dump it upon Papa.

"Come, darling." Papa evidently saw the worry etched in her face and put his arm across her shoulders to lead her out of the room, Helen and Mama trailing behind. "Don't concern yourself over it. This is something for me to worry about, not you."

"But you're not worried!"

"Of course not."

"We're not *that* wealthy," she said, aghast at his lack of care. "We live well enough, but we can't afford a factory. In fact, the men successful in industry have far more money than most in the *ton!*"

Papa beamed. "There, see, you're being positive now!"

She shook her head. "No! My point is they can pay for…well, whatever they have to pay for! If they make so much, surely that means it must incur a lot of cost to run. And we know nothing about how to run a mill. In fact, my only knowledge about textiles is types of fabrics. And that's it! I have no idea how they're made."

Papa gave her a small smile. "You're truly that worried about it?"

"Yes, of course!" She watched Mama and Helen walking arm

in arm, still discussing evening wear, completely unaware of their conversation. "How can I not be?"

"Because it's not a woman's place to worry about men's business."

Unable to help herself, she narrowed her eyes slightly.

Papa grinned. "If you're truly that worried about it and really have questions that I cannot answer, why don't you take a look at what's in those boxes? See for yourself?"

Julia ignored the unexpected thrill that went through her. "Really? You would let me do that?"

"Of course. Weren't you asking earlier if you should get a job?"

"Yes."

"Well, now you have one."

She stopped walking. "What are you saying, Papa?"

"I'm saying, have at it. It's open-ended. See what you find and dig into it. Do whatever you like or deem reasonable."

Julia tried to force back the excitement. In truth, this appealed to her greatly. Perhaps because it would help calm her nerves by letting her be more in control of the situation. She never did like relying on others to take care of what she could herself. While she shared a lady's maid named Walsh with her mother and sister, she was known to sometimes start the dressing process on her own, as she was always the last one to be assisted. There had been a few times where she'd made her own bed after waking and a maid had scolded her. Or had set the family's empty plates to the side for them to be cleared away quicker. She never took over the servants' jobs, as they would not be too happy about that, but if she could do one or two things here and there to help, why wouldn't she?

It was several hours before Julia was able to sit with the boxes. First, she had to take a nap—which wasn't too successful, as she kept thinking about the duke visiting her home. Revisiting all of the utterly humiliating moments, like when he'd caught her looking at his bottom and instead of realizing what she'd been doing, had thought there'd been something stuck to him and tried to brush it away. Honestly, was the man truly so naive?

When the nap hour was over, she bathed and dressed, finally feeling well enough to cooperate with Walsh. They entertained a few of Mama's friends from her stage days for an hour.

Then it was time to get ready for the evening.

Julia let out an audible sigh as she rifled through one of her armoires with Walsh. Their fashion budget meant they could only afford one lady's maid for all three Honeyfield women, but the thin, blonde- and gray-haired woman had been in her position for so long, she'd slipped into the role without a single bump.

Amongst Walsh's fast-paced chatter about gloves and hats and dresses, Julia's mind couldn't stay on task. She loved dressing up in sparkling evening gowns yet tonight found herself unable to focus on anything fun.

The mix of worry and curiosity over the boxes kept tugging at her. Finally, after twenty minutes of indecision on her evening outfit, she left her bedroom to find her family downstairs waiting for her in the foyer. They were all dressed elegantly and ready to depart. Meanwhile, she was still in the yellow afternoon dress she'd worn for Mama's friends.

"Why aren't you ready yet?" Helen asked, tugging the end of one long, white glove that went up to her elbow. "We're ready to leave!"

Julia stopped in front of the family, all of whom wore matching frowns and quizzical expressions. "I'm not going tonight."

Mama and Papa exchanged a glance. "But you have to! We always go everywhere together!" Mama replied.

"I know. And I know you will think this is silly, but I can't stop worrying about those boxes."

"'Boxes'?" Mama asked. "What boxes?"

But Papa jumped in quite quickly, winning a scornful look from his wife. "Is that what you wish to do this evening?"

Julia lifted a shoulder. "I can't even pick out a dress because it's distracting me so. I'm sure everything is fine, but..." She didn't want to admit that she was worried for her family financially now. And for whatever reason, she was the only one who seemed to care. Mama and Helen not caring, she could understand that. Women were generally kept ignorant of such matters. But Papa? Admittedly, he wasn't exactly the most responsible man, but he was hardly wasting an ounce of thought on it. She would expect something like this would at the least cause his brow to furrow. It could have a detrimental effect on the family as a whole.

But she had the overwhelming, nagging feeling that there was something awful hidden in the paperwork. Apparently, it was up to her to find it.

Papa quickly kissed Julia on the cheek before Mama could argue further, and said, "If that's what you wish," before letting out a strange, little "hee hee" of glee.

Helen shot Julia raised eyebrows, which Julia understood to mean, *"Maybe he's already sloshed."*

As soon as they were gone, Julia ran into the library and opened one of the boxes. Inside were numerous folders. At least it appeared organized.

The folders had tabs and about half of them were labeled. Most folders were invoices for wool and flax—which she quickly concluded were the two materials the mill worked with—plus parts for machinery, machinery repairs, and notes surrounding that. There was an old letter from a Mr. Fitzhugh to the former duke that read, essentially, *"Rumor is a few of the women tried to join a local union, but they don't allow women members. That settles that silly business."*

There was also a notebook that appeared unlabeled. Curious, she pulled it out and opened it. There were several columns on the page. The columns contained women's names, addresses, and dates. Some of the dates contained one calendar day. Others would be a week, perhaps a month. There was no explanation of what the dates were for or why these people were in the entry.

Were they the dates the workers had begun their jobs? That didn't make sense. Julia flipped to the next page and found one person had a red X in the date column. Fired? Quit? That made the most sense.

She kept the notebook out but stacked the folders back together and set them neatly back in the box. Nothing stood out to her admittedly untrained eye, so she went over to the other box to go through it.

The contents of this box were similar. Mostly invoices and other general business-related papers.

Two "in and out" notebooks made her go cross-eyed. There were two columns, one which was written in red ink and one in green. Each one had a corresponding date and a note section. There was payroll, which was written in red. Machinery repairs, also written in red. Notes about wool and flax paired with men's names—presumably the local farmers who provided the material—also in red. In green were names of men, sometimes women, with corresponding business names. Fabric stores, tailors, dressmakers, sewing shops, even one of those department stores the middle-class liked to shop in. These were purchasers of the manufactured textiles and fabrics, she gathered.

At the bottom of the page were sum totals. The red total was larger than the green. Julia frowned deeply. Sure this was merely a bad week, she flipped through some more.

Unfortunately, there wasn't anything reassuring to be found. The mill had been running that way for over ten years. It hadn't made a profit in ages. No wonder the duke had wanted to get rid of it! Speaking of, at what point had the former Duke of Rivenhall gotten involved? She tried flipping through the pages but gave up quickly, as there was no way for her to know.

Julia supposed that wasn't important. What mattered most was right now. The mill was hemorrhaging money, even when it'd had the current Duke of Rivenhall as its owner. He must have been propping it up with his own funds.

Anger colored her vision. The duke was far, far wealthier

than the Honeyfields. He'd dumped a money leech onto her poor father without a single care!

A money leech that would quite literally ruin her family. There was no way they, unlike the duke, could afford to hold up this failing factory.

Julia had to sit down and rest her forehead in both hands in order to think. But as much as she tried to will reality away, the truth was stark.

Within months, they'd lose everything. No wonder the duke couldn't sell it. No one with any sense would want it. And that was precisely why the duke had dumped it on her father.

He couldn't find a buyer.

Wouldn't he have simply shut the factory down, then? Perhaps his ego refused to let him, seeing it as a failure. Or maybe he felt bad for the workers who would be out of a job. At least now they remained employed, even if the mill wasn't doing well. But that didn't make sense either, he didn't strike her as someone who would give any consideration to those below him.

And then there was her father. Why would he agree to this? He'd accused the duke of ruining him, so he was aware this was bad business. Of course, there was no way Papa had any idea how dire the situation truly was. The duke had swept over the details—she was confident in that assumption. Papa had probably gotten caught up in the moment. Distracted by the idea of something new and interesting.

She glanced up, and there was a portrait of her father twenty years younger hanging on the wall. He wore a grin that had always caught her attention since she had been a small child. It was slight and knowing, as if he were up to something mischievous and she would have to figure out what it was.

Taking a calming breath, Julia looked back down to the mess he had gotten them into and reached in the box to see what else was there. Out came the payroll record book. Skimming through it, she saw that most of these workers—notably all women—had "3s" for each day they worked. Six days a week. Did that mean three shillings per day? That was so incredibly low, it *had* to mean something else. She would figure that out later. But even if that was their pay, at least they were receiving it despite the mill's problems.

After reaching in again, Julia found one last folder at the bottom.

It contained numerous documents related to the building, mostly dry legal papers. She learned it had been built in 1845 and taken a year to construct. The company that had built it had been called "McManus." The name tickled at her brain, so she filed that away for the moment because on the back of one of the papers, something was stuck.

Carefully, she managed to separate two papers from each other. The top paper was yet another document about the factory building.

But the second one? It was a piece of paper labeled "land deed."

Land?

Julia twisted her mouth as she read it over. When she'd reached the bottom of the page, her mouth fell open. A rush of excitement swept over her body as she comprehended what she had discovered and she slouched in the chair with a heavy, cheek-puffing exhale.

And she laughed aloud, utterly elated. The duke had *no clue* what a fool he was. He thought he would be rid of the Honey-fields, did he?

The poor, poor cad had no idea what he was up against. *Whom* he was up against. With a renewed vigor, Julia jumped to her feet and gathered the few items she would need, then rushed out of the room.

Chapter Six

Twenty minutes later, Julia was ready to leave the townhouse. Every woman had one or two dresses that made her feel like the queen of the world, and Julia had Walsh ready her in one such dress. It was emerald-green silk with a large, black velvet bow at the lower back, and smaller, black bows on the front bodice, on the sleeve cuffs, and in a few sporadically placed spots on the skirt. It was a dress she wore that never failed to win her looks of admiration from passing gentlemen. It was the dress she always wore when she needed a confidence boost. It was the perfect dress for her plan.

She topped off the look with a black-and-green hat upon the top of her hair. Walsh had done her hair halfway up, the rest hanging in long ringlets. The hat was set in place with two crystal-topped hatpins. She adjusted a spray of silk flowers set upon one side and ensured the hair ringlets had not lost their bounce.

Satisfied by her appearance, she hurried downstairs and came across Tomlins in the foyer.

"Are you leaving, Miss Julia?" the young man asked with a frown. "Why, it's ten in the evening. You mustn't leave without a chaperone, especially at this hour."

"Oh, Tomlins, you worry too much." Julia of course knew

this was uncouth, especially at this hour. However, she did not need anyone meddling in what she was about to do. Instead, she went over to the hallway table she had set a notebook and folder upon. She lifted them up and held them close, then turned to make her way out of the door before she realized something.

She turned back to Tomlins, who was doing his best to straighten his perpetually crooked necktie. "Do you happen to know where the Duke of Rivenhall's residence is?"

Tomlins straightened. "Surely, you're not planning on visiting an unmarried gentleman alone at ten o'clock at night!"

"It's business-related."

Tomlins sputtered. "B-But—"

"Mama and Papa won't be home for several hours. I highly doubt I'll be away more than one, and anyway, Papa is well aware of what I'm doing. And you know I'll simply go out the door right now and try to find the duke myself if you don't tell me. Then I'll be wandering London all alone, lost, and quite frightened."

Clearly resigned, and no doubt knowing the Honeyfield family far too well to not recognize the truth of her statement, Tomlins told her the address with a regretful tone. Thankfully, it was only a few blocks away, so she declined the offered carriage ride and accompanying footman.

When she'd arrived at the residence, she couldn't help but admire the building. It was in a beautiful part of Mayfair, private and quiet. And it was wider than most townhomes, with five windows across and sitting on the corner, when so many were only two or three windows across. The Honeyfields' townhome, for example was two windows across.

There was no sign of candles or gaslights in the windows, however. Perhaps he wasn't home.

But of course he wouldn't have been! Why would a young and unmarried duke be at home at this hour? He was likely at a gentleman's club or some dinner party.

Or, perhaps, he was somewhere a bit more risqué. Like a

gambling den. Or wherever it was that men found courtesans.

She swallowed, not liking that thought.

Not that it was any of her business.

Regardless, Julia willed herself forward and knocked on the duke's door. A moment later, a footman answered, his uniform crisp, a butler at his side. The butler stood tall, thin, with gray hair and a menacing frown, just how a butler should look in a proper townhouse.

"Good evening," she said, feeling a bit nervous. "My name is Miss Julia Honeyfield. Is His Grace in at the moment?"

The butler stared at her with a near snarl, as if she had turned the same color as her dress.

"Are you mad, young lady? Do you realize what hour it is?" He spoke with as much disdain as the duke would have if he had been the one uttering the words.

"It's a pressing business matter, sir, I assure you." To provide evidence of this truth, she showed him the folder and notebook she had brought along.

"Absolutely not. Shut the door, Francis."

The footman slammed the door in her face, the brass knocker banging loudly from the movement.

Julia stood there stunned, her mouth hanging open. She debated knocking again and offering up some choice words to the men but didn't feel brave enough to stand up to them, especially that terrifying butler. Instead, she quickly gathered herself and retreated down the steps while looking back up at the dark windows.

She could try again tomorrow during the daytime, but she had a feeling the butler would refuse to help her after the way she'd shown up tonight alone, uninvited, and late. Plus, she might lose her nerve, which she needed to confront the Duke of Rivenhall about this pressing matter. She even had on her favorite dress and couldn't wear it two days in a row, either. That would be ghastly.

And then she had a thought. A bit mad, yes, but it could be effective.

She went around the corner of the townhome and found a long line of privacy hedges dividing the sidewalk from whatever was behind the townhouse and hedges. She walked along the greenery hoping to find an opening to look through, but in the darkness, it was difficult to see anything. She doubled back and eventually found a gap between the hedges. It was a door—a wrought-iron fence was hidden behind the greenery, and this was the way in.

Glancing around to make sure no one was watching, Julia wedged herself in, found the knob, and turned it. The knob turned easily, but the door wouldn't budge.

She swore to herself when she found it had a keyhole. The door was locked.

Perhaps the fence could be scaled? She wouldn't be above climbing her way over. But from what she could see, the top of the fence consisted of protrusions that were pointed quite sharp to prevent exactly that.

Putting her attention back on the keyhole, she crouched down to study it, and a curious idea crossed her mind. Surely, it wouldn't work…but it was worth a try, wasn't it?

Gently, she removed one of the hatpins and stuck the sharp point in the keyhole. It took some finagling, but she found if she angled it a certain way, she felt something metal press against it and start to give way.

And then it clicked back.

"Oh. Well, there we go, then," she mumbled to herself, pleased. But the gate remained locked.

Perhaps there were more prongs, so she poked around again.

Not one minute later, she found herself on the other side of the fence. And gasped loudly at what she'd found.

It was paradise. This block of townhomes was large enough to have an enormous shared green space. But it wasn't just flat lawn. There were pergolas. A pond with a willow tree. A fountain in the pond. A garden path!

But this was not the time to lose focus. Hidden in the shadows, Julia slid down the line of hedges toward the duke's house.

Light illuminated from the second floor. She resisted the urge to let out a squeal.

All right. Now she was here. And he might, in fact, be home. What should she do, throw rocks at the window?

It would be just her luck that his butler would be the one to find her.

No, she had to see who was in that room before deciding what to do. As she had no clue what that room was, anything could have been happening in there. He could have been hosting a party. He could have been dining with friends. He could have been with a woman.

Her face heated at the thought. That would be rather humiliating to find. And she *really* hoped she wouldn't.

There was a balcony up on the second floor, and a large tree at the corner of the house. One could climb onto the balcony from the tree and it looked easy enough to climb up, even while holding the papers.

Julia crossed the last bit of lawn and reached the tree without issue. Wedging the papers in a narrow gap between two branches, she climbed up carefully, moving the papers along with her and setting them in a level or tight spot while she moved up after them. It was difficult. Her hat kept bumping into branches and her skirt got tangled a few times, but she eventually made it to a branch level with the duke's second floor. Ensuring the light still glowed in the room, she then grabbed the papers one final time and carefully inched along the large branch that crossed over to the balcony.

Unfortunately, Julia made the mistake of looking down and terrified herself. She was now almost twenty feet up in the air. Had she gone mad doing something so foolish? If she fell, she would be lucky to survive. Her heart was beating quite hard now, and sweat began to dampen her brow.

She could turn back. It would be hard, yes, but she could do it and stay safe—and alive. She could return to her family, her comfortable life, and drop all of this silly mill business, giving the problem back to Papa to figure out.

Except that wasn't an option to her. Papa didn't seem to worry about it; she seemed to be the only one who saw the mill as a pressing issue. And she was determined to see it through, show both herself and her family that she could do this. Prove to the duke that he couldn't ruin the Honeyfields, not without some resistance.

Plus, she really wanted to see his face when she told him what she had discovered. And she didn't have the patience to wait until tomorrow for that. He thought they would be an easy family to take advantage of, did he? Well, she would prove him wrong.

Julia swallowed her nerves back down. She wasn't going to quit. Instead, she took a deep breath and continued crawling along the branch, slow and careful. When the stone balustrade came within arm's reach, she slid the papers between two balusters and hoped a gust of wind didn't take them away.

Just as she thought she had made it, though, and moved to set her foot on the branch to step over, her right foot slipped and twisted in a not-so-comfortable way. Trying not let out too loud of a yelp, she overcompensated her balance and almost lost her hold of the tree. Her heart nearly jumped out of her chest as her body weight caused the branch to wobble violently.

She was falling!

By some miracle, though, she was able to fall in the direction of the balustrade and held on for dear life, hoping that the duke— or anyone else—couldn't see her.

Letting out a puff of breath, Julia managed to pull herself up and climb over to safety.

Allowing herself a moment of triumph for making it and not plummeting to her death, Julia then crouched into a dark corner with a view of the lighted window.

The room was empty of occupants.

"Blast," she whispered to herself. An ache on her right leg

caught her attention and she moved her green skirt to stick out her foot. The stocking on her right leg had been ripped and she had been scratched by tree bark underneath. Her ankle was also rather sore. She tried moving her foot around. It didn't seem to be sprained or broken, at least.

Gathering up the papers, she stepped up to the window to get a better look in the room.

It was a sitting room and beyond open double doors, a bedroom.

A rather handsome bedroom, obviously the duke's. It was three times the size of hers and painted a dark green. A large, four-poster bed draped in dark-emerald velvet with hunting scenes embroidered in gold thread sat regal against a wall. The plush bed with green bedding also happened to be void of women *and* still made up, she couldn't help but notice.

Off the balcony where she stood, however, was the sitting area. The opposite wall from her view had a desk. The room also had a stone fireplace with a nice crackling fire already lit for this cool, late spring evening, and one single leather wingback chair with a round, wood side table holding an oil lamp. A book lay atop its surface, along with an empty crystal glass.

A few rugs—in various shades of green and brown—were placed around both the sitting room and bedroom to frame out the different spaces.

Several enormous paintings adorned the walls, also, all very green outdoor scenes with horses or hunting.

The duke, apparently, really liked the color green.

Julia looked down at her green dress. "Oh, blast," she mumbled to herself.

But there was nothing she could do about that now. Instead, she watched the room a minute longer, but still no sign of the duke caught her attention. Or any women, Julia secretly noted happily.

The balcony door was, to her pleasant surprise, unlocked when she tried the handle and it opened noiselessly. With the papers tucked close, Julia tiptoed in and began to meander around the room.

She sniffed the air. It smelled nice enough, like a man's soap or aftershave or whatever men used that had fragrance. She ran a finger atop the mantel of his fireplace and it came away clean. Nothing of interest on the mantel caught her eye other than a few books and trinkets. She studied the titles. A collection of poetry by Henry David Thoreau. *The Legend of Sleepy Hollow* by Washington Irving. *The Raven* by Edgar Allan Poe. A few more she recognized as American authors but didn't know the books offhand. And then Jane Austen's *Pride and Prejudice*.

Curiosity tugged at her and she slid over to the round side table and picked up the book sitting there, waiting to be read. *The Three Musketeers* by Alexandre Dumas.

"Interesting," she mumbled to herself. The duke had a curious range of literature in his possession. Were these clues into true character of the mysterious man? If so, she couldn't decipher what they told her.

A sound caught her attention, causing her to still. It sounded like…water? With a sudden rush of fear, realizing she could get into some rather awful legal trouble for her antics, she spun toward the noise, her heart hammering hard in her chest.

Through the open double doors into the bedroom, she spotted someone appear from out of sight.

The duke!

But he hadn't seen her yet in the adjoining room. He was rubbing a towel over his face and hair. And he had not one stitch of clothing on.

"Oh!" She couldn't help but shout out loud before slapping her hand over her mouth.

His towel fell to the ground and the duke stared at her with enormous dark eyes. His face went dreadfully pale, and they both froze in place. It was impossible to ignore the man's physique now.

What in the world had he *done* in America?

Shocked silly, she couldn't help but quickly look him over, as if unbelieving that he stood before her in such a state. Her gaze quickly swept over his hard form, but her attention was taken by strange marks across his right side. Scars? She clutched the papers tightly against her chest as her mind and eyes caught up to each other and she fully comprehended that the Duke of Rivenhall, Sir Crabby, the surliest man she had ever known, now stood before her fully nude.

"What in the blazes are you doing here?! Do you know how to turn around?" the duke shouted as he hastily picked up the dropped towel to wrap it back around his waist.

Julia yelped and for once did as asked.

Chapter Seven

HUMILIATION LIKE NATHANIEL had never felt before slammed into him like a boulder falling from a cliff.

To think only minutes ago, he had been soaking his sore body in the bathtub, relaxation and calmness flowing through him like gentle waves. His book and night cap had been within reach, his comfortable bed, where he would be gloriously alone, had waited for him. The incessant buzz from too much talking, too many people, too much socialization that had rung in his head had desperately needed to be silenced. He was to call his valet for dressing, and that had promised to be the last human interaction for the day.

He needed to be alone. He needed the quiet.

Instead, the most irritating woman alive stood in his bedroom, that ignominious Miss Julia Honeyfield, and she was staring at him naked. How the blazes had she even gotten *in* here? Absolutely no chance had his butler, Poole, let her in.

Nathaniel grabbed his towel off the floor and wrapped it around his waist with jerky movements. Strangely, he was most embarrassed by her seeing the scars that marred his body. Probably because she would pepper him with questions about it, as if it were any of her business.

A big reason he'd willingly returned to England had been to

move on from that traumatic day, to live a life where it didn't shadow him and people didn't give him pitied looks every time they stopped him to check how he was doing whenever he left the general store or the post office or anywhere he was minding his blasted business.

He hated talking to people. Had ever since that horrible day ten years ago. Ten blasted years and they wouldn't leave him in peace. England was supposed to be a respite, a new beginning. But he arrived and that godforsaken Brumstock Mill had laughed in his face, as if God found his life to be a joke. Of all the businesses to be saddled with, why did it have to be a textile mill?

With a clench of his jaw, he pulled his mind away from that day and to the absolute last woman he would ever want interrupting his private chambers.

"What in the blazes are you doing here?! Do you know how to turn around?" He hadn't meant to shout as loud as he had, but he didn't want her looking at the scars any longer.

Miss Honeyfield made the most ridiculous squeak and spun around fast.

Had he seen her holding something? No, surely not.

Nathaniel stormed over to his bed to grab the nightclothes his valet, Timms, was supposed to dress him in. As Nathaniel had always dressed himself in the past, having a valet had taken some getting used to. However, he knew it to be expected for his new ducal role—and didn't care to put the competent man out of a job, either. Tonight, though, he dressed himself in the mirror. As he buttoned up his nightshirt, he couldn't help but look at Miss Honeyfield over his shoulder, still huddled in the adjoining room. A black hat sat atop her head, but it looked like it had been knocked crooked by something. Her green dress had a few dirt smudges on the hem, and a black bow on her lower back hugged her form. He wanted to rip off the blasted bow and throw it off the balcony. But the green, he had to admit, did look becoming on her.

Grumbling to himself—nothing about that woman should

have been becoming to him—he returned his attention to his nightshirt, quickly ran a comb through his damp, raven hair, then grabbed his black silk housecoat and tied it on over his nightclothes.

He made his way to his chair and Miss Honeyfield, who stood near it.

"You may turn back around, Miss Honeyfield, and promptly explain why you are in my private chambers and how you got in here." Nathaniel stopped at a respectable distance from her.

Miss Honeyfield turned back around and looked up at him, her cheeks flushed cherry red. Her brown doe eyes met his for a moment, but she quickly looked away. She held a notebook tight against her front.

Somewhere far in the back of his mind, he noted that despite what looked like leaves in her hair, when Miss Julia Honeyfield was actually dressed for the day, she was actually quite beautiful. Those round, falsely innocent-looking eyes could easily trick a man into doing her bidding. And her hair, shiny with long curls a perfect chestnut color, tempted his fingers. The curves of her body made him swallow. She didn't have the wasp waist so many women strived for, and he personally preferred a woman with extra softness to her.

Then again, there was also something alluring about her just-out-of-bed look, too.

What in the blazes was he doing? He mentally kicked those idiotic thoughts away.

Miss Honeyfield cleared her throat. "I, erm, tried to come in through your front door, but your door was slammed in my face."

He narrowed his eyes as he studied her dress further. Why did it have so many bows? "And you didn't take the hint?"

She stammered. "I-I needed to speak with you immediately. So I—"

"Broke in?"

She closed her eyes and lifted her chin. "Technically, I suppose if you want to put it that way, you could."

Letting out a sigh, he grabbed his crystal decanter and poured into the glass beside his sitting chair. "I would offer you a drink, but seeing as you're an unwelcome guest, I won't be." He lifted his glass to her as a mock cheer and took a sip. "How did you get in?"

"Through your balcony door. It was the only room with light, but I didn't know this room led to your bedroom. And then once I was up here and realized it did, I said to myself, 'Well, I'm already here. May as well go in.'" She made a show of shrugging. "I apologize for catching you in such a moment."

He ignored that. "What do you want, Miss Honeyfield?"

She took this as her cue. "I was looking through the boxes you left with Papa and made some interesting discoveries."

Nathaniel took another sip for his nerves and set the glass down again on the side table. "Why are you looking through them and not your father?"

"He wasn't interested," she replied a bit too quickly. "My suspicions were that you dumped a money leech on us and I looked through the boxes, quickly concluding I was right."

He forced a mocking smile. "Congratulations."

"Why didn't you simply shut it down when it was yours?"

"Because I'm not keen on putting hundreds of people out of work, even if it may be an inevitability."

She narrowed her eyes and appeared to be considering this. Perhaps she felt the same way. "You do realize that you have essentially ruined my family."

"Not my concern. Your father should never have agreed to the wager. Take the issue up with him."

"While that may be correct, you *knew* what you were doing, Your Grace. You knew he wouldn't say *no* and you used him to weasel your way out of bad business."

He looked off for a moment to mull over her accusation. "Correct."

She took a deep inhale through her nose.

"I am beholden to my tenants, Miss Honeyfield. I care about myself and them. And aside from my staff, I care for no one else."

"And the factory workers." She smiled like a cat who'd caught the cream.

He ignored her. "This mill business"—he gestured toward the notebook she clutched—"was preventing me from tending to my tenants' needs. And I couldn't get to that because the mill was taking up so much of my time and money. Roofs need repairs, windows need reglazing, their walls need patching and repainting. And many of my tenants need to upgrade their farming equipment. Do you know what happens if I don't tend to all of those needs?"

"What?"

"They leave. They are my main source of income. And the number of farmers in this country drops every year, which means no one is filling in those vacancies. And then I lose *my* income and become ruined. But my ruin takes many families in the process. Not just one."

She narrowed her eyes again. "You really think the queen would let that happen?"

"Yes," he replied immediately. "It's happening now to others. Plus, she doesn't like me much and I'm sure would express glee over my failure." Queen Victoria had called him, *"Basically an American,"* when he'd returned, and even he knew it hadn't been a compliment.

"Imagine that," Miss Honeyfield replied dryly. "You know, my being here right now is almost me doing you a favor."

He let out a single, unamused laugh. "Oh, I would love to hear the explanation behind this."

There was a challenging glint in her eye. It energized him. "Perhaps I will let you figure it out for yourself, then." Miss Honeyfield set the notebook down on the side table. She had also been carrying a folder, which she handed to him. "I'm going to time how long it takes for you to figure out why I'm here."

Feeling hesitant, he took the folder and they stared at each other down. They then both glanced at the clock at the same time. Without another word, he sat in his chair and opened the folder to find a small stack of paper inside.

Out of the corner of his eye, he saw her start meandering around, studying her surroundings. The woman was rather nosy, wasn't she? But he wasn't about to lose time worrying about that.

He had gone through the mill documents countless times. But he'd spent most of his time doing so examining the money that had come in and the money that had gone out, as that had been his main responsibility over the past six months: taking the money in and sending far more out.

These papers, he had skimmed over. Property records. Those were self-explanatory, aren't they? Hardly worth more than a sweeping glance.

He lifted his glass and took a sip, then set it back down. Peering up at Miss Honeyfield, he watched for a moment as she studied a painting of the farm he had lived on in America. Miss Honeyfield seemed interested in it but didn't ask about it.

Attention back on the papers, Nathaniel flipped through them. And then he reached the back of the stack.

Land deed.

Land?

Not once had he heard or seen anything about the land the mill sat on. He had never seen this paper before. And, in fact, he had never given any thought to the land the mill sat upon. Surely, it was tied to the building?

He let out a *hmm* and at the edge of his vision saw Miss Honeyfield turn toward him.

The land belonged to McManus Enterprise. Who, or what, in the blazes was that?

"What is McManus Enterprise?" He looked up as he asked. Before he could work through that question, though, he was horrified to find Miss Honeyfield examining his copy of *Pride and Prejudice.*

"Put that back!" He jumped out of his chair, nearly scaring

her out of her skin before ripping the book out of her hands to put it back in its place on the mantel.

Her hand was over her heart. "My word, Your Grace. I had no idea you were so passionate about romance. And look how tattered it is."

He gave her a death glare. "That is not mine, Miss Honeyfield. It belonged to—" But he cut himself off when he realized what he was about to divulge.

"Who?"

"Never you mind."

"Your mother?"

He looked down at her again and saw that her face had softened with pity. He despised pity. "Back to the task at hand," he said. "What is McManus Enterprise?"

She handed him the notebook. "It's been five minutes, and you are only halfway there."

He snatched the notebook out of her hand and sat back in his chair, fully annoyed now. Opening to a random spot in the notebook, he skimmed through the payments he'd made last month—the red column—and quickly found *McManus* at the very top.

"Hmm," he said again.

"You're getting closer," Miss Honeyfield replied in a singsong tone.

He ignored her and kept pouring through the columns, finding *McManus* again at the very bottom on the green side.

He sat up straight. "What the—"

"Curious, isn't it?" she said, and he could hear the grin in her voice.

Nathaniel stared into the fire, sorting through everything he could remember about the mill. He would read the invoices, write the checks, then give them to his solicitor, Mr. Frankfurt, who would send them out. Then when checks came in for the duke, Mr. Frankfurt would bring them, Nathaniel would sign them, and Mr. Frankfurt would have them deposited.

And as Nathaniel rubbed his temples, he recalled writing checks for a few hundred pounds for a McManus Enterprise. At the beginning of the month. And then a few weeks later, he would sign the same blasted checks, working automatically and without examining closely what he was signing, as he was just happy money had come in, and Frankfurt would deposit them in the bank.

With a rigid spine, Nathaniel looked Miss Honeyfield square in the eye, utterly horrified.

She grinned from ear to ear. "Ten minutes."

"I own the land." He was going to throw up.

"That's right. And you still own it right now." And then the blasted woman giggled. *Giggled!*

"I had more time than you to figure it out, but, essentially, the original owner of the mill who owned both the land and the building, that was Seamus McManus. Both the land and the then under-construction factory were one entity under McManus Enterprise. After the mill was constructed, Mr. McManus sold the building to someone else—unused—and that was when the building became a textile mill all those decades ago. Since then, the building and land have been separate entities with separate owners. But then Mr. McManus died in 1865, and the mill happened to be put up for sale at that same time. That's when your father bought them both: the Brumstock Mill, *and* McManus Enterprise, which is the business the land falls under."

Nathaniel's mouth dropped open.

"Now, this is my favorite part." There was a faint turn of her mouth, the slightest gleam in her eye.

He had seen that same expression before on the baron and it made his eye twitch.

"This means, we're leasing the land from you," Miss Honeyfield continued. "We are supposed to pay you rent each month, for our building to sit on your land."

There was no beating around the bush. Finally, he understood why she was here. "And you're not going to pay, are you?"

She gave him a deep chuckle. "No. But while there is no loan on the land any longer, *you* still have to pay taxes on it. I don't know if you've even lived here long enough yet to have to pay them, but you'll find the taxes quite astronomical."

Nathaniel swallowed. "So, I'm not rid of the mill, then."

She gave him a noise of pity. "No, you're not, I'm afraid. It also means you're in business with us now. You were so happy to leave my house today, to ruin us and leave us behind with your mess. But now, you're stuck with us."

He closed his eyes and inhaled deeply. When he felt calmer, he opened his eyes again to find Miss Honeyfield smiling at him with her head cocked to the side. Infuriating. "I would like to meet with your father tomorrow morning, then, and determine how to move forward," he said.

"There's no need for that. He's given me full rein of this."

He paused. "Sorry?"

"He wants nothing to do with the mill. He's put me in charge of it. Exclusively."

Nathaniel furrowed his brow. A woman in business? Then again, she was the only one who had figured out this whole mess. Blast, how did his solicitor not know about this? Had he missed it himself? He had been hired on after the former duke had purchased the whole mess, so perhaps he had missed it as well.

Add find a new solicitor *to my never-ending list of tasks.*

"I don't understand how I've never seen this before," he said, indicating the land deed.

"It was stuck to the back of another paper."

Nathaniel let out a sigh and rubbed the bridge of his nose. "Very well, Miss Honeyfield. I'll happily sign the land over to you as well. Free of charge, just like the mill. You could sell it as a bundle."

She pursed her lips and tilted her head. "No. We are not interested in owning the land, and it was not part of the wager. I'm not going to make this easy for you, Your Grace. In fact, I plan on making this as difficult for you as I can."

His eye twitched. *Stay calm.* "You said you were on the brink of ruin because of this."

"Like I said, I don't plan on paying you rent. That helps considerably."

He paused as he considered his next move. "I could take you to court for that."

"But will you?"

He wouldn't. It would create a circus amongst their peers and the newspapers. And evidently, she knew this as well.

"What do you propose, then?" he asked.

She looked over at the fire and crossed her arms. "Honestly, I'm not sure myself. I think it's hard to really do anything with a business you've never set foot in before, though, don't you agree? I think we should go see it for ourselves and figure it out from there."

He raised his eyebrows high. "*We* should go there? Who do you mean by *we*?"

She furrowed her brow at him as if *he* were the daft one. "I mean you. And myself."

"Unchaperoned? This is madness."

She shrugged. "We could see if my father would join, though I doubt it. He has a busy social calendar these next few weeks. Why do you think I'm unmarried?"

He glanced off to the side, unsure how to respond. Another one of those rules he didn't understand? He knew a young woman of the *ton* walking about on her own was frowned deeply upon, but he supposed he never really thought in depth about why. There must have been more to it that he didn't know. "I'm not following," he admitted.

She rolled her eyes. "I am unmarried partly because I have been caught going about on my own."

"People have seen you on your own and...that's why you can't marry?"

"Yes, that's right."

Nathaniel thought back to America and how the rules on this

seemed looser over there. Then again, he hadn't exactly associated with the upper classes and social rules were far less rigid for the average person.

Or perhaps he was simply ignorant of the rules that applied to women. Did these types of rules apply to married women or only unmarried? Because he personally wouldn't think anything of his sister or daughter, if he'd had either, going off on her own at a ball or a walk. Or any situation, really.

Not that he planned on having a wife anytime soon, of course.

He needed to bring his mind back. "You truly want to go all the way to Manchester?"

She looked back over to him. "Yes. Don't you think that's wise?"

Frustrated, he ran a hand through his hair. "I suppose it is."

"Excellent. We may take a train tomorrow, then."

Dread filled him at the mention of trains. He swallowed. "No trains."

She blinked. "No trains? That's absurd!"

"No. Trains." His heart was already hammering by merely saying the word.

"But it would take days to get there by carriage!"

"Yes, it would. I would estimate about four days, in fact, if we break it up into eight-hour trips. Five or six days if we do shorter trips. Now you know why I have yet to visit."

She swept a hand at him. "I suppose I can travel by train then."

His mouth went dry at the thought and he shouted out without thinking first. "No!"

"No?" Her eyes were enormous at this sudden and severe reaction. "You are quite panicked at the mere suggestion."

"Trains are notoriously unsafe." Sweat began to bead at his brow. "I don't care how irritating, how long, how uncouth, or whatever adjective you choose to describe the situation. You will not travel by train. You will travel with me. And that's not up for discussion."

She put her fists on her hips. "This is ridiculous! You really want to spend a week traveling with me, and that's not to mention however long we stay there on top of it?"

The panic subsided. She would make sure he knew how unhappy the situation made her, of that he was certain. But she wouldn't be on a train and that was all he cared about.

He now had the upper hand and gave her his own smug smile. The resulting flames in her eyes told him the smile irritated her. *Good.* "You are the last person I'd want to spend that amount of time with," he said. "Would you like to begin paying rent, then?"

"No." It came out sharp.

"Then I refuse to budge as well. Unless we choose to sit this way forever, which I don't think either of us want." He gathered the documents together and handed them over to her. "And we leave at eight in the morning. Tomorrow."

She scoffed. He knew enough about the woman to know she wasn't a morning person. "You can sleep on the way there," he added.

"I plan on talking the entire time," she replied in a haughty tone. Desperate for quiet to let all of this settle, Nathaniel stood up, placed his hand on her upper back, and guided her out his private chambers, down the stairs, and into the foyer.

Not surprisingly, she chattered the whole way, complaining about him and the mill. Poole appeared to see what the commotion was.

"Wh-What in God's name is this?" the lanky Poole sputtered out, glaring at her. "I told you to leave, young lady!"

"Yes, and she instead broke into my bedroom," Nathaniel explained. "Poole, the next time Miss Honeyfield dares to appear at my front door, ensure that it doesn't slam in her face. But that it closes gently. We do not wish to cause offense."

After a brief hesitation, Poole promised he would make sure of this, bowed, and hurried over to open the front door. Due to the late hour, Nathaniel presumed the footmen was abed.

Nathaniel gently nudged Miss Honeyfield through it and out into the night to return home however she had arrived. As he did so, he noticed even *more* ghastly bows at the cuffs of her sleeves. Merely reacting, he stepped closer to touch one, accidentally brushing his hand against hers. "I utterly despise your bows, Miss Honeyfield. I would like to rip them off and flick them away, or better yet, send them straight into an inferno." He lifted his gaze to her face, angled up to his, while he slid the bow between his ungloved fingers. They stood just a few inches from each other. And she wore the most curious expression on her face. Wide eyes, parted lips.

"Oh, well…" Her voice was low. "In that case, my bows utterly despise you as well."

It struck him then how strange the moment was. He didn't like her yet found himself fondling her dress. He met her eye again and felt a strange tugging sensation at the corners of his mouth. He stepped back, reminded her he was prompt with schedules, thus she best be ready by eight in the morning, and had Poole shut the door before she could respond.

It was only once she had gone that he realized his heart raced. And this time, it hadn't been caused by talk of trains.

Chapter Eight

J ULIA HAD ALWAYS wondered where she would end up in life.

To satisfy this curiosity as a young girl, she'd often partaken in silly games of fortune-telling with Helen. Once, they had attempted to create their own fortune-telling cards, but Mama had gotten rid of them, explaining that she had known a fortune-teller and the woman had died after a flowerpot had fallen on her head. As far as Mama was concerned, fortune-telling cards were bad luck and the house didn't need any of that.

The girls had ended up resorting to reading tea leaves as their preferred method of predicting their futures, as it didn't require any extra paraphernalia to be discovered by curious parents.

Of course, their futures were strictly tied to the men they would marry, as girls in the aristocracy (even the lower-ranked ones like the Honeyfield sisters) rarely worked and could even more rarely own property. Neither of the girls had truly believed in reading the tea leaves; it was clear their minds had been finding patterns and shapes in the leafy debris, not unlike seeing animals in fluffy clouds. But it was still a fun way to pass an afternoon.

Once, Helen had sworn she had seen a man with no teeth in Julia's cup.

"I wouldn't marry a man with no teeth," Julia had whined back.

Helen had then shrugged. "Maybe he gets kicked in the face by a horse after your wedding."

Julia laughed to herself as she recalled this old memory while watching the white clouds outside the carriage window.

Beside her, the Duke of Rivenhall turned his head to look at her, likely wondering what she was laughing at. His black top hat sat prim and proud upon his black hair. And he had had a fresh shave this morning, which highlighted his sharp cheekbones and masculine jaw. Even though she couldn't stand him, at least she had a nice view for the foreseeable future. She took a very covert sniff. He also smelled quite nice, like balsam and lemon.

But he didn't deserve to know what had made her giggle, so she ignored him and let her mind trail back to her fortune-telling days.

The girls had seen other pictures in their tea leaves. Hearts, flowers, houses, dogs, cats. Once, Julia had thought she'd had a headstone in her teacup.

She tensed and straightened up. She had forgotten all about that one.

The duke's voice interrupted her thoughts. "What's the matter?"

"Hmm?" Julia replied a bit absently.

"You keep squirming. And you won't stop moving your foot."

Julia looked down at her right foot as if suddenly remembering it was there. She rolled her ankle. It was the foot she had hurt climbing the tree the night before and it had been sore this morning when she'd awoken for the day. "I don't like being stuck in here is all."

The duke folded his newspaper and set it upon his lap. "We're only two hours into our trip, Miss Honeyfield."

"With one thousand to go," she replied with a dramatic sigh. "Then who knows how many days we stay there. And then the return trip! I'm honestly surprised you are willing to spend so much time with me, Your Grace, especially when far quicker modes of transport are readily available."

"It's not a matter of being willing to spend the time with you," he replied, terse. "I think I've well established how unsafe other modes of transport are *and* how much I am not looking forward to all of this time with you. I really do wish your father had agreed to join like I asked him this morning, and I cannot believe I'm saying that."

Julia turned her foot in a circle again. "I told you, he's leaving this all up to me." In truth, Papa had seemed more concerned with not missing out on parties he had already planned to attend. It wasn't unusual for her to go about on her own, but she had to admit she was surprised her father allowed extended travel unchaperoned. Even Mama, who had been far wilder than Julia or Helen in her younger years as an actress, seemed to want to argue. But Papa had put his foot down on the matter, ending the conversation for the whole family. Julia even got the strange feeling he almost seemed *pleased* by her traveling alone with the duke, which was odd. "And anyway, you don't have your valet."

"He was violently ill this morning. I could hardly force him to come along and I didn't wish to delay this issue further. It still doesn't change anything, though. Regardless, this is not proper in any way."

She shot him a coy smile. "Do I need to worry if you will be improper, Your Grace?"

The newspaper slid off his lap and his body jerked awkwardly as it started to fall and he hastened to catch it. She couldn't help but laugh. He was so strange sometimes.

"Absolutely not, Miss Honeyfield." His voice was strained. "Not that you will believe me, but that's not the kind of man I am."

The carriage jostled over a divot. "What kind of man are you, then?"

"Are you asking as a jest, or genuinely?"

She considered the question. "I *was* jesting, but I would genuinely like to know since the opportunity to ask has presented itself."

The newspaper had come apart and he was attempting to line up the pages and refold it. "I like to think I'm a man of honor. At least, I hope I am. It's difficult to judge oneself; even the most reprehensible man on Earth could explain away his worst actions. A murderer could claim the murders were justified for some fiendish reason, even if the reason only makes sense to them."

"That's a good point." Julia watched his hands refold the newspaper and noted how masculine they were, unlike those of most of the other men with whom she was acquainted. The duke had taken his gloves off earlier, presumably for a more comfortable read. His hands were large, his knuckles slightly calloused. Unlike the rest of his appearance, his hands weren't elegant. They were rough, as if he were used to working with them. This piqued her curiosity.

"I suppose if I have to boil myself down to something," he said, seemingly unaware of her study of him, "if I could, I would always keep to myself. I've never been one to have many friends. One or two close ones at the most."

"Don't you get lonely?" Though Julia was only truly close with her family, she still enjoyed attending parties where there were lots of people around her.

"No. It's rare when I truly enjoy another person's company." He paused. "I'm always uneasy when others are around."

Interesting. "Why?"

Surprisingly, he was willing to explain. He scratched behind his jaw. "I worry too much about how I act, what I say. It's worse now, being an outsider. Mannerisms between everyday Americans and English aristocrats are quite different. I feel more guarded around the latter, and I don't care for that feeling."

"Are you uneasy with me? You surely know me well enough by now to know I wouldn't begrudge you an error of my name. If you called me 'Lady Honeyfield' instead of 'Miss Honeyfield,' instead of being upset by the error, I'd likely be flattered."

"That's because an error like that benefits you. What if you were a viscountess and I called you 'Miss Honeyfield'?"

"It depends. Are we at a party and others are around? Either way, I suppose I'd hardly care and likely would correct you during a private moment for your benefit."

He glanced at her quickly. "Perhaps you are right. But most others would find offense in the error."

She nodded slowly as she thought about this, deducing that he was likely correct. Her silence stretched as she studied his profile. He had a strong nose and nice lips; they weren't thin like many others'. "*Are* you uncomfortable around me?"

He looked over at her, one dark eyebrow lifted. "You broke into my private chambers in the middle of the night."

"Hmm. That's fair, I suppose."

He continued to fiddle with the newspaper but now looked away. "What kind of person do you consider yourself to be?"

Julia twisted her mouth in thought. The urge to give a silly response was strong, but he had taken her question seriously and answered it.

What kind of person was she? Well, deep down, she was a hopeless romantic. Wasn't that what her entire life and existence revolved around? She loved reading romance books and hearing about and attending weddings. Nothing was better than those flutters of excitement when a handsome gentleman asked her to dance. Admittedly, though, those moments had become rarer and rarer as she'd aged.

But her life wasn't purely rosy. There was the matter of her brother, the eldest sibling of the family. Some time ago, he had gone to see friends for an evening, but no one had seen him or heard a word from him since. Either he was having the time of his life and had forgotten all about them, was in prison under an assumed name or in an entirely different country, or was dead.

"Miss Honeyfield?"

The duke's voice brought her back to the present and she forced a smile. "Sorry, I was trying to think how to answer that. Did you know I have an older brother? Evander?"

His eyebrows lifted as if surprised by this, so she briefly told him what had happened with her brother. "We used to wonder when he would come back, but I think we've accepted he won't be. Maybe that's why we enjoy parties so much, to help us not think about him. I don't know. But I like having fun. I love a big, loud party. The atmosphere of all those people, the loud music and hum of people conversing. It energizes me. I suppose what you get from silence, I get from noise."

He studied her as if he could see through her. And maybe, through those words, she had unknowingly made herself transparent.

"I'm sorry about your brother." His voice had gentled. "If there ever is anything I can do to assist your family with that, you must let me know."

She tore a look in his direction, caught off guard by this. Was he being earnest or simply polite? But all she could do was give him a silent nod. Sadly, there wasn't anything he could do to help. They'd already tried everything.

Her foot started to bother her and she turned it again, wishing she could stretch out her legs. But the seat across from them had one of her traveling trunks on it, as it wouldn't fit in the storage rack outside. That already held his one trunk, and her other one.

Obviously, she'd ensured more clothing packed than deemed necessary, not knowing what to expect being away from home for likely a few weeks.

Julia shifted again. This was going to go on for days and days. All because the duke was a stubborn mule about not going on trains and terrifying her into going with him. What was that about, anyway? Despite his protests, she was sure there was a reason behind it. She promised to get to the bottom of the cause at some point.

"Why do you keep massaging your ankle?" the duke asked.

She resisted the urge to sigh. "I hurt it a bit while climbing your tree last night."

The duke snorted. Then after a moment, indicated to her foot and said, "May I?"

She arched an eyebrow. "You want to see my ankle?"

He nodded.

What else could she do? With a turn in her seat, she set one leg over his lap, causing the newspaper to slide off again and fall to the floor.

The duke cleared his throat but put his attention on her shoed foot and white-stockinged ankle. With gentle fingers, he pressed her ankle lightly in different spots while watching her face. "Does any of this hurt?"

"No."

Nodding, he then began to gently massage her ankle, circling his thumb and the pads of his fingers over it. "We often had minor injuries that would have to be treated at home. Pulled muscles, sprained ankles, minor cuts, and abrasions."

Julia studied him upon this interesting tidbit of information. Was he talking about America? Why would they get minor injuries? And who was '*we*'?

Unfortunately, he did not expand on it. Instead, she allowed herself to watch him since he was handling her.

This was all quite strange, admittedly, but it also felt like heaven the way his hot, large hand and gentle, careful touch sent tingling sparks up her leg. Julia had to resist the urge to let out a contented sigh and close her eyes.

"What did you do in America?" she decided to ask after a long bout of silence, needing to distract herself from his touch.

The duke lifted his attention away from her ankle and to her face. "Sorry?"

"America. You said you had to treat injuries there. And you were there for quite a while."

The gentle massaging continued. "Nearly twenty years."

"We're going to be together for a long while, Your Grace. And no one knows what your life was like since you and your mother left. I must say I'm quite curious what you were doing there."

The duke looked down at her leg again. Was he nervous? "We lived in upstate New York," he said after a hesitation.

"Oh?" The rising excitement had to be shoved back down. Up until now, he had been resistant to talk about his past to anyone.

"Yes." But he kept his gaze averted.

"Where in upstate New York? What was the name of the town you lived in?"

He let out a sigh. "Peekskill."

"Peekskill," she repeated with awe. She held on to this little nugget of information as if it were a found gem.

"It was right on the Hudson River. Woodsy. Rather nice place to grow up."

"I'm sorry you had to leave it behind."

Now he stared at her intensely, and it made her heart palpitate. He looked as if he were about to say more, but ultimately, he didn't.

So, she prodded further. "America was at war with itself while you lived there. Did you see any battles?"

"The war was several states south from where we lived. We never saw any battle, thankfully."

"Did you have to go fight?"

"No. I'm not an American, and I could help the country better where I was."

Her eyebrows lifted. "How so?"

"Do you always ask so many questions?"

"Yes."

Humor glinted in his eye, and the massaging stopped. Instead, his hand rested over her ankle, warm and comforting. "I'm a rather private man, Miss Honeyfield. It's in my nature."

"And I'm a rather curious woman. Which is also in my nature."

Nathaniel laughed, his eyes crinkling with it. It was a genuine laugh full of humor, deep and raspy and, oh, it was the most seductive sound she had ever heard in her life.

As her heart quickened and she realized the effect he had had on her, she forced herself to move past it quickly.

"We lived on a farm," was all he offered up, however.

She studied his dark suit; perfect, white necktie; and black top hat and tried to imagine this handsome duke knee-deep in muck on an American farm. She couldn't see it, but it *did* finally explain his physique. "Do you miss it?"

He opened his mouth to respond and it hung open for a moment. "I miss the happy parts," he finally said.

If he was trying to keep her curiosity tempered by providing short and vague answers, he was failing terribly. She had more questions than ever now. But she could tell he wasn't in a mood to divulge more at the moment. His past would have to be dug into another time.

Silence washed over the cabin and the gentle sway of the carriage and clip-clop of the horses' hooves began to lull Julia into slumber. As they still had many hours ahead, she settled back into the corner and let herself drift to sleep, forgetting that her leg remained propped up on the duke's lap.

NATHANIEL WATCHED MISS Honeyfield as she slept deeply, leaning back against the sidewall, and he wondered what a pampered woman like her required for dressing each day, especially evenings. He imagined an hours-long routine, bathing with freshly-made rose water, requiring exactly one hundred brush strokes through her hair before being fussily styled, and only the finest dresses with sequins and beads. And, of course, bows. With the carefree partying lifestyle she lived, it was no wonder her family treated late afternoon as early morning. What would it be like to not have a care like that? To go to parties and actually enjoy oneself there? Nathaniel tolerated it, as it was required of him, but he would eventually hit a sudden wall where he would have to leave, either a conversation at hand or the party in its entirety. The stress, otherwise, would become overwhelming.

He tried to imagine being a part of a family that was sociable like that and it made him shudder.

But that life also wasn't the life he was accustomed to.

He used to always get up before dawn, every single day. Didn't matter if it was Monday or Saturday, June or December, the horses had the same schedule nearly every day. The animals didn't care if he was tired or ill from a late night, or if he had stayed out late with Caroline and wanted to lie in bed dreaming about her.

Miss Honeyfield's question kept gnawing at him though. Did he miss America? He missed the life he'd had before the accident. His life had seemed set, and the dukedom had been something to worry about sometime far, far in the future, when his father had died of old age, and Nathaniel was old as well.

Back when everything had been planned out and his life made sense, he had talked to Adrian about keeping up work at the farm and moving down the road into his own home after he married. Both Adrian and his mother had been supportive of that. They had gotten along well with Caroline. What more could a man want in life? He had his family, the woman he loved, the horses, and the farm. It had been perfect.

Then his life had taken a complete tumble in the most literal sense. And with that, Caroline had been gone.

It seemed like ages since it had happened, and he had long ago accepted it and moved on as best anyone could. He didn't wonder "what if" anymore. But he did sometimes miss that old life of his, when everything had been full of hope and his future had been bright.

Miss Honeyfield mumbled in her sleep and shifted. He looked down at her little shoed foot, still propped up on his lap. Gently, he lifted it and set it on the ground. In her sleep, she frowned, as if displeased he had moved her off of him, and shifted so that she was now leaning against the wall instead of back into the corner.

The woman never stopped moving, not even in her sleep. In the unlikely event she managed to marry, God help the man she ended up with—if he could even keep up with her.

After removing his hat and leaning forward to set it upon Miss Honeyfield's second trunk, Nathaniel let his head fall back against the seat and watched her for a bit. Thought back to that morning. As soon as he had pulled up in his carriage, Miss Honeyfield had practically come prancing out of her home, fresh as a daisy, while servants had brought out three trunks after her.

Three trunks! What did she think they were going to be doing on this trip? Visit every viscount and earl between London and Manchester?

When her family had trailed out after her and the three Honeyfield women sang that ghastly welcome song at him again, Nathaniel had gone over to the baron and all but begged the older man to join them on the long trip.

But Lord Odstone had refused. *"My daughter is perfectly fit for such a matter,"* he'd said, stubborn. *"She's more knowledgeable about the whole issue than I am!"*

Which was, of course, true, but that did not make her fit for the matter, either. Even the mother had recognized this. In vain, Lady Odstone had tried to get their lady's maid to travel with Miss Honeyfield, but the baron had put an end to that at once. *"Everyone is in town. They will not see anyone we know on their travels,"* he had argued. *"Walsh needs to be here for you and Helen. We have important engagements coming up you two must attend with me. No further discussion about the subject will be humored."*

Nathaniel couldn't help but wonder about the idiotic baron's intentions.

Or perhaps such behavior would be seen as normal in her family. They were known for being a bit wild, after all. Perhaps he simply hadn't defined their version of *wild* as wild enough.

After all, Miss Honeyfield's entire life had revolved around drinking and dancing. She had never had responsibilities, though she likely had received a decent education. And she had grown up doing whatever she'd wished without consequences, it seemed.

Though finding out about her brother had been sad to learn, and he wondered what had really happened to the man. Clearly, he was dead, but the Honeyfields weren't fully ready to accept that yet, which he understood more than they could ever know.

Despite that, he was sure he would never understand the family.

But back to the task at hand, what exactly did Miss Honeyfield expect to find once they arrived at the mill? He did have to admit she was right in that it made sense to see the factory in person.

The pampered woman began moving again, evidently trying to find a more comfortable sleeping position. To his abject horror, she shifted in a way where she now leaned on him.

Deep asleep, she rubbed her cheek against his shoulder, snuggling into him, and let out a contented sigh.

He stared with his mouth hanging open. Once he'd shaken off his shock, he tried nudging her. When that didn't work, he gave her a gentle shake.

"Miss Honeyfield," he said. But she didn't stir. He repeated her name, much louder this time. He gently tried prying her off, but she furrowed her brow and pouted in her sleep and wouldn't let go.

With a deep sigh, Nathaniel gave up. At least she was quiet. And had stopped moving. Trapped, he closed his own eyes and succumbed to slumber.

Chapter Nine

THERE WAS THE scream of metal against metal.

Nathaniel startled awake and realized the carriage had stopped. Against him, Miss Honeyfield stirred, awaking as well.

Bewildered, glassy-eyed looks of confusion were exchanged between them. She blinked several times, seemed to realize she had been sleeping on him, and scooted away while wiping her mouth with the back of her hand.

Normally, he would have made some sort of wry comment. But something about the air felt and tasted dangerous.

He looked out of the window, hoping to find a village that would indicate they were stopping for a break for the horses.

Unfortunately, they were only surrounded by trees.

"Something is wrong," he mumbled to himself.

"What?" Miss Honeyfield replied in a panicked voice. "Where are we?"

"I'm not sure."

Outside, the overlapping sound of men's voices penetrated the carriage walls. Nathaniel's coachman, Mr. Moss, always carried a pistol on him and the man had an excellent shot. It tempered Nathaniel's nerves slightly.

"What are they saying?" Miss Honeyfield whispered as she inched back to his side, though this was surely to hear better, as the sound was coming from his side of the carriage.

Nathaniel put a finger to his lips to indicate quiet and listened as well.

"We have nothing of interest, sir." Mr. Moss's voice was muffled, but Nathaniel could still understand. "Too much women's clothing, that's about it." Mr. Moss ended this with a chuckle, evidently trying to diffuse whatever was going on out there. However, there was no responding laughter.

But what Mr. Moss had said was true. Nathaniel wasn't foolish enough to travel with anything of overt value. They had taken the plain black carriage that needed a good polish and some cosmetic repairs. He would never dare long-distance travel with the fancy carriage. In truth, he even hated using that one around town. It had the Rivenhall emblem on it in gold, like a smug announcement wherever he went. *Look at me! I'm the duke and you are not.*

Whoever was outside didn't know they were anything but ordinary travelers.

There was more overlapping conversation and Mr. Moss's voice picked up a panicked pitch. "Is that really necessary? We truly don't have anything!" Mr. Moss's voice was now traveling around to the back of the carriage.

Which meant they were coming toward the door on Miss Honeyfield's side.

Nathaniel's heart beat hard. If he was right, they were being robbed by highwaymen. *Blast!*

Immediately, his mind began to calculate risk. There was no telling who stood outside with Mr. Moss. It was good that the coachman was still well and on his feet. Some robbers would simply swoop in and kill everyone to take their belongings without a fuss.

Whoever was out there had some modicum of honor, however small.

With that understood, his mind scrambled over to Miss Honeyfield. Protecting her at all costs was most important.

Where could he hide her? He glanced around, but, of course, there was no hiding in a carriage.

If he had to, he would give them his trunk of clothing to keep her safe.

Hopefully, it wouldn't come to that.

He gripped the edge of the leather seat and looked over at Miss Honeyfield again to find panic reflecting in her wide eyes. Hoping to reassure her, he squeezed her arm. "If we get out, stay close to me," he whispered. "And let me do the talking."

She swallowed and nodded.

The carriage door flew open, causing Miss Honeyfield to yelp, and a man with graying whiskers and a red, sun-burned face leaned in. He grinned from ear to ear upon seeing them, though most of his teeth were missing.

But the grin fell away, leaving a tense expression behind. "Out," the man demanded.

Nathaniel considered what to do. He could refuse, forcing the robber to go into the cabin if he wanted to reach them that badly. In that case, Nathaniel would be able to overpower him and get the situation back in his control. But there was one key unknown fact: if the man was armed or not. Nathaniel couldn't see, and that was likely by design.

With a mental curse to himself, he decided compliance would be the best way out of this. Nathaniel climbed out and found Mr. Moss off to the side, unharmed, but his face etched deep with worry. Nathaniel also recognized this moment as an opportunity to keep Miss Honeyfield separate from this nonsense and went to shut the door—but the man immediately put his dirt-smudged hand out to stop it.

"The woman, too," the robber said gruffly, tapping the wood end of his rifle against the side of the carriage.

Now that a rifle was added to the equation, everything changed. Nathaniel nodded at Miss Honeyfield and she hastened out. He immediately moved her behind him, and she latched tightly on to his arm, causing his heart to skip a beat.

He had to keep her safe; she was relying on him for that.

The robber held the rifle with little care, the wood stock end leaning against his shoulder. Nathaniel took a few slow steps to the side to get closer to Mr. Moss.

"Is that your wife?" the robber asked while looking over Nathaniel's shoulder.

Saying *no* was the obvious reply, as it was the truth, but he caught himself. There was more risk for her if he said *no*, as the robber could see her as an opportunity. "Yes, she is," he decided, getting a flinch from her in response.

She would definitely be bringing that up later. If they made it out alive.

The robber spit on the ground and took a few slow steps forward. "Let's make this easy for all of us, then. What do you have that I would want? Valuables? Money? I think we all know what I'm looking for."

Nathaniel didn't have any valuables, but he did have coinage. Not enough to give away his station, but enough to cover food and sleeping arrangements for a few weeks for three people, since Mr. Moss would be staying with them the entire time, as Nathaniel wasn't sure how quickly he would finish his business and wanted the freedom to leave at a moment's notice.

But that cash was not disposable by any means.

Somehow, he had to get them out of this situation without losing their money. The coin purse was, perhaps stupidly, in his pocket. But there was only one robber against the two of them—he would absolutely not allow Miss Honeyfield to get involved in this—so the odds were in their favor.

But with two weapons involved—the robber's rifle and Mr. Moss's pistol, which remained hidden under his coat—and being unarmed himself, that made risk a bit muddier. Regardless, if the robber got the coin purse, they would be in trouble. The sun was getting lower in the sky. A village was surely close, but if they had no money, they would have to turn back and return to London, with most of their travel being done in the dark.

And if they were being robbed in broad daylight, what would happen at night?

"We really don't have anything other than clothes," Nathaniel offered. "And if you don't believe me, you're welcome to look."

As he said this, though, he realized he had no idea what Miss Honeyfield had had packed. A woman who loved to dress up and go to parties surely had jewels in her luggage.

What a fool he was!

The robber narrowed his eyes but looked over Nathaniel's shoulder again. "What's your name, Mrs.?"

"Don't talk to her." Nathaniel growled and clenched his fist.

But the robber only looked amused and patted his gun in reminder. "I asked you a question, lass."

Miss Honeyfield cleared her throat. "My name is Julia."

"Julia. What a pretty name."

"It's all right." She shrugged one shoulder, no sign of worry anywhere.

"You know, I often let people go by this point." He grinned and shook his finger. "But not you two."

Neither of them responded.

"You two are quite curious. I'm a very observant man, you see. I have to be able to judge people within seconds. If I decide within those seconds that people aren't worth my time, they think nothing of me waving them down. I make up some excuse, perhaps lie and say their wheel looks loose, and they go on their merry way. No police get involved."

There was a long pause, the only sound a gentle breeze rustling the leaves above.

"But you're worth looking into." The robber cocked his head while looking at Miss Honeyfield.

"Why?" she asked.

Nathaniel clenched his teeth. Had he not told her to keep quiet?

The robber chuckled and stepped closer, pinched Nathaniel's

sleeve, and lifted his arm. "What a curious pair you make. Your husband looks like a toff but doesn't sound like one. But look at his hands." The man studied Nathaniel's ungloved hands, permanently callused from two decades of hard work.

"And you." The robber looked in her direction. "You sound like one. But you don't look it."

"*Hey!*" She pressed her fists into her hips.

Nathaniel gently nudged at her from behind. What in the blazes was she doing?

But the robber seemed to think nothing of it. He rubbed his hands together and began digging through their trunks. After a few minutes, disappointment settled on his face.

There was nothing of value.

Unfortunately, though, the robber wasn't going to give up that easily. "What's in your pockets?" the man asked as he returned to Nathaniel.

Nathaniel didn't respond, but his stomach fell. The robber had no problem shoving his hands into Nathaniel's pockets.

The man let out a loud, long whistle when he opened the coin purse. "That's a lot of coin there, mister. What are you doing carrying that with you?"

"We're traveling for a few weeks." Panic rose inside him. "We *need* that money!"

The robber grinned from ear to ear again as he shoved his hand into the opened purse and let a large handful of coins rain back down. They made a rich, clinking sound. "You know something," the robber said, his eyes greedily latched on to the money. "For years, I worked for a steel mill. Poured liquid metal into different shapes. Those pieces of metal were then used to create railways. Or locomotives. And those locomotives drove on those railways to move important things. People sure got rich on that kind of thing."

Clink.

"People sure got rich on me breaking my back for a few shillings. Wild, isn't it? Work twelve-hour days. Hardly a break to eat or relieve myself. Guy next to me falls asleep at machinery 'cause he works twelve-hour days then has a newborn waking up all night, nearly loses an arm when his sleeve gets caught in something. All that…for a few shillings."

Nathaniel kept quiet as Miss Honeyfield adjusted her hold on him and pressed closer.

"It would have taken me months to make this kind of coin." *Clink.* "Months of back-breaking labor, risking my life." *Clink.* "Lost that job a year ago. Couldn't pay rent. Couldn't feed the family. And you know what I realized? Rich folk steal from us by barely paying us an amount *they* set, keeping what we *should* get. Why shouldn't I take what I'm owed? Make my life better and easier in the process?"

"I'm not sure you should be too smug about getting involved with something that requires putting a rifle barrel to someone's face and killing them if they don't cooperate." It was stupid of Nathaniel to say, he knew that. But he was furious. They had lost their money. He was sorry for the man's past misfortune, but what could Nathaniel do about it? He hadn't even lived in this country when it had happened! He'd been doing his own back-breaking work back then.

Even as the Duke of Rivenhall, he couldn't eradicate poverty. He could drain every last pound, every last shilling, give it to every single working-class citizen and it wouldn't even make a dent.

The robber took a step forward at Nathaniel's boldness.

"You want to steal from the wealthy and keep it for yourself?" Nathaniel held up his rough-looking hand in a show. "Do I look like the type of person who sits around all day eating little tea cakes? Do you think I don't know what working my own hide off is like?"

But the robber was unaffected. He simply laughed and shoved the coin purse into his pocket.

Without thinking, Nathaniel lunged at him. The robber was so surprised by this that he dropped his rifle. Miss Honeyfield rushed forward to nudge it away. The two men scuffled on the ground while Miss Honeyfield shouted at them to *stop* as she tried to get away from Mr. Moss, who was attempting to pull her away.

Nathaniel flipped the man on his back, then got in a good punch to his jaw. It wasn't the first time he'd needed to overpower an out-of-control man. But the robber dodged at just the right moment, took a cheap shot, and kneed Nathaniel right in the groin, nearly paralyzing him with pain.

The tides turned. The robber now had the upper hand and was a lot stronger than he looked. He got another good blow into Nathaniel's stomach and knocked the air out of Nathaniel's lungs. The robber then rolled over, panting and holding his fist as if it hurt.

Pain radiated all over Nathaniel's body. And while he curled up in the fetal position, gasping desperately for air, Miss Honeyfield crouched at his side. He looked up at her hovering over him.

"Are you all right?" She'd hurried out the question.

He could feel the achy location of every hit all over his body. Unable to respond verbally, he did his best to nod between gasps.

"You complete fool," she said lowly between clenched teeth. "*That* was your idea of a solution?"

He closed his eyes. "I lost my control."

"And now I have to go clean up the mess."

"Don't you dare—"

But it was too late. She was already out of sight.

Chapter Ten

"Have you ever seen a play before?" Julia knit her hands together behind her back and asked the robber as he pushed himself up to his knees.

He looked up at her, his mouth gaping. "Have I *what*?"

"Have you ever seen a play before? My mother used to be a stage actress. She sings *all* the time, at *all* hours of the day!" An exaggeration, but he didn't need to know that. "It's quite lovely. Never a moment of silence in our house! In fact, I can sing anything you would like. Do you have any requests?"

The highway robber blinked at her, then glanced over at the duke, still collapsed on the ground nearby. "Are you serious right now, lass?"

"Oh, yes! Any opera, any vaudeville song—my mother was the best. She's older now and has been off the stage for years, but she was such an accomplished singer that she could sing Mozart's "Come scoglio" aria, from his *Così fan tutte* opera. Are you familiar with it? It has several rather difficult leaps, where the singer must go from a deep note to a high one and repeat it in quick succession."

The robber stammered a few times. "I-I—"

"I'll sing it for you. But first, I should tell you a funny fact about that song. Mozart wrote it for a specific singer that he rather disliked. An Italian soprano named Adriana Ferrarese del Bene. Perhaps he thought her exceptionally arrogant, or simply disliked the way she moved her head when she sang. I've heard both explanations. Anyway, with low notes she pulled in her chin and high notes, she lifted it. Mozart created this aria specifically so her head would bob like a chicken when she sang it."

The robber blinked. "Lady, you're mad."

Julia belted out the aria without advance warning. She had not inherited Mama's perfect pitch, but she had inherited Mama's volume. The song was both ear-piercingly loud and painfully off-key. The robber covered his ears and begged her to stop, but she pretended she couldn't hear. She clasped her hands together at her breast and reached a high note—except she couldn't get anywhere near it and her voice cracked and made a horrific noise. She resembled a screaming alley cat more than an accomplished—or in truth, unaccomplished—singer.

"The hell with the lot of you!" the robber shouted, snatching his rifle off the ground to run away. As Julia continued squawking, the robber made a hand gesture at the forest and two armed men came stumbling out. The trio promptly ran for their lives, covering their ears as best they could while also holding weapons.

The song cut off once the highwaymen were out of sight and Julia was sure the fiasco had ended. Julia turned to the duke, still on the ground and staring up at her with eyes wide with horror, while his coachman crouched beside him, attempting to brush off the dirt from the scuffle.

Julia shook her head at him and said, "Leave it to a woman to clean up men's messes."

The duke sputtered. "Th-There were two more. In the forest. Armed!"

She knew that. She'd spotted them just after she'd exited the carriage and the duke had put her behind him. By that point, the duke had been trying to reason with the robber and hadn't been paying attention. "I know," she said. "But I couldn't really tell you, could I? And the man you were dealing with was perfectly amiable until you attacked him! Really, what were you thinking!" She set her hands on her hips.

With the coachman's help, the duke stood up and stumbled as he got his footing. A small twig fell from his sleeve. And his black hair was mussed in several different directions, with blades of grass and specks of dirt and gravel all over it. "'Perfectly amiable'? He had a rifle!"

"Yes, but he didn't *use* it."

The duke pinched the bridge of his nose. "Miss Honeyfield, you are aware of how bad of a situation we're in right now, yes?" The duke began to pace, rubbing his hands over his face. "That very fine gentleman, as you seem to think him, took the coin I brought. What do we do now?" He spun around to face her and turned his palms up in the air. "A village shouldn't be too far ahead, but we have no way to pay an inn. That *perfectly fine* robber took all of our money!"

Appalled by his unraveling from an elegant gentleman to what looked like a rake emerging from a wild night, she removed her gloves and shoved them in her traveling dress pockets before reaching up to fix his hair—it really was a horrific sight—and combed her fingers through it to dislodge the grass and dirt until it looked relatively normal. She ignored how nice the thick, silky strands felt. Her hands then moved to his chest and she began brushing off the road debris still stuck to the fabric, secretly enjoying the hard feel of him. After a few swipes, she could feel his eyes boring into her and she stilled and looked up. His cheeks were red and his stare piercing.

"I don't need your help, Miss Honeyfield, nor did I ask for it." He seemed to snarl.

Her eyes briefly widened in a mocking way. "Oh. My mistake, then." She reached back up to his hair and roughed it up again until it looked worse than it had before, then crouched down to the road. She took a large handful of dirt and gravel, stood back up, and pressed the dirt onto his dark coat.

The coachman let out a loud gasp and faltered a few steps back.

With flair, she began to rub it in all over his chest, shoulders, and arms.

Finally, she stepped back to admire her work, pinching her chin thoughtfully between her thumb and forefinger as if studying an artistic masterpiece. "Much better," she said with a nod of satisfaction. Noticing her palms were dirty, she then wiped them on a clean spot on his sides.

Realizing that maybe she had done it a bit overmuch, she looked up at him and realized that she stood far too close to him in the moment.

For a moment, their gazes locked together. The duke didn't look angry, but she could see that the wheels in his head were turning. She realized far too late that she had been having fun with a man who had laughed one single time around her. There was no chance he would see this as the good fun it was meant to be.

Oh, he was going to be so furious with her.

She considered apologizing profusely, but before she could, his eyes lowered to her mouth, causing her heart to flutter oddly. He lifted his hand to her chin, tilted her head back, and slowly swiped his thumb across her bottom lip. When he'd dropped his hand and met her gaze again, she could still feel his touch burned onto her.

"Dirt," he explained in a low, rough voice.

She swallowed, and of course this was the moment her mind decided to recall his towel dropping last night. Heat rose in her cheeks. "Apologies, Your Grace. I was just trying to have a bit of fun is all."

There was a hint of amusement in his eyes and he turned away from her and to his coachman. "What do you think, Mr. Moss?" The duke gipped his lapels and looked down at himself. "Is it an improvement?"

The coachman was evidently so confused, he merely stared back open-mouthed.

The duke chuckled lightly and turned back to her. He cleared his throat. "Like I was saying, we're in a bit of a bind."

She glanced up at his hair, which was still wild and sticking up and odd angles. She shifted. Was he going to *leave* it like that? She crossed her arms, trying not to react. "What kind of bind?"

"We have no money for an inn. But traveling back to London now, we would be doing a lot of traveling in the dark. The sun will be setting soon. After what just happened, I worry about doing that."

She furrowed her brow. "I have money of my own. You do know women can and do carry coinage with them all the time. Right?"

He stared, dumbfounded, as if this had never occurred to him.

She pressed her lips together as the duke directed the coachman to continue on the road they were heading, and she followed him into the carriage. Moments later, they were moving again.

Finally.

"How much coin do you have on you?" the duke asked, looking down his shoulder at her.

She told him the amount. "And," she added, "unlike you, I didn't stash it somewhere a robber could easily get to."

The duke's attention went to her trunk taking up the other seat.

"Not there," she replied.

"Where is it, then?"

She looked up at him as she patted her thigh over her skirt.

A long pause. "You…have it in a dress pocket?"

"No, silly. I have it strapped to my leg. That way, I have it on my person at all times while also keeping it safely hidden."

He tilted his head. "If you have it that well-hidden, how do you get it off without exposing yourself to everyone?"

"I—" Julia stopped, realizing she hadn't considered that part. She stood up, bending over a bit so that she didn't hit her head on the ceiling. "Avert your eyes, please." With a finger, she made a circle in the air.

The duke obliged and turned his body fully toward his window.

As she propped one foot on the seat, there must have been a divot in the road because the carriage dipped and shook, throwing her into him.

"Oh!" She let out a little yelp. "Sorry!" She pushed off of him and swayed a bit once back up on her feet.

"Are you all right?" He looked up at her, his face reddened.

"Just fine. Yes. Let's be quick about this, shall we?"

As soon as he'd turned away again, she lifted the hem of her skirt all the way up and past her knee, exposing white, lace stockings with a frilly band and a bow on the front. The stockings ended just below her knee and, for comfort during the warmer months, her bloomers weren't long but short, ending above mid-thigh.

At mid-thigh, she was completely bare, and this was where she had affixed the small leather bag.

When she'd set it in place this morning, she'd made sure it had been buckled tight enough to not slip, but loose enough that it did not cut off circulation. But as she went to unfasten the buckle, it wouldn't budge. Letting out a sigh of frustration, she tried again to no avail.

Wiggling it down didn't work, either.

Perhaps being out in the warmth of late afternoon, coupled with the stress of the robbery, had caused her leg to swell just enough that the band couldn't be removed.

With her eyes closed, she dropped her head back. "I can't get it off."

The duke didn't move an inch.

Releasing another puff of air, she tried one final time, but her small fingers merely fumbled at the thick, leather strap. "I need help."

"You're sure?" He didn't sound very confident.

"Yes. Please, turn around and help me. I've tried several times. Unless you find a woman's leg highly offensive and cannot handle seeing one?" In truth, though, she was saying this more to make herself feel better.

He turned around to find the lace-covered leg propped up directly next to him, and his eyes homed in on the bow. He reached out to touch it and rubbed the silky ribbon between his fingers.

She watched him, curious. He had done the same thing with the bow on her dress last night. But, oddly, she didn't want to stop him. There was something rather intimate about it, about watching him do that, and it wasn't unpleasant to her, either.

He seemed to realize what he was doing and cleared his throat, pulling his hand away. Finally, he looked up. "What's the issue?"

"I can't unbuckle it. Or slide it off."

The duke tried unbuckling the leather strap himself, being careful not to touch her bare skin. But it didn't work. "We need something metal and flat." He paused. "Do you have anything like that?"

"I have a pair of small scissors. Bottom corner of that trunk, there's a small canvas bag. It should be in there."

She watched as he gently pushed garments aside and removed the bag. He gave the bag to her and she found the small scissors that she used for trimming errant button threads or hairs or even her nails if necessary. Not knowing what he planned to do with it, she handed it to him.

He took it and tried sliding the closed point of it under the tongue of the strap. "I used to take care of the horse's tack at the farm. Repair or replace anything that became worn." When it didn't slide in, he went to reach out but hesitated. "I'm sorry, but I might touch you."

Her heart faltered at the mere suggestion. "I don't care. Just get it off."

He gave her a nod and both his hands now worked on the strap. "Leather can be finicky, especially if it's not used and is stiff. Like this strap. I would have to get creative with removing parts that refused to come off." With a gentle hand, he managed to wedge the scissor point underneath the leather tongue and began working it out of the metal loop. As he did this, the rough calluses on his palms and fingers brushed over her soft skin and she took in a sharp inhale. The reaction was totally out of her control. But the sensation of his hot, rough hands brushing against such a soft and intimate part of her body—despite the fact there was absolutely no attraction between them whatsoever beyond her mild visual appreciation of him—completely overwhelmed her nerves.

No doubt unaware, he looked up at her. "Does it hurt?"

Her heart was surely about to burst out of her body. "No."

He glanced back down at her bare leg, swallowed, and seconds later, the bag fell away, leaving the skin it had sat upon feeling free but raw.

"Your skin is bright red," he said with genuine concern, and he ran a slow, gentle finger along the line of raw skin.

The sensation of his light touch against the sensitive skin set her aflame.

"I'm fine." She moved away from him to put the scissors away and threw the skirt back over her leg. "It's simply irritated." Afraid to look him in the eye, lest he discover he had set her on fire, she took the bag and sat down, putting her full focus on her window, where she was met by a wonderful sight.

Finally, they had arrived in a village! Relief spread through her.

It shouldn't have surprised her that the duke could cause her heart to race. It was foolish to deny any longer she was physically attracted to him. What woman wouldn't have been? At least it was only visual appreciation and nothing more.

Keeping her distance was crucial, though. He was actively trying to ruin her family. And in turn, she was trying to ruin him. They were at complete odds with each other—enemies—and she had to remember that.

Chapter Eleven

NATHANIEL SIGHED WITH relief as he collapsed in the tiny chair of his tiny room at a tiny inn. It had been an excruciatingly long day, but he was alone and freshly bathed. And it was quiet.

He lifted a glass to his lips and relished the burn of the liquor sliding down his throat. The flames in his fireplace crackled and leaped. It was the perfect way to top off the day.

Lifting a book he had found in the room—some guide about local birds—he tried to read but couldn't focus. After reading the first sentence about the greenfinch for the tenth time and still not grasping it, he set the book to the side and glanced over to the bare wall to his right.

On the other side of that wall was Miss Honeyfield's—*Julia's*—room, and every so often there was the subtle sound of gentle footsteps.

When they had arrived at the inn earlier, Nathaniel had requested they use more familiar forms of address. He hadn't been called anything more than "Nathaniel" or "Mr. Blackwell" for his entire adulthood until his return to England, so for him, it was a trifle. Julia had struggled with it, though, tripping over herself a few times. But after the highway robbery from earlier, she understood the need for obscuring his title. But she had made it clear these more informal names were *only* to be used when they were around people. Proper address was to be used when it was the two of them, such as in the carriage.

But now, they weren't in the carriage and the last thing anyone needed to know was that a duke was staying under the roof of this small country inn. Not that he had anything worth taking any longer.

He chewed on his bottom lip in irritation. He didn't like being beholden to Julia in such a way. It was already tense enough with them stuck traveling together while essentially being rivals.

He still couldn't believe he had put himself in a spot with the mill so badly. He had been so close to brushing his hands of the issue! If only he had known beforehand that the land and building were separate entities. It hadn't even occurred to him that they could have been.

Now, he was in an even tougher position. The taxes on the land were one of the biggest expenses. And Julia refused to let the baron pay what was basically rent to have her father's building sit on his land. Which meant he would have to cover it with his own funds, or the courts would come pounding on his door, making this into an even bigger, more expensive mess than it was.

With a sigh, he ran a hand through his hair. He would have to worry about that later. If he worried about it now, he would be up all night.

As he took another sip of his drink, there were gentle footsteps next door again.

He stared at the blank wall once more and wondered what Julia was doing. He imagined her back to him, bare, while a nightgown slipped over her head and fluttered down, her chestnut hair curling down her back.

"I am depraved," he mumbled to himself.

Clearly, it had been far too long since he'd enjoyed the company of a woman if he was being tempted by his nemesis. Yes, Julia was pretty, but that was nothing more than fact. And as a man, it was only natural for him to be drawn to her from purely appearance.

He hated to admit it (and she would surely kill him if she knew of his depraved thoughts), but seeing that long, shapely leg in tempting white lace, her bare thigh soft and warm in his hand... It had unleashed something in him that he'd been struggling to wrangle back ever since that moment.

"Pathetic," he scolded himself.

And the way he was drawn like a magnet to those blasted bows of hers. He hated bows! What was it about Julia Honeyfield's infuriatingly cheery bows that turned him into a brainless moth going after a flame?

In fact, that was the *perfect* analogy. He was a moth and for some godforsaken reason, Julia, of all women, had become the flame—all because he had neglected a key part of being a man. If he weren't careful and flew toward that flame, he would burn himself.

But still, his fingers had itched to touch the bows. To feel that silk ribbon slide between his fingers, then up to her bare skin.

He had been so taken by her blasted leg and blasted bow, he couldn't even unbuckle the blasted leather bag because he'd been such a blasted, quivering mess.

He buried his face in his hands. If she got even an *inkling* of what was running through his head right now, she would have the upper hand in everything. She would—and could—use it against him.

And he would be left a confused, dizzy, sputtering, panting fool who agreed to whatever she wished.

Nathaniel downed the remainder of the liquor, flew to his feet, and began pacing around the cramped room. He had to keep his distance from her. Physically, that was impossible for the foreseeable future, but mentally, he could keep his distance. He knew how to put up a cold stone wall.

But how to tamper the flame within when she gave it a rush of air?

He froze when it hit him.

Her singing voice.

Good lord, her singing voice had been *traumatic*.

He couldn't help but chuckle to himself, remembering how she'd actually scared off highwaymen—hardened criminals—simply by singing.

Admittedly, that was quite funny.

He came to stop at the window and peered out into the dark, cool spring night. Soon, he would give in to slumber and couldn't wait.

A knock on his door pulled him out of his thoughts. Mr. Moss. They still had to determine what time to leave in the morning and were supposed to figure that out hours ago. He figured Mr. Moss had fallen asleep, but perhaps he had been enjoying being awake in his own room alone as well.

Or perhaps it was housekeeping. All three of them had decided to eat dinner in their rooms as opposed to the dining room.

He opened the door expecting Mr. Moss or a maid but was crestfallen to find Julia standing before him in a silk housecoat, her long hair in a thick braid hanging over one shoulder, staring up at him with those doe eyes, a notebook clutched close.

He scowled. "What do you want?"

"My, my, is someone tired and crabby?" she asked as she walked past him and entered his room.

Uninvited.

"Should you be walking around like that?" he asked.

She gave him a funny look and glanced down at herself. "No one saw me in my housecoat. And anyway, it's pertinent and could not wait for me to redress."

"I didn't invite you in my room."

She fluttered a dismissive hand at him. "I'll only be a moment, I promise. I wanted to show you a few things I don't understand about the mill."

"Why should I help you?" He didn't mean it, but his voice grated with irritation.

She furrowed her brow. "May I remind you, *Nathaniel*, that the only reason I'm here right now is because you got my family sucked into a Blackwell family mess."

He pulled back at that.

"Can we talk about this so you can get your precious rest?" she snapped.

He scowled again. "Fine. Let's get it over with. What do you want to know?"

The rooms unfortunately didn't have much in the way of seating and instead of having a standing conversation like a normal person would, Julia went and sat on the edge of his bed and patted the space next to her.

Moth to a flame.

He recalled her head bobbing like a chicken as she'd screeched out Mozart's aria. Surprisingly, it kept the depraved thoughts her being on his bed would have normally roused.

"This notebook here," she began once he'd sat next to her. Though not too close, he made sure. "It looks like it's payroll."

He resisted the urge to sigh. "That's because it is."

She gave him a bored look before opening the notebook in a random spot. "Right, but, here, look. I'm clearly misreading something. Does this say all of these people get paid three shillings a day? That's not possible."

He studied the paper. That was, in fact, what it said. "Why isn't that possible? That's what it says."

Her face twisted in concentration. "It must mean something else. That is far too low. How could anyone live on that?"

Nathaniel took a moment to consider how to explain without making her feel or seem foolish. "Granted, I'm not an industry man," he began, cautiously. "I have no idea how to run a business. I have no idea how any of it works. Which is why I want to get rid of it. But I did live in a working household, where I worked and received pay for said work."

"You did?"

He nodded. "The thing about farm work is you can be paid

well, but it's very much seasonal and the pay can be unreliable. I lived there, so I had to help year-round, no matter whether there was a boon like during the war, or if there was a drop in demand. It was hard work, but as a whole, I suppose I enjoyed it well enough to stay. We bred work horses, and we had to breed enough to keep the farm running and people getting paid. If we didn't sell enough, or if the horses became ill or were stolen, then guess what was affected first?"

She waited for him to continue.

"Pay. We still needed to take care of the horses above everything else. They were animals reliant on us."

"Of course."

"With factories, a lot of farm families are leaving farmwork behind for the factories. I personally knew people who did that in America."

"But why? I've never understood that."

"It's reliable pay. It's low, but you know what you're going to get each week. You'll get paid even if the barley crops fail. You'll get paid even if a flood washed out all of the season's crops, or a deadly illness spreads through the equine population. It's easier to budget. Less stressful in its own way. That's appealing to a lot of people, to know what one's income will be this week and the next and the one after that and even months from now. Meanwhile, farms can lose an entire season of crops, and the income that would have come with it."

Julia twisted her mouth in thought and studied the page once more. "But why isn't it higher?"

"Honestly, that, I don't know. Maybe three shillings is the going rate for factory work. I have to imagine it is. I'm sure there's a lot we don't understand. But we both know the mill is bleeding itself dry." Without thinking, he placed his hand over hers. "Don't worry too much about it just yet, Miss Honeyfield. There's nothing we can do about it until we get there. I'm sure it will make more sense once we're able to talk to the foreman."

She glanced down at his hand still on hers and looked back

up. The tension in her face eased. "You're right." She smiled. "I could worry myself to tears thinking about it all night."

"There's going to be lots of worry, I'm afraid, in the coming days. Try to save it for when it is needed or unavoidable." He gave her hand a gentle squeeze then pulled it away.

Julia looked up at him with those big doe eyes of hers and bit her lush bottom lip. "I should get back to my room, then." She quickly rose to her feet and grabbed the notebook, then gave him a onceover as he stood. "Nice to see you finally freshened up," she added with a small laugh.

He couldn't help but grin back and started to lead her to the door. "I can't imagine what went through the innkeeper's mind when I walked in earlier covered in road debris."

"I'm sorry I made you so messy earlier."

They stopped at the door and she turned to face him.

"I'm sure I deserved it," he said.

"Oh, you definitely did."

He laughed gently, and a curious thing happened. She blushed.

No. Certainly, that wasn't right. The woman detested him. She could never be charmed by him.

Confounded, he opened the door for her. "Goodnight, Miss Honeyfield."

She paused as she walked through it and turned back to face him. "Goodnight, Your...I mean, Mr. Blackwell."

He wondered, in the way she seemed to be stalling or hesitating, if he was forgetting something. Some obscure rule he should be following.

"Is there anything else?" he asked.

"Oh, no. Sorry. Nothing else. Goodnight." And with that, she was gone.

He waited until he heard her entering her room before shutting his door. As he readied for bed, he absently listened to her soft footsteps padding around next door. If her room's layout was the same as his, then she was climbing into bed.

After a few minutes of silence passed, he was reassured that she was tucked away safe for the evening and fell asleep himself.

Chapter Twelve

THE MORNING AFTER the highway robbery, Julia tried to engage the duke in conversation. Perhaps he had not slept well the night before—the beds had been hard and lumpy, so she wouldn't blame him if that were the case—because he was rather stubborn about *not* talking to her.

At first, she'd tried talking about the mill. After all, that was why they were traveling together in the first place. She was curious as to what it looked like. If it was big or small. Curious what Hamwich looked like, if it was a small village or blended into Manchester seamlessly.

His response to her questions had been, "Not right now, Miss Honeyfield." And that had been it.

For the hour after that, she'd tried asking him questions about America. About horses. She was too afraid to ask about his mother—it remained to be explained why the dowager duchess had not returned to England, so Julia assumed something had happened to her—but she tried everything else she could think of.

He would either grunt in response or redirect.

Finally, he'd said in an annoyingly quiet and deep voice, "I am really looking forward to a quiet drive today."

She'd frowned at him. Why would he want that? There was hardly any space between them. How could two people sit so close to each other for such a long time and not talk?

It wasn't even fathomable, as far as she was concerned.

After the duke had stopped responding to her—which was decidedly quite rude—Julia had given up for the time being and pulled her embroidery from her trunk.

He wanted quiet? Then he would get quiet.

For a whole day, she worked on her embroidery hoop and didn't talk to him, except for a few curt words when necessary. Not in the carriage, not at the inn they stopped at.

Once they had left London, their trip had been through the countryside and this time of year, many beautiful wildflowers were growing. She'd decided to embroider them using her brightest silk floss.

It was a blank canvas and she worked freehand. She didn't follow any patterns, didn't really have anything particular in mind except covering the canvas in wildflowers.

She filled it rather quickly.

And now, today, they were in their third day of travel. Manchester was getting closer.

Julia pulled the needle through and pushed it back in. She wondered what her family was doing right now. Wondered if they missed her. If they were having fun without her. For a moment, she felt a pang of resentment. When she'd set off on this trip, Papa had seemed quite eager for her to go, which had been surprising. Even though taking care of this mill business had been somewhat of a family emergency and she had been the only one willing to handle it, if anyone discovered she and the duke had traveled together without a chaperone, her reputation would be far worse than it already was. But she'd figured Papa had seen how interested she'd been in this mill business, so maybe he'd looked past it for that reason.

Now, she began to wonder if perhaps he was happy to unload the problem of the mill onto someone else, even if that someone else was his own daughter.

But at the time, she had seen the adventure in it. Though she traveled with the duke trying to ruin her family, at least she could be the first to learn all about where he had been the last twenty years and squelch her curiosity about it. It was the hottest gossip of the decade!

But still, the duke remained tight-lipped about it.

Needing to rest her hand from her craft, Julia secured the needle into the fabric and placed the hoop atop her trunk.

Beside her, the duke—*Nathaniel,* he'd gone so far as to insist she start calling him, and she supposed it better for her own sake to pretend they were married when in public—napped soundly. His arms were crossed over his chest, his hatless head leaned back against the seat. A slight furrow dragged his brow. She watched him for a moment. Now that they'd been around each other for several days, her rigid dislike of him had admittedly softened.

But *only* a little.

He still irritated her, just a bit less than before.

She stuck her tongue out at him and felt a bit of satisfaction from that.

Outside, the sky had become quite dark. When had that happened? Pressing her forehead against the glass, she watched the slate-gray clouds drag across the sky like waterlogged blankets.

Then the downpour began.

Never before had she seen rain fall so violently. She couldn't even see the fields any longer.

A sudden bright light turned her vision white for a moment while an earth-shaking boom of thunder followed.

Frightened, she let out a loud gasp and placed her hand over her heart. Hopefully, the coachman and horses were safe.

Nathaniel startled awake. As he looked around with confusion, his face was hard and pale, while his hands clenched in fists. His eyes met hers and she thought she saw fear in them. But once he seemingly realized where he was, his stance softened and color returned to his face.

The urge to ask if he was all right was immediate, but she had to oblige his request that she stop talking. He was a duke, after all.

"My word, look at that storm," he said with a gruff, sleepy voice.

She didn't respond.

"Did this just start?"

She closed her eyes, lifted her chin, and turned away.

"Miss Honeyfield?"

But she ignored him. Just following his ducal demand, after all.

He let out a sigh. "Since you are apparently still not speaking to me—"

She whipped her head around and glared at him. Hard.

Evidently uneasy, he shifted in his seat and lifted his hands. "Very well. Not sure what you're angry at me for. All I was going to say was, this better let up soon or we could have trouble."

⁂

ONE HOUR LATER, they got stuck in the mud.

The rain had not letup at all. Nathaniel had never seen such a storm ever before in his life, and the storms in America could easily get more intense than those here in England.

At the moment, he and Mr. Moss were trying to get the back right carriage wheel free while Julia watched them from the window inside the vehicle. The road had flooded, practically becoming a creek at this point, and there wasn't a dry spot on his shirt or waistcoat as the water sluiced down his face and body.

The two men had managed to find a fallen tree branch large enough to set in front of the sunken wheel and, hopefully, lift it out.

Nathaniel set the branch in place and motioned to Mr. Moss to get the horses moving.

Mr. Moss did and the horses tried, but to no avail.

Nathaniel pushed back the damp hair plastered to his face.

The wheel had sunk too deep. He swore.

While he tried to figure out what to try next in the middle of the isolated, soaking-wet countryside, he looked up at the window and found Julia watching him with a frown.

He scowled back.

She disappeared from the window.

Irritation surged through him. Why had she been acting different lately? This wasn't the first, or the tenth, time he'd been stuck in a rainstorm while trying to solve a problem. And he didn't mind it too much. But still, she was in the dry cabin while he was out here.

Mr. Moss appeared again, just as drenched as Nathaniel. "What do you suppose we do?"

Nathaniel shook his head. "We keep trying. If we can't get it free, one of us will have to go on ahead and find help."

Mr. Moss looked up at the window. Out of the corner of Nathaniel's eye, he could see Julia was back. "I'll volunteer for that."

"Are you sure? I don't mind."

But Mr. Moss nodded.

The carriage door creaked open and Nathaniel sighed.

"Can I be of any help, Mr. Moss?" Julia's suspiciously innocent voice asked.

Mr. Moss looked at Nathaniel with a bit of surprise. "Erm, Miss Honeyfield, I don't think so."

"Could you please tell His Grace that perhaps if someone pushed the back of the carriage while the horses pulled, then it would roll over the log?"

Mr. Moss met Nathaniel's eye again with a questioning look.

"Thank you, Miss Honeyfield," Nathaniel said, making sure annoyance rang clear in his voice. "I was about to try that."

"Oh, excellent. Glad I could help." She paused. "Mr. Moss."

Mr. Moss leaned over to him once the carriage door had slammed shut. "Why isn't she talking to you?"

"I have no idea."

"Did you do something?"

Nathaniel gave him an incredulous look as rain poured down his face.

The older man smiled, his cheeks round. "May I offer a bit of advice, Your Grace?"

"It's pouring out and we're frolicking around in the mud. But, yes, let's stop for some advice."

Mr. Moss didn't pick up on the sarcasm and pulled Nathaniel off to the side for extra privacy. "Excellent," Mr. Moss said. "Why don't you, I don't know, apologize? Sometimes the Mrs. gets in a tizzy about something. I've been married twenty-five years, and I've come to learn that sometimes a man doesn't know what he did, but the wife has every genuine reason to be mad about it."

Nathaniel crossed his wet arms. "It sounds to me like you've been propagandized by your Mrs."

Mr. Moss let out a bark of laughter. "It's all part of keeping up the marital bliss, Your Grace. And she's a fine lady."

Nathaniel paused. "Who is, your wife?"

The coachman laughed again. "No! I mean, yes, but also your lady friend. I know I'm up front all day long, but when we stop for the night, you always watch her walk away with a funny, wistful expression on your face. I guess I just assumed, and seeing how she's here without a chaperone—"

Nathaniel pinched the bridge of his nose. "Whatever you are assuming is incorrect, I assure you. The woman drives me utterly mad. I am merely reassuring myself that she is heading to her room and not doubling back to pester me further."

But to Nathaniel's irritation, Mr. Moss merely chuckled and shook his head. "If you insist, Your Grace."

The pair returned to the carriage as more thunder cracked above. Julia now watched them from the open door with a curious expression.

Not curious enough, however, to break her wall of silence against him and ask what they had been talking about. Maybe said silence wasn't so bad, after all.

Nathaniel and Mr. Moss agreed on the next plan of action. Mr. Moss would be up by the horses, while Nathaniel pushed from the back.

As Nathaniel headed toward the back of the carriage, he barked at Julia to get back inside. She let out a loud "hmmph!" and slammed the door shut.

Finally.

At the back of the carriage, he positioned himself to push. Once again, her face appeared at the window to watch him.

Irritation bloomed. He didn't care for being watched like this, as if he were on stage for her amusement. He shot her a narrow-eyed look.

And she gave one back to him.

For some reason, he found this amusing, even though it should have added to his ire. But he refused to let the amusement show.

He readied his position and shouted over the loud storm to Mr. Moss. The horses began to move. He grit his teeth as he pushed with all his might.

It still didn't move.

As he took in deep, restorative breaths he considered his next move. What if he tried lifting it?

After Caroline's death, he'd made a point to be as strong as he physically could be in case he was ever needed for rescue. After leaving the farm, he'd had to improvise at his home with logs and other heavy objects.

This seemed to be just the kind of situation where that strength was needed.

He glanced up at Julia and watched her for a moment, hoping he could get them out of here and into the next village posthaste. Manchester would not be today's destination, unfortunately.

Julia might not have realized this yet, but with as muddy as the roads were, they were going to be stuck in the next town until the roads were safe to drive over.

That could be a few days.

As he looked at her, she made a show of pulling out a fake pocket watch and tapping at its face.

This time, he couldn't help but grin.

Julia's mouth opened with surprise, but then she grinned back.

When the horses started pulling again, Nathaniel mustered as much strength as he could and gripped the bottom edge of the carriage. With all of his concentration on the task, he lifted and pushed as hard as he could. His feet sunk into the mud. His legs and arms shook violently.

This wasn't going to work.

But then he felt movement. With a renewed spirit, he yelled out and lifted as hard as he could.

The carriage jutted forward a few paces and came to a stop while Mr. Moss made a celebratory *whooping* sound. The stuck wheel was now free.

Julia leaped out of the carriage, ran over, and jumped on him, causing him to stumble back. Mud from him smeared all over her dress.

"You did it!" she shouted, ending with a joyful laugh.

She placed a big, wet kiss on his cheek.

Nathaniel froze, as he had not been expecting that.

Humor glinted in her eyes as she continued to look up at him and then turned to thank Mr. Moss, placing a kiss on his cheek as well. Mr. Moss turned bright red and thanked her sheepishly.

Once they were on their way again, Nathaniel looked over at Julia and found her working on her embroidery. She was wet and muddy from the rain now, too, but didn't make a complaint about it.

He was growing weary of traveling. Perhaps being stuck in an inn for a few days wouldn't be so bad.

Chapter Thirteen

THE ROAD EVENTUALLY came upon a river, turned, and followed parallel to the waterway, leading them to a quaint, little village called Cloverly. Though the heavy rain continued, Julia was able to see the carriage pass numerous stone cottages with abundant gardens, smoke curling from their chimneys. Eventually, the cottages turned into small shops: a butcher, a tailor, a dressmaker's shop, and finally, an inn.

When they stopped, both Julia and Rivenhall let out sighs of relief. Both were wet and cold and muddy—him much more than her—and desperate for any semblance of warmth.

Inside, they were met with an inn packed tight. Loud groups of drenched people huddled together, tried to talk over each other to the innkeeper.

"Oh, dear, I hope they have enough rooms," Julia said, now worried. Surely, they wouldn't have to find another town in this weather! That would be foolish and dangerous.

"Looks like we're not the only people trying to get out of this storm," the duke said. He placed a hand on her midback, leading her through the crowd. "I'm sure it will be fine."

Julia, however, wasn't as convinced.

When it was their turn to talk to the innkeeper—who was quite flustered at this point, his white hair messy from stress—all he said when he looked at them was, "Married?"

Julia frowned. "Are *we* married? No. No, absolutely not!" She laughed heartily but immediately realized her error. "We are siblings, of course!"

The innkeeper adjusted his glasses. "Well, I've only got one room left. Next!"

"Wait!" The duke pulled the man's attention back. "I want that room. For my coachman."

"All right." The innkeeper nodded. "There's another inn just up the road. You may have better luck there, but I can't make any promises."

"How far is the next town?" Julia asked. If nearby, then that would tamper her worry. Her shivering was out of hand now, and her voice shook when she talked.

But she was crestfallen to learn the next big town, which would have a better chance of vacancies, happened to be Manchester. And travel took two hours on a good day.

Back in the carriage, while Mr. Moss argued with Nathaniel outside over taking the only available room, she tried her best not to cry. Home felt impossibly far away. She missed her family. She was cold and tired and hungry.

This had started out as something different, fun. Kind of an adventure. But now she grew rather sick of it.

"Miss Honeyfield." The duke's deep voice pulled her out of her misery as he climbed into the carriage. "We'll figure it out."

"But what if—"

"None of that." After taking his seat, he placed a hand on her knee, giving it a gentle squeeze while the carriage jerked into moving. Oddly, he did manage to comfort her the tiniest bit. "Save that worry for when it's needed. Remember? Mr. Moss is taking us to one more inn to check. Perhaps this time, though, we start with the siblings explanation."

"I'm so cold." Her teeth chattered as infuriating tears began welling in her eyes against her will. "I'm miserable and mad at you and so blasted cold!"

Rivenhall studied her for a moment and began lifting his arm—was he going to put it *around* her?—but then the carriage came to a halt.

He pulled away and put his attention out of the door's window. "You stay here. I'll go in quick to see if they have anything. If they don't, we'll figure it out. But don't worry until then."

She wrapped her arms around herself as he climbed out, closed the door, then gave her a small smile through the door window.

And then, he disappeared inside the building.

Julia shivered as she sat in the cabin, the sound of rain pelting the carriage unrelenting.

From her side, the window looked out at the river. It seemed to be moving a bit more swiftly than it had when they had first come across it sometime ago. Of course, there was significantly more water in it now than there had been before. She began to wonder if flooding would be an issue, but it didn't look anywhere near that risk yet.

And surely, this rain would stop soon. It had been a downpour for nearly half a day now.

With a shudder, she leaned forward to get a better look at the inn. It reminded her of the little stone cottages she'd spotted when they'd first come through this town. Except, as an inn, it was much larger. Most of all, she hoped that they had two rooms available, but she wouldn't complain if the rooms were bigger than the last few had been. She was growing weary of hard, lumpy beds and cramped quarters.

The duke seemed to be taking a while. Hopefully, that was a good sign.

Unless he was asking for directions to another inn.

Julia rolled her head from side to side to stretch her neck, trying to keep her worry down like he had said she should.

Though for part of their travel, she'd refused to talk with him, Julia was surprised at how quickly she and the duke had grown comfortable in each other's presence.

He still fit his nickname Sir Crabby, but she was beginning to realize he wasn't often in a sour mood like she had assumed. He just looked like it.

She hated to admit it, but he was growing on her a little.

Emphasis on *a little*.

The duke was still, for all intents and purposes, her business rival, though she technically didn't own the mill, her father did. But she *was* the family business representative.

The door to the carriage flung open, revealing a harried Duke of Rivenhall. Julia inhaled sharply and straightened in her seat.

"We're married," the duke forced the words out in a low voice. He briefly looked back over his shoulder. "You're Mrs. Honeyfield and I'm Mr. Nathaniel Honeyfield. I couldn't use my name, as it would be too recognizable. So, we're using yours."

"I thought we were going to say we were siblings!"

But he didn't respond. Instead, he disappeared from the doorway and a young man of about fourteen years with a gap between his front teeth popped his head in.

"Hello, Mrs. Honeyfield!" the young fellow said with exuberant cheer. "What a day!"

"I suppose." What was going on?

"Come on out, then." He waved her out. "I'm Benny Smith, and I'm to bring your trunks inside." As she emerged, Benny Smith made far too upbeat chatter about the weather. She exchanged as pleasant a word or two as she could and headed over to the duke, or *Mr. Honeyfield*, who waited for her under the awning waving goodbye to Mr. Moss. "I demand to know what is going on," she said low.

"Upstairs." The duke held a shuttered expression on his face.

With a huff of annoyance, Julia spun away from him and entered the inn.

A blast of warm air hit her—the most incredible feeling to her chilled, wet body—and she shivered violently in response.

The duke led her past a crowd surrounding the innkeeper, a middle-aged fellow with a shock of orange hair and not one piece of it out of place, and then past what looked to be a tavern and dining room, to a creaky stairwell leading up to the second floor. Stopping at Room 25, he put the key into the keyhole and turned it with a loud click.

Eager to get out of her wet clothes, Julia rushed in to find an inviting room, its fireplace already roaring with fresh logs. A large, plush bed sat against the back wall, and there was even a sitting area near the fireplace.

It was much nicer than the last few rooms she'd had to stay in.

"Oh, this is *very* nice," she said as she angled over to the fireplace. She extended her palms out toward the fire and closed her eyes with a smile. "I could get quite used to this."

The sound of trunks being set down caused her to turn. The duke handed Benny Smith a tip—using her money—and Benny shut the door behind him, leaving Julia alone with the duke.

"Do you…need something?" she asked. It was curious that he remained in the room. Perhaps he wished to discuss business, but couldn't that wait until they had changed their clothes at least? "There is nothing I would love more in the moment than to spend even more time with you." The words were clearly sarcastic and caused the duke to press his mouth in a tight line. "But if you wish to talk business, I must change first. So, please leave. Thank you."

The duke's white shirt and dark waistcoat were covered in mud splatter, so he had put his dry suit jacket over the ensemble before he went into the inn to get their rooms. But now, he was removing it.

"Yes. About that."

The way he said it didn't sit right with her. She looked over to their trunks and counted out four of them.

But she only had three.

"Excuse me," she said, "but why did Barry put your trunk in here?"

The duke let out a long sigh as he laid his jacket over a small table. "Because this is my room, too."

There was a long pause before she let out loud laughter and crossed over to her trunks. She snapped open one of the lids and began removing clean clothing. "You are a very funny man. But I am not in the mood for jests right now. Especially jests such as that one. As you may imagine, I'm not exactly in good humor at the moment."

"Miss Honeyfield, I wasn't jesting."

Horrified at this realization, Julia spun around lightning quick. "I am not spending the night in the same room as you, Your Grace. It simply cannot and will not happen."

He rubbed a hand over his stubbled cheek. "Yes. About that—"

"Oh, no. Oh, no, no, no." Julia set her clean and dry clothing on the bed before stomping across the floor toward the door.

"Where are you going?" Nathaniel called after her.

"I'm getting you your own room. I don't care what the cost is!"

"Miss Honeyfield, wait!"

But she didn't wait. She stomped down the hallway, stomped down the stairs, and then came around a corner to where the innkeeper's desk was. The loud throng of people was still there.

Coming to a halt, she wondered if she should come back later. But that wouldn't do; she needed to change! How could she do that with *him* in her room?

"But, Mr. Baker, sir!" one of the women in the throng cried out and gripped the top of the innkeeper's desk. The innkeeper appeared to be seated in a chair because all Julia could see was the top of his orange head. "I need somewhere to stay. Every place I've checked within miles of here is completely booked up!"

"I realize this, ma'am." The innkeeper, Mr. Baker, was likely doing his best to be understanding. "But I am completely booked up. I'm so very sorry, believe me!"

The crowd continued its clamoring, numerous people arguing back with him.

A break in the crowd allowed Julia to see him better. He was younger than the last innkeeper, perhaps in his mid-forties. "You could try heading south down the road again. A few hours south of here, you might find something!"

For a moment, Julia hesitated, but she was a guest, after all, so she went to take a step forward despite the odd looks people gave her filthy clothes.

A hand lay on her shoulder, causing her to tense. She didn't need to turn around to know it was the duke's.

"Julia." He leaned down to her ear, causing her skin to prickle. "Can you not see the man is busy right now?"

"I don't care." She pulled her shoulder away from Nathaniel and looked up to find his jaw clenched. Leaving him behind, she stepped over to the innkeeper, who did his best to smile warmly to her, but his eyes were weary. "Ah, Mrs. Honeyfield. Is everything all right?"

"Y-Yes," she stammered and paused. The crowd continued to clamor. "I was wondering—"

"I've already talked to your husband about it, Mrs. Honeyfield. Don't you worry."

She furrowed her brow. "About what?"

The innkeeper glanced at the crowd and then motioned to her to get closer, glancing at the duke, who was standing off to the side. "He's already reserved the room for the next three days to ensure you don't lose it."

"Three days!"

The red-haired innkeeper frowned and scratched at his jaw. "Yes. Did he not tell you? To get to Manchester from here, you have to keep taking that road out there, north. And it goes over that river." He nodded toward the entrance. "But there's a bridge in town that falls into disrepair when we get heavy rain."

A bridge that fell apart during a rainstorm? Who was in charge of such a thing?

"I don't understand," she said stupidly.

The innkeeper glanced back over his shoulder. "I'm sorry. I

can't talk long right now. But, with the roads being impassable and the bridge being out of service, you're going to be here until it's repaired."

"*What?*" she nearly shouted. But before she could argue with him—as if that would solve anything—that hand fell upon her shoulder again, causing her teeth to clench.

"Come now, sweeting. I know you're chilled to the bone but, look, a maid passed out warm cloths." It was the duke's annoying voice. He dropped a wet, hot cloth in her hand before making a show of cleaning his own dirty hands off with his own cloth. "Let's go get you dried off."

"Oh, you would like that, wouldn't you?" she snapped back while furiously scrubbing her hands. Wait, had he called her "*sweeting*"? Two could play that game, and he was sorely underestimating her right now in her anger. "My little pookie muffin."

The duke made a choking noise but cleared his throat to cover it up. "Now, now, I know travel puts you in a sour mood—"

"Pookie muffin, you are always so terrible at reading my moods." She ran a slow finger down his chest while pouting. "This isn't a sour mood." Training her eyes up to him with a coy expression, she found him staring down at her with reddening cheeks. *Good.*

Julia went to walk past him, but he grabbed her free hand instead, forcing her to stop. She whipped around, angry, only to be met by a challenging glint in his eye.

With fluid grace, the duke brought the back of her hand up to his lips. His bare hand felt hot, the calluses rough against her own soft hand. A woman with less control would have faltered, but she gave him a look of smugness. A kiss on the back of her hand was hardly anything at all.

But he let his lips linger upon her skin, and he refused to turn his smoldering eyes away.

Through her pounding heart, she gave him a narrow-eyed look. It occurred to Julia that she could tell him to stop, and he would, likely with an apology, even.

But in a strange way, she didn't want him to stop.

Instantly, she regretted that decision, though, when he broke eye contact to look down at her hand.

What was he doing now?

Gently, he turned her hand over. Her fingers curled into her palm. And he kissed the inside of her wrist.

Without warning, she gasped, giving away how true her surprise was. The duke, making it worse, volleyed her reaction with that deep, raspy laugh that made her stomach do funny flips.

And then he let her go.

She pulled her hand against her chest and gripped it as if it had been injured. It hadn't been, of course, unless there were truly burn marks left behind. It sure felt like there were. "There are *people* here," she hissed, tempted to throw her wet cloth at him. But the Duke of Rivenhall merely clasped his hands together behind his back, stood up straight, and gave her a smug, triumphant smile.

The infuriating man utterly glowed in the moment, knowing that he had flustered her first.

"Why, Mrs. Honeyfield," he replied, "we're just a happily married couple. Doing happily married couple things."

"You're a pig," she whispered.

He laughed heartily.

Remembering there was a crowd, Julia looked over to find them all watching the show. Some of the people looked on with shock, while others covered their mouths, clearly trying not to giggle.

But upon being noticed by Julia, they all turned back to the innkeeper and the cacophony of arguing and begging resumed.

"I, um…" The humor on the duke's face fell away. He looked off to the side. "I asked them to prepare a hot bath in the room for you. Go ahead on up there. Warm up, change, whatever you want." He held his hand out presumably for the now dirty cloth. "I'll be up in an hour."

She frowned. Why would he send a bath up for her? She gave him the cloth to return. "But you're in a far worse state than myself."

"While I will admit I've never seen a rainstorm quite like this before, being soaked in water and mud was once a frequent occurrence for me." He glanced over at the room with the tavern. "A drink can warm me up for about an hour, and then I'll come change and wash up." He looked back over to her. "Does that sound agreeable to you?"

She shifted. Why was he being so considerate? Then again, it was only a hot bath.

Which *did* equate to heaven in the moment.

Was he trying to put her guard down for some nefarious reason?

She looked him over with skepticism but found no sign this was anything other than a thoughtful gesture. "Thank you," she said cautiously.

He gave a small nod. "I'm sorry about all of this. But that was quite literally the last room within hours of this place. We had to take it. And they would never let an unmarried man and woman room together.

"And you heard what he'd said, the roads are impassable now. We're going to have to pretend to be married for a few days now that we will be around people. But then afterward, we can go on resuming our usual mutual dislike of each other."

Though he did say that playfully. But the way it made her feel left her wondering if maybe she was, kind of, sort of, growing a tiny bit fonder of Nathaniel.

Chapter Fourteen

THE INN'S TAVERN smelled of smoking pipes and cold humidity, and the hum of low conversation intertwined with the sound of rain that permeated the spacious room. Tudor-style windows, with small diamond panes, lined one wall and looked out toward the dark-gray sky pressed against the emerald-green grass of the English countryside.

Nathaniel went over to the oak bar and ordered a whiskey, then made his way to the large fireplace in the dining area. There were several tables nearby, but all were occupied. One such table was occupied by a man with round spectacles in as much of a sorry state as Nathaniel.

The man noted Nathaniel and briefly raised his glass in acknowledgement, as if to say, *"Same story here, lad,"* before returning his attention to the fire.

Chilled and dirty, Nathaniel was glad there was room to stand by the fire at the very least. Maybe he'd even dry off a bit.

Nathaniel took a sip of his drink and was glad for the small comfort it provided. There had been many a time when he had worked through the rain on the horse farm, his clothes drenched in mud and water (or worse), so his tolerance for it was much higher compared to that of others.

"They say it will be down for a week," a nearby man's voice

said, capturing Nathaniel's attention. "As if this has never happened before!"

Another man replied. "The blasted thing is always breaking down at the sight of one raindrop. That bridge was probably built in Shakespeare's day! Even the nails on it are rotten. And it's our only way to head north to Manchester. Do you know one family here that doesn't rely on that? We don't even have locomotives out this way yet. Which is another thing!"

Apparently, the inn's tavern was popular with the locals.

"All right, Henry, that's enough. Can't you see this isn't the time?"

But Henry wasn't having it. "I send an ungodly amount of grain up north on a weekly basis. I was supposed to send some out today, but obviously—" There was a pause. Nathaniel didn't turn to see but assumed the man was indicating the windows. "And so, what, I'm out a week of that income because no one wants to fix the bridge?"

"It's not so easy, Henry." This time, it was a woman. "We're a small, rural village. Replacing a wooden bridge with a stone bridge is not only significant work, but how many weeks would we not be able to head north while it was constructed? You would be even more unhappy then."

Nathaniel lost interest in the conversation. He'd known about the bridge when he'd reserved the room. The innkeeper had warned him that every time it rained, something on the bridge fell apart and would have to be fixed. Nathaniel, of course, had no idea how big this bridge was, but an all-wood bridge on a well-traveled road seemed like a recipe for disaster.

But, like the woman had said, replacing it with stone would be a headache in its own right.

Thankfully, that wasn't a concern of his. Hopefully, the bridge would be repaired soon enough, though, so he and Julia could move on to deal with their own problems.

Nathaniel took another sip of his drink as his mind went to Julia. The fury that had gone through that woman when she had realized they were stuck sharing a room for the next few days and had to pretend to be married for an extended time—it admittedly amused him despite his own frustration with the situation.

He smiled a bit to himself as he recalled their playful little tiff just outside the tavern room. He'd probably taken it a little too far when he'd kissed the inside of her wrist. But the way she'd reacted—it was almost as if…

No.

They were merely blowing off a little steam by irritating each other. That look in her eye hadn't been heat. It'd been annoyance.

Though his promise to himself to keep his distance from her was now a spectacular failure, it didn't mean he was attracted to her.

He frowned to himself.

That was also a bit of a lie; there was no use in pretending otherwise. Julia was pleasing enough to look at—he knew this. And he might even have liked the rare moments he was able to touch her, as brief and innocent as the moments had been.

As he took a sip of the whiskey, he watched the flames in the fireplace dance and spark. Somewhere above him, the fire in his room was doing the same dance.

And in front of that fire was a bathtub.

His mind meandered over to what Julia might have been doing in the moment. Perhaps she was still undressing. Unhooking the small buttons on the front of her bodice. Or letting the skirt drop to her ankles.

Then those lace stockings she wore. The short bloomers. The rest of the contraptions women wore under their dresses.

Perhaps a tavern maid was there helping her and would take the clothing away to launder.

Julia would then be alone and would remove the pins securing her hair. Her chestnut hair would tumble down her back, sliding over her shoulder as she stepped into the tub, her toes and dainty little foot first, her long, shapely leg following. Once in, she would lower slowly and the waterline would slide up past her knees, her thighs, her bare hips, and tapered waist. Up, the warm waterline would go.

Knowing her, she would then make some kind of noise of satisfaction as the hot water engulfed her chilled body. She always had to make sounds.

The thought of Julia Honeyfield making noises of pleasure caused heat to throb through his veins.

Realizing that he was now fantasizing about *Julia Honeyfield*, Nathaniel threw back the remainder of his glass and shivered as the burn slid down his throat. He closed his eyes. Christ, he was a wreck. This was now the second time he'd thought about Julia in a way that would send her open palm across his face if she had the slightest inkling of his thoughts.

No, he was not attracted to Julia. He was attracted to *women*, and she happened to be the one nearby. He was never one to be overtly sexual like so many other men he knew. Often, he didn't see what his friends saw in their wives or, when they'd been younger, their sweethearts. He never "lady hopped" as his friends had so crassly called it.

Which of his friends had been the one to coin that term? Ah, yes, Will Barnes.

Will Barnes. Now that was a name he had not thought of in a very long time.

Will, in fact, had been the one who'd introduced him to Caroline.

Immediately, Nathaniel had known Caroline had been different. He had finally understood why his friends lost their heads over women. She had been kind and beautiful, and he had fallen in love with her because of it. They had ended up being together for many years and had shared many intimacies. But despite being from the American working class, which didn't concern itself about the matter anywhere near as much as his fellow English peers, she adamantly wanted to wait until marriage for them to lie together.

Of course, that had never ended up happening.

Nathaniel returned to the watery present and looked down at his empty glass. If anyone, least of all Julia, found out that he had never been with a woman in that regard, he would be a bigger laughingstock than her father, Lord Odstone.

But it *did* explain his attraction to Julia. She was pretty. And ever-present. And maddening. So maddening! His body took the fiery annoyance he felt toward her in a totally incorrect way because he had deprived himself of that intimacy his entire life and mistook annoyance for desire.

Glancing at a nearby clock, he realized that the hour had passed. He was growing tired of being in wet clothes. It was his turn to change.

Chapter Fifteen

JULIA HAD NO idea how long she had been asleep when the sound of the door stirred her, but it only woke her the smallest amount.

The bed was so cozy. The room so warm. Her clothes so nice and dry.

With her eyes remaining closed, she snuggled further into her pillow. Somewhere in the depths of her mind, she recalled she had only put on short bloomers and a chemise before giving in to the temptation of a warm, dry bed.

It was probably the inn's housekeeper or maid coming to take her muddy dress.

Slumber soothed her mind again.

"Julia? I mean, Miss Honeyfield?" a pleasant man's voice asked.

She sighed, her eyes remaining closed. "Mmm?"

"Are you awake?"

"Not really," she replied, her voice scratchy. "Go away and don't bother me."

A throat cleared. "You're, ah, naked."

Her eyes tried to fly open, but she squinted because her vision was blurry. "What?" She sat up, horrified and confused. At some point, she had kicked the blanket off, but she was very much *not* nude. She squinted again in order to see the towering, dark form standing directly next to her side of the bed. "If you consider this nude, then what did I see of you back in London?" she asked.

But then she briefly looked down at the low-cut chemise to make sure she hadn't fallen out of it unknowingly.

Thankfully, she hadn't.

As Julia rubbed her eyes, Nathaniel moved away and went to his trunk, snapping it open. "Do you mind if I change?" he asked from across the room. "I can't stand another minute in these clothes."

"I'm going back to sleep." Her head hit the pillow once again. After shutting her eyes tight, it took her a moment to comprehend what he had said and realize that she had not in fact told him she did mind if he changed now. Too lazy to move, however, she decided she would simply stay put and not peek at whatever he was doing.

Really, the duke's current activities were none of her business.

But then, the blanket pulled up over her, presumably to cover her up. Was he truly that offended by her?

She opened her eyes again and moved to say something snide, but then he put a hand to her forehead and frowned. "Are you not feeling well?"

Annoyed, she pushed his hand away. "I'm fine, Your Grace. Just tired and comfortable." She gave him a fake, forced smile. "Why, are you worried about me?"

"I'm responsible for you. If anything happens to you—"

"I'm responsible for myself, thank you." Her nose flared.

"I'm sure that would be a great comfort to your father if you died of fever. Right before he murders me."

She considered this scenario. She could see it. "I'm fine. Merely taking an unplanned nap."

"All right."

Though she was secretly grateful to have the blanket back over her—though she would never in a million years admit that to him—she closed her eyes, preparing to fall back to sleep.

Instead, her curious mind focused on noise. Not slumber.

She could tell by the rustle of fabric that the duke was digging through his trunk seeking out a change of clothes. The trunk snapped shut, and the sound of wet clothing being removed and dropping to the floor made her shut her eyes tighter.

She had already seen him nude once. No need to see that again.

Do hurry up, Nathaniel, she thought to herself.

But then she heard the water splash.

Oh, no, was he taking a bath?

"What are you doing?" she asked, horrified.

"The water isn't yet completely cold. I'm covered in mud. May as well wash off. Do I need to ask you to leave the room?" He spoke in a teasing voice.

Obviously, he was trying to irritate her. He lived for it.

But why did he dislike her so much? Was it the mill business, or was there more to it?

Oh, it didn't matter. She didn't care. Most people disliked her, anyway.

Except, deep down, she *did* care that Nathaniel disliked her.

Best to ignore that unexpected realization. Because hadn't Lady Georgette set her sights on him?

Lady Georgette possessed a better social position as a viscount's daughter, and far better physical attributes. Much more appealing in every way to Nathaniel than Julia.

The gentle lapping of water told her he was now in the bathtub. Water was probably dripping down his bare skin, possibly tanned from the sun, over the corded muscles of his back—

She laid a hand on her forehead. Maybe she *was* fevered. This was madness, utter madness!

Her memory of the duke with just a towel flashed in her memory. Her brain was obviously exaggerating everything she remembered because none of *that* seemed possible.

It was silly to get all flamed and bothered over something her mind had embellished, so she decided to very, very gently open one eye just enough to prove to herself she was wrong.

He was in the bath, his back to her.

She opened both eyes and secretly watched as he rubbed a bar of soap into his hands, set the soap to the side, then rubbed his hands over and through his black hair, gently massaging the suds into his tresses and scalp.

Every single muscle flexed in his arms with the movement. His shoulders and biceps. His forearms. Even his hands.

Absolutely mesmerized now, Julia watched as he continued washing himself, running the soap bar all over his body, rubbing the suds with a washcloth in his large, masculine hands.

Oh, to feel those hands sliding over her.

He leaned forward to rinse his hair in the water and then came back up.

Horrified by the wildness of her mind and how she had zero control—the size of him and his muscles were, unfortunately, quite accurate in her memory—she slammed her eyes shut.

This wasn't acceptable in any way. And he would be furious if he knew she was watching him.

"Oh, blast," he mumbled.

"What's the matter?" she replied, her eyes still tightly shut.

"Um…" There was the sound of water splashing. "Do you have the faintest idea where a towel is?"

Inwardly, she sighed. Sitting up, she used a flattened palm to shield her view of him. "Yes, just a second." She crossed the room to where the inn had placed the towels, grabbed one, and angled over to the tub while covering her eyes.

As she held out the towel, her heartbeat began to quicken.

Which was silly. This was Nathaniel, the most irritating man in the entire world.

A man who was also very handsome and who kissed the inside of her wrist sensually with soft lips.

She cleared her throat as he grabbed the towel and there was the sound of him rising out of the water.

The scent of the soap swirled around them. She backed away and hurried to the bed, throwing herself atop it, facedown.

"I don't know about you," his voice said from somewhere. She wasn't about to discover from where. "But I'm absolutely famished. Should we go downstairs for dinner after this?"

"That sounds good," she replied with a high-pitched voice. She grimaced at herself. It sounded far too forced and cheery.

Once he said it was, "Safe for her to look," adding an annoying laugh after, she quickly dressed and put up her hair. Trying to move her mind off of the Duke of Rivenhall in a bathtub, she forced conversation.

"About the sleeping arrangements," she began.

"What about them?"

"I refuse to share a bed with you. I don't care that you're not really my middle-class husband and are, in fact, the Duke of Rivenhall. I will not share a bed with you."

"I…wasn't expecting you to."

She looked over to him as she put up the last tuft of hair. "Oh." She paused. "You're sure?"

Nathaniel shrugged on a clean, dark waistcoat. She hated how nice he looked in dark colors. It should look severe and displeasing. "I was planning on sleeping on the floor near the fire. The bathtub is there right now, but they'll remove it once we go down to dinner."

She eyed the spot. "You can't sleep on a bare floor. That's ridiculous."

"Why? I've slept in worse places."

Did she even want to know? Of course she did. "Where?"

"Floor of a horse stable. I can't even count how many times I've done that. Mares giving birth in the middle of the night, or if one's ill. We took shifts, but I still had to sleep on a stone or hay-covered floor plenty of times."

Julia tried to imagine what Lady Georgette would think of that. "Sounds uncomfortable."

He gave her a small, crooked smile before rubbing the towel

over his hair one last time. Combing it back with his fingers, a strand fell forward over his forehead. She resisted the urge to push it back.

"I still don't think I can, in good conscience, let you sleep on the floor," Julia said, still not convinced.

"If I have to, I'll sleep in that chair." He tossed the towel to the side and lifted his dark suit jacket and shrugged it on over his shirt and waistcoat. "Now. I don't know about you, but I can't go on longer without food." He held out his elbow to her. "Shall we?"

Chapter Sixteen

NATHANIEL WAS CRESTFALLEN to find the dining area packed. Unlike earlier, the low chatter now was raucous. Laughter filled the air. Chairs squeaked as people adjusted their seats. Waitresses were flitting around the room laying out plates.

The mouth-watering scent of roasting meat filled the air.

"It smells like heaven." Julia had her small hand in the crook of his elbow. She looked up at him with wide doe eyes. "I didn't realize how truly hungry I've been until now."

"Neither did I. And I haven't eaten well in days." Because of his daily activity level, his appetite was usually larger than most, and it hadn't been fully satiated in days.

Nathaniel led Julia through the room, but he quickly began to feel nervous trying to find a table. Everyone watched them walk by, looking like fools while circling through the room, lost.

But there weren't any tables available. And they'd had to vacate their room for the removal of the tub, so no dining up there tonight. He clenched his jaw. What would he do?

A movement out of the corner of his eye caught his attention.

"Oh, look, someone is waving us over," Julia said while turning him to see.

It was the muddy gentleman he had seen earlier by the fireplace, with the round glasses. The fellow was now clean as well, and he appeared to occupy one table with, presumably, his wife and two empty chairs.

"I'd rather not dine with strangers." Nathaniel lowered his face down to speak privately to Julia. The day was already taxing enough. Now he had to force conversation with people? All he wanted right now was to eat with Julia in peace and then go back upstairs.

"Don't be silly," Julia replied in a low voice. "We're going to be here for a few days, aren't we? Do you want me to talk to *you* the whole time?"

He frowned. "No, I really don't."

This pulled a laugh from her, causing a surprising leap of pleasure within him. "Then let's go make some friends, shall we?"

She went to move forward, but nerves forced him to remain in place.

"What's the matter?" She looked up, eyebrows drawn together.

"I'm not the most sociable person, especially with people I don't know."

"What do you mean? You're a d—" She caught herself. "You spend almost every day socializing with people."

"Yes, I do. And it takes a long time for me to warm up to others. It's also why I need to have my quiet evenings to unwind. Otherwise, I'd go mad."

She twisted her mouth in thought. "How about this? We go and eat with them and then, if you decide you've had enough and must leave, just give me a little nudge. I'll stay behind. That way, there're no prolonged goodbyes or too many questions for you."

Relief flooded him. Would she really do that? It sounded awful to him, but Julia was so opposite from him that maybe it wouldn't even faze her. "As long as you're all right with that, I would appreciate it."

She confirmed that it was nothing at all and they headed over to the couple, who looked to be in their forties or so, not baby-faced any longer, but any lines on their faces were just starting to show. The man with the round spectacles and thinning hair stood and reached out to shake Nathaniel's hand heartily, grinning widely. "You're that fellow I saw looking utterly lost earlier!"

Nathaniel felt heat spread over him.

Julia gave his forearm a barely perceptible squeeze. "Oh, my husband is always completely lost whenever I'm not around! If it weren't for me, he'd never be able to find his shoes in the morning!"

Nathaniel was about to ask her what in the blazes she was talking about, but the couple chuckled.

And then the wife, her brown hair tied back in a low knot, threw in her own anecdote. "Earlier, my husband said to me, 'Martha, I'm going for a walk to get some fresh air.' He said this from his chair next to a window—I had to remind him we were nearly underwater!"

As the group laughed again, Nathaniel glanced down to Julia. He gave her a small smile as a way to silently thank her, and he swore she reddened.

The couple invited them to sit and introduced themselves—Joe and Martha White, in Cloverly to visit family. Martha—the pair insisted on dropping formalities—had grown up here, and her parents still lived nearby. But, according to her, it was best for everyone if they slept in different buildings.

They ordered their meals—roast beef—and the plates were soon after placed before them. "You see, my mother…" Martha began. "She absolutely quibbles over everything. I love the woman, but my goodness, I can only handle a few hours at a time."

"What does she quibble over?" Julia asked after taking a sip of water.

"Last time we visited, she said to me, 'You know, Martha, if you rubbed a little rose hip oil around your eyes, it would keep that puffiness from getting worse.'" She paused. "Those was the very first words she had uttered to me at that visit, by the way. Right as I walked in the door. No *hello*, no kiss upon my cheek. I hadn't seen her in months, and that was how she greeted me!"

Joe stuck his fork into his dinner and began sawing into it with a knife. "She said the same thing about my belly." He looked down at his round stomach.

They all laughed.

"Thankfully, my mother doesn't fuss to that degree," Julia said. "But she sometimes sings in place of talking."

"Oh?" Martha asked with obvious curiosity.

Julia nodded as she chewed her bite, then swallowed. "She used to be a singer. And will bellow a song at random moments in the middle of a conversation. If you enter a room, she will sing out, 'Hello, my darling,' as if it were the line of an opera."

Nathaniel gave her a funny look.

Julia noticed and grinned. "You haven't experienced that yet, have you? I know you've heard the welcome song, but not that. You will. Don't worry."

"Oh, so you're newly married!" Joe said jovially. "That explains the show you gave everyone earlier. Congrats are in order, then."

Nathaniel exchanged a knowing look with Julia. "Thank you," they both replied.

Martha wiped her hands on her napkin. "How did you meet?"

"Oh." Nathaniel shifted. He hadn't given any thought to their fake history together.

"It's a funny story, actually," Julia jumped in.

He could see a gleam of mischief in her eye. Whatever she was concocting in the moment, he could already tell he was in for it.

"I was out for a walk with my sister, minding my own business, when my hat started thrashing around. My sister shrieked—a bird was attacking me. Well, my hat."

"A bird attacked your hat?" Martha placed a hand at her cheek.

"Oh, yes! It was frightening. Of course I screamed, my sister screamed, the bird screamed, we all screamed together as my sister and I tried to shoo the bird away. We didn't want to hurt the poor thing, but I was afraid it would go for my face."

"Naturally!"

"As luck would have it, it was also a windy day. In the commotion of the attack, my hat loosened and blew off my head!" She threw in some wild hand movements for affect.

"Oh, my!"

"The hat went airborne and blew straight across the street, like it were a balloon. Without thinking, I went running after it and nearly got ran over by a carriage." Julia turned and met his eye. She plastered a wobbly, crooked-grin on her face and let out a sigh.

Nathaniel lifted one eyebrow.

"And then *he* appeared out of nowhere like a guardian angel and pulled me to safety."

Nathaniel shook his head at her as he tried not to grin.

"That is quite the story," Joe said, but he seemed pleased by it. "I've never heard something so dramatic before."

"It is rather dramatic the way she explains it," Nathaniel replied dryly, winning a mischievous grin from Julia.

"How did *you* meet?" Julia turned back to Martha and Joe.

"Our mothers knew each other." He paused. "That's pretty much it."

A few chuckles went around the table.

For a little while, they ate and exchanged polite conversation. Many complaints about the weather were shared, of course.

"You're from this town," Nathaniel said to Martha, getting a responding nod. "What is the deal with the bridge?"

Martha rolled her eyes. "It's the most awful thing. It's one of two ways out of town, the only way north for anything with wheels, and it's incredibly old. It's all wood for some ghastly reason, and it's falling apart." She forked the greens on her plate. "Bits and pieces are always having to be replaced and when it rains heavily, floorboards seem to disintegrate."

Joe crossed his arms and leaned back in his chair. "A group of us are going out tomorrow to check it out, if you'd like to join? Hopefully, we can get it fixed quickly. I would imagine the rain will let up before then."

Surprised at being included, Nathaniel looked up from his plate. "If I can offer any assistance, I would be happy to."

"You look like a fellow who would be good to have around for such a thing. That's settled, then." Joe smiled. "Where are you headed, anyway? I'm assuming Cloverly wasn't your destination?"

Nathaniel took a moment to reply, unsure of what to say. "We're heading up to Hamwich."

"Hamwich!" Martha said with sheer surprise. "Why would you be going there?"

Julia replied, "You know of it?"

"Of course. My sister used to live there. Lives in Liverpool now. There isn't much there. Though it's right by Manchester, it's still rather rural." She paused. "Why are you going?"

Julia looked to him to answer.

"Business reasons," he decided on.

Martha lifted her eyebrows. "I suppose that would be the only reason to go there. Outside of some farming, it's pretty much just manufacturing. Not many people live there. Most live in Manchester and bicycle or take the tram to work. It's going the way of the ghost, if you ask me."

Nathaniel frowned. This was the first he had heard that. "'Going the way of the ghost'? I don't understand."

Martha glanced at her husband. "Like I said, few people live there. The factories there are starting to fall apart." She tapped her chin. "If I remember correctly, there was a glassworks, which is still doing well. Two or three others, though I don't remember what they are. Oh, and the textile mill, of course! Brumstock Mill, I think it was called. My sister Anna used to work there."

He leaned forward a bit, eager. "Your sister used to work at the textile mill?"

"Oh, yes. A few years ago." She gave him a onceover. "You

seem rather curious about it."

He had to act quick. Delaying his response would be suspicious. Would she know who he was? But how would she? It was her sister who'd worked there. A while ago, supposedly. "I've been curious about dabbling in industry." He was partially lying. "We've been looking into failing businesses, perhaps to buy at a discount."

This seemed to satisfy her. "Well, you won't find a bigger failure than that place. I would caution against it, though."

"Why?"

"The foreman there is a brute. Mr. Fitzhugh." She spoke the name with a pinched face. "You seem like nice people. I wouldn't want my name tied in any way to him if I were you."

Lovely. Nathaniel had so far been glad for the foreman, as he had been working there for several decades. He'd been hoping the man would be a good ally and someone to rely on fully.

Martha continued. "The workers are all women and he treats them like dirt, but it got much worse when they tried unionizing a few years ago."

"'Unionizing'?" Julia asked, sounding surprised.

Martha nodded. She had been mindlessly poking at her food with a fork but now set it down. "Not in an official capacity. Did you know trade unions are exclusively for men? Women cannot unionize. Or at least, they can't join the already established men's unions, as they don't accept women members, which kind of leaves the women in the lurch, doesn't it? Can't have much of a union with only a few people. But they've organized their own walkouts before. Things of that nature."

"Over what?" Nathaniel asked, feeling tense. Did this tie into why the mill's output had dropped off in recent years?

Martha looked directly at him and something about it felt pointed. "The foreman likes to bother the ladies." Martha's eyes went over to Julia. "If you understand what I mean."

"Oh," Julia replied, nodding slowly in understanding.

Nathaniel frowned to himself. He would have to ask Julia

about that later.

"Anyway," Martha said in a brighter voice. "In other words, I wouldn't get involved in it if I were you."

"Why doesn't the owner fire him?" Julia sent Nathaniel a pointed look.

"According to my sister when she worked there, the owner did try to. Some fellow all the way from London, I think. But he has no effect on Mr. Fitzhugh. He's not present. And Mr. Fitzhugh has refused to leave in the past. The owner doesn't live anywhere nearby. What's he going to do? I doubt he even has a spare shilling with that place to get solicitors involved in booting that wretched foreman." She tapped the table in thought. "I would guess Mr. Fitzhugh knows he won't be hired anywhere else, which would be why he refuses to leave. Too many bad things have been tied to him."

Nathaniel couldn't help but wonder if the owner she spoke of had been his father, or someone before him. Regardless, a pang of guilt hit that he had been so removed from the mill that he had not heard of this issue with the foreman.

Chapter Seventeen

FOR THE NEXT hour or so, Julia and Nathaniel stayed at the table with Martha and Joe. They were an engaging couple, quite funny, Julia thought, and were even able to get the duke to talk extensively, which wasn't an easy feat.

None of them knew how long they would be stuck at the inn, between the muddy roads and the broken bridge. So, she felt glad there were others to whom they were warming up.

Nathaniel seemed to be sucked in to a story Joe and Martha told about their neighbor's piglet. "What had the piglet done?" he asked after they'd called it a thief.

"The animal had broken into the house one afternoon and had gotten into a bag of flour," Joe explained.

"We'd been out," Martha added, "and when we had returned home and found flour all over the kitchen, we'd been sure someone had broken in. It was dreadfully frightening at first."

"But it had not been a robber"—Joe pointed a finger for effect—"but Petunia the piglet. We'd found a trail of little footprints that led right to the criminal, who had been fast asleep on the cold, tile floor covered in flour. Never seen such a satisfied swine in my life."

Nathaniel laughed and slapped the table, as if he understood firsthand a piglet's behavior could be unusually mischievous.

For Julia, the story reminded her of her sister.

Not that Helen was a little piglet, of course. But when Helen had been a child, she had found a stray kitten wandering somewhere outside their country home. He'd been gray with bright-blue eyes. Mama was, unfortunately, allergic to cats, so they were never able to have any. But Helen had fallen in love with the kitten and decided to hide him in her room until she figured out what to do.

In the time she'd had him hidden, the kitten had learned how to climb the bedding.

And the bed canopy.

And the curtains.

One afternoon, a maid had entered the bedroom the find the entire room ripped to shreds. Helen had gotten into a lot of trouble for that one.

Julia smiled inwardly, remembering how Mama had fainted upon the discovery—but only once she had reached a chaise in an adjoining room.

Though at the time, Helen and Julia had thought it had only been a kitten, Julia understood a bit better now that there had been damaged trust, plus a major expense and mess. She didn't run her own home and might never. The thought put a pit in her stomach, but she ignored it. There wasn't much she could do in her circumstances.

But she couldn't help but think about her family right now. What were the doing? Were they having dinner as well? Were they preparing to attend a ball that Julia would be sick with jealousy over if she'd known about it?

Did they miss her like she missed them?

Or were they having too much fun to notice she was gone?

Maybe they'd even forgotten about her.

She swallowed the lump that began to form in her throat and forced a smile when Martha made a compliment about "what a lovely couple they made."

This fake marriage was the closest she would ever get to

being married, to having companionship. It was quite sad, really.

But, again, she had to brush those thoughts aside. Her attention then focused on Nathaniel. He was at ease now, leaning forward with his elbows on the table and his hands clasped together as he discussed bridge repair with Joe for the following day.

He seemed to be genuinely enjoying Martha and Joe's company, which was something she had never seen from him before. Usually, he had short conversations with people, cutting them off suddenly and hurrying away. She had witnessed that countless times.

Though it made sense, in a way. Martha and Joe were probably far more similar to the people Nathaniel had befriended back in America than the aristocrats he was forced to be around now.

"What do you think about that, Julia?" Nathaniel's voice pulled her out of her thoughts.

She shook her head to focus. "I'm so sorry. I must be getting tired. I didn't catch that."

"The rain should be letting up overnight. I'm going to head to the bridge with Joe and a few others tomorrow morning and see if we can get it fixed. That way, it's ready whenever the roads dry out. He's told me the types of repairs we would do and it's something I should have no trouble with."

"Oh. All right."

Nathaniel furrowed his brow. But his attention was pulled away from her by the waitress asking if anyone needed anything else.

Another minute passed. Five. Ten.

Julia began to get strangely impatient and kept looking at a wall clock. It was nearing ten o'clock at night, which was still quite early. Yet after this day, she wasn't so surprised to discover she was looking forward to bed.

And without realizing what she was doing, she nudged Nathaniel.

He looked over at her. She didn't say anything but gave him a slight eyebrow-lifted stare that she hoped communicated, *"I'm done for the evening."*

Thankfully, he seemed to understand and gave a small, private nod, though it didn't escape her that his furrowed brow indicated that he was still concerned.

As they both stood, he leaned into her ear, his deep voice rumbling low. "Are you not well?"

"I'm fine. Merely tired after a long day." Julia gave him a reassuring smile, or so she hoped. She said goodbye to Martha and Joe, promising to have breakfast with them in the morning if they ran into each other, and turned to give a final nod to Nathaniel.

He was distracted by the waitress, who had come to bring pudding for the table.

She placed a hand on his arm. "I'm going up now. No need to wake me when you—" But as she said this, he, still focused on the waitress talking about the pudding, leaned over and kissed her.

It was hardly more than a prolonged peck, but his lips touched hers.

His lips. Touched mine.

His stubble. Grazed my skin.

And for some horrifying reason, she wasn't angry by this. No—her heart galloped with excitement.

She inhaled sharply and her eyes went wide. He didn't need to go *that* far for the act!

For the briefest moment, he cocked his head slightly, as if confused by her reaction, but she saw the exact moment he realized what he had done. His eyes went as wide as hers, all color drained from his face.

What did that mean? Had he kissed her on accident? How did one do *that*?

She gathered herself. It didn't matter why he'd done it. Without another word, she hurried out of the room.

A few steps down the hallway, and once out of view of the dining area, she stopped to lean against the wall to fully absorb what had just happened.

With her eyes closed, she tried to put herself in his position. Would kissing her perhaps be needed to prove they were married? Perhaps someone had questioned him about it and he hadn't thought to tell her.

Or maybe it had been an accident. But how did someone accidentally kiss someone? Nathaniel was odd, but he wasn't without a brain.

The whole moment made no sense. He must have had a good reason for kissing her. He didn't like her—he had made that quite clear many times over. Which should have comforted her.

In fact, she should have been shuddering with disgust over the moment. This was the Duke of Rivenhall—Sir Crabby—and she disliked him just as much as he disliked her! And yet instead, she was remembering the feel of his rough hands brushing against her thigh when he'd helped her remove the hidden coin purse. The sensation of his hands massaging her ankle, his thumb and the pads of his fingers gently pressing into her sore ankle and circling slowly, soothing the pain.

That time he'd brushed his thumb over her lip to wipe away dirt, standing so close.

A fantasy of him kissing her neck burst forth into her mind, causing her to gasp at the vividness of it. Her lips began to tingle and she placed her fingers right where his warm, soft lips had touched hers just moments ago.

It shouldn't have been so enticing. But it absolutely should *not* have been rousing vivid fantasies!

And yet it was.

"Julia?" Nathaniel appeared from around the corner. He halted upon finding her and his gaze slid down to her mouth, where her fingers still touched the spot he had kissed. Quickly, she pulled her hand away and pushed off the wall, forcing loose shoulders and lowered eyelids. Though if it looked convincing, she didn't know.

He took a hesitating step toward her. "Forgive me. That was

a mistake that I did not mean to make."

Boiling heat rose in her veins. "How do you *not* mean to kiss someone?"

"I wasn't thinking. Old habit. Please. I'm very sorry."

Old habit? Old habit with *whom*? Someone secret here, or in America?

A wave of nausea hit her as she imagined Nathaniel kissing some unknown woman passionately, both of them panting and sweating. Blast it all!

"Very well, then," was all she could say before turning to walk away. But his hand flew out to grab hers.

She stopped and yanked her hand away. Would the man please let her leave in peace?

He swallowed, checking over his shoulder, as if ensuring they were still alone. "Are you upset with me? Because I would understand if you were."

She let out a long sigh. "It was a mistake, yes?"

"Complete accident."

"Then all is forgiven."

He let out a long breath of relief and ran a hand through his dark hair.

"Really." She waved a dismissive hand, but for some reason, the back of her throat had become tight. Was she really so ugly? Or that awful? She knew he didn't like her, so why did she give such a blasted care now? Oh, the whole thing was humiliating! A gorgeous man had kissed her and it was only because it had been a *mistake*!

She forced a smile. "Go back to what you were doing. I'm just going to collapse face-first into bed. And I'll see you in the morning?"

But without waiting for a response from him, she turned around and fled.

Chapter Eighteen

A S JULIA READIED for bed, the taste of defeat clung to the back of her throat, and the lump that had been there since dinner was starting to grow even bigger.

Ignoring it, she brushed her long hair in the mirror, observing her high-necked, full-sleeved nightgown with the little bows all over it. Quite utilitarian. Perfect for the woman who slept alone each night.

As she pulled the bristles through her hair, she watched the rain stream down the window.

If she were home right now, she and Helen would be gossiping in front of the fire. Helen would tell Julia about the latest men who had asked her to be their mistress. Julia would be picking apart the dresses spotted at a recent ball.

So many aristocratic women had more money than taste.

Julia stopped brushing her hair and set the brush down with a sigh. She missed her family greatly.

But those tender emotions were quickly replaced by irritation as her thoughts turned to the duke. It seemed he wouldn't leave her thoughts for more than a short moment. She stood up and paced the room. It wasn't as if she were *fond* of him, but in spending the last several days together, she had come to realize there was more to the man than being Sir Crabby. Even though he didn't like her, he was at least thoughtful and considerate. Protective. Patient, for the most part, at least. He possessed more humor than she had ever expected him to. Though there was still much to know about him, she—quite unfortunately—found that she liked him.

Julia began to flex her hands. Oh, whom was she kidding? All of this hair brushing and pacing and melancholy thoughts were a cover for the raw humiliation that clenched her stomach like a vise.

She wanted him.

"You foolish woman," she mumbled to herself. She had her pride! They were foes, set out to destroy the other financially. He was trying to destroy her family, for heaven's sake!

A storm of emotions toiled inside of her, but she shoved them into an abyss to be ignored.

Hurrying over to one of her trunks, she threw open the lid in a huff. There was only one way to work through this: needlework.

Julia pulled out an embroidery hoop and sat in the chair near the fire.

She had been working on it here and there when she could and it was coming along well. She stabbed the needle into the fabric and pulled it through. Stabbed hard and pulled. Stabbed again and pulled.

It was helping—marginally.

That was, until she stabbed it right into her finger.

"Oh!" Julia yelped as she pulled her finger away. Sharp pain throbbed on the pad of her finger in time with her rapid heartbeat, and she stuck her finger in her mouth, hoping to alleviate the pain.

Julia's bottom lip began to quiver and tears welled in her eyes.

The hoop dropped to her lap and she buried her face in her hands and began sobbing uncontrollably.

What an utter emotional mess she was!

Here she was stranded in the middle of wet, muddy countryside, hundreds of miles away from home, on her way to a failing factory her foolish father had been stuck with in a drunken wager. A failing factory filled with workers so unhappy that they wanted to unionize and would inherently despise any new owner of the business, including her. And she would have to deal with a foreman who was a pig. If he hadn't followed any direction from the former Duke of Rivenhall, or whoever had tried to fire him in the past, there was no way the foreman would respect *her*!

And on top of it all, Nathaniel, whom she wanted despite knowing better, had kissed her on accident. Not because he'd wanted to, but because he'd thought she'd been someone else.

Loud sobs echoed in the room. She should *not* have been in this position. Her true feelings about her life, about her future, were impossible to ignore now with the sorrow that spilled out of her against her will. She had always been someone who wished to move about on her own. As a girl, she'd run off at every chance, either to play by herself or climb trees because adults wouldn't follow her up there. She had an independent streak that her mother and father may have tried to quell at first, but her stubbornness had won and by the time she'd been old enough to know better, she hadn't known any other way. Either Mama and Papa had given up on the fight by that point, or that had just been the way life had unfolded. They had always been a bit lax about chaperones with Julia and Helen. But in thinking about this, Evander and Helen had always been two peas in a pod until he'd disappeared. They had gone everywhere together, and Julia was a few years younger than them and Helen held a spinster label now. Julia was the truly unchaperoned one. How had she not had this realization sooner?

But she liked her independence, liked going about without a chaperone breathing down her neck all the time. That, she wouldn't be able to change, as it was too ingrained in her. But that had led to her being truly alone. She had convinced herself that she was quite fine with this, actually. For a long time, she had thought spinsterhood would be ideal for her. That no, she did not want to be married and was glad to have her own special sullied Honeyfield reputation to protect her.

But she was beginning to realize, perhaps now that she was getting older and could see how long the rest of her life could stretch, that deep down, that wasn't true.

She didn't want to be alone. At least, not anymore.

Right now, like most others her age, she should be at home with a husband, maybe even children. Comfortable and set in life.

She should *not* have been stuck with a man she was so ashamedly attracted to, one who had never even glanced at her once at any ball.

And why would he? There were many women far more beautiful than herself. With more money. With more respect!

Julia didn't have any of that. She had no beauty, no money, no respect.

She was the *ton*'s silliest woman. Even her family thought her a joke—wasn't that why Papa had her on this business errand? Papa knew they were in a hopeless situation with the mill. There was no getting out of it. He signed papers. It had all been done legally. May as well humor that silly girl Julia for a few weeks at least.

She sobbed harder.

Then, to her utter horror, the door opened. Julia hurriedly forced her melancholy down and wiped the tears away.

"Julia?" Nathaniel's voice cut through the quiet. He crossed the room in a quick succession of steps. "What's wrong?"

Embarrassed, she flew up to her feet and the embroidery hoop tumbled to the floor. The duke leaned over to pick it up and held it out to her. The needle hung by its thread and twisted, glinting in the dim firelight.

"I stuck my finger with the needle," she said with a shaking voice as she took the embroidery hoop. Still reeling from the flood of realizations and emotions that had just engulfed her, she focused on fussing with securing the needle to the fabric.

"Those were quite the sobs for sticking a finger."

She looked sideways, still avoiding eye contact. "Were you eavesdropping?"

"I was already coming in and heard you when I was at the door. I stopped for a second because I wasn't sure if I should enter or come back later."

Julia hurried over to the trunk and tucked her embroidery away. "And you decided not to mind your own business."

"I decided something was wrong and wanted to help."

She let out an unhumorous laugh, closing and latching the trunk lid as two infuriating tears slid down her face. "Why? You despise me. What do you care?"

Nathaniel stayed in place for a long beat before crossing the room to her side. "What's upset you?"

"I told you, I stuck my finger."

"May I see it, then?" He held out his hand and waited.

In no way did she want him to be observing her stuck finger. But it was better than digging into why she was truly upset. "If you insist," she said with a haughty voice, and she took two steps toward him to offer her open palm.

Gently, Nathaniel took her hand in his and lifted it. She swallowed at the sensation, and the way he put his attention on her with such pointed focus.

She watched his face for the first time since he'd come in the room. His black hair was starting to grow out too long, and his stubble was becoming a visible beard. He frowned slightly at her pointer finger.

"Right here?" he asked, gently running his thumb beside the injury where the skin was still tender.

"Yes," Julia replied, quieter than she'd meant to.

Nathaniel made a noise of pity and put his gaze directly on hers. It caused her heart to skip a beat, idiotic thing. "Unfortunately, I'm going to have to take you to the surgeon. They may need to amputate."

She ripped her hand away. "That's not funny!"

"That *was* funny, actually, and you would have laughed if a stuck finger had been the real reason you were crying."

Annoyed, she wiped the infuriating, still-falling tears with the heels of her hands. "Fine. You really want to know? I'm upset because I miss my family. I've never been away from them before. But I'm also realizing I never will be fully away from them, but I mean I'm *truly* realizing it. Fully understanding what my stubborn independence takes from me. How pathetic does that sound?"

"It doesn't, but I don't really understand, either."

She glared up to him. "Nathaniel, I should be married and in my own house, but it's my own fault that I'm not. You know, my refusal to be chaperoned? I wish I could be more independent than I ever can be. And I've actually lost independence by doing so. I've lost the ability to go on and start my own life."

"Well," he finally said after a moment, "I live completely independently and it's not as great as it sounds."

She narrowed her eyes. "You said you loved it."

The corners of his mouth twitched. "I do. I'm trying to make you feel better."

"Brilliant work."

He looked over to the fire. "Well, I do understand missing people. Probably more than you realize." His dark eyes returned to hers as more tears slid down her face. Without any hesitation, he pulled a crisply folded handkerchief out of his pocket.

It occurred to her then how close they were standing.

"When I was twelve…" Nathaniel lifted the handkerchief to her right cheek and dabbed the tears dry. "My mother woke me in the middle of the night. We were at a ball in the country, someone else's home, and my father was passed out drunk. With very few belongings and the help of her most adored and trusted servants, we fled."

Her heart seemed to still at this admission. "Why?"

He hesitated. "I didn't know it at the time, but my father did not treat my mother well. He made sure this mistreatment occurred behind closed doors so no one knew."

"What did he do?" Immediately, she regretted asking, as it wasn't any of her business.

But Nathaniel didn't seem thrown off by the question. "He…mistreated her. And he also had several mistresses. All of this, he had told my mother, was normal. She was an object to him, not a person. And he said so in so many words."

"But it is normal." Not that she approved, but it was the truth. Many men of the *ton* treated and saw their wives this way. Fortunately, through her father, she knew it wasn't always that way.

"It's not normal where I come from," Nathaniel added.

She blinked, confused. But of course, he meant America.

"But it was more than that," he continued. "I learned that when they married, my mother laid down a few rules. Mistresses were not allowed in her home, and all of *that* should be completely invisible to her. He agreed, naturally. And for a few years, he did as she had asked, but then there started to be signs that poked through. Lingering scents of perfume, makeup on his shirts, clues of that nature. He became bolder. Anyway, long story short, she walked in on him with a friend of hers one night. And she decided between that and the way he would get physical when drinking, it wasn't worth it for her to stay. The night we left, she decided she was tired of it, didn't want to raise me in a life like that, and took me to America."

"Isn't that, I don't know, criminal?"

He nodded. "It is, but he couldn't find us, and we were in a whole different country, so his power was pretty negligible there. Those servants who helped her leave? She wasn't foolish enough to think they wouldn't tell my father something. She gave them false information, told them we would be settling in California because of the boom from the gold rush. There was a lot of wealth out there at the time. But we actually went to New York."

Julia lifted her eyebrows high. "So you two just, what, started over there with nothing?"

Nathaniel shrugged. "She took enough money to keep us afloat. We rented a small house in Brooklyn for a year; it was owned by an older couple who were Spanish immigrants. My mother had no skills, of course, but helped them with odd jobs that she could handle, like cleaning the windows. We met their son, Adrian, a few times. I liked him well enough." The duke looked her right in the eye. "Like I said, I understand you missing your family. I missed my father. I didn't know the full story of why my mother had taken me away until I was much older. She had told me that he wasn't a good man and she didn't want him to influence me, but I was old enough to understand that he had done something she found unforgivable. A few years after we left, he tracked us down and sent a letter. He had asked that I be sent back and threatened to send someone after me, but no one ever came."

Julia waited patiently to hear the rest and was buzzing with interest over it.

"My mother let me read it. She said it was best to see it right from the source." There was a flash of anger in his eyes. "It was just paragraph after paragraph of excuses. Excuses for his drinking, excuses for his infidelity, excuses for his heavy-handedness and long absences I had always thought were business-related but then realized he'd been holed up with mistresses. For months at a time."

"Oh, you must have been so upset." Julia reached out and touched his arm. "Did he ever come to get you?"

Nathaniel shook his head. "Not that I know of, at least. We did leave at one point to keep me hidden from him, so maybe he failed to find us again. Or maybe he got lazy. I've always thought someone told him that me living in a poor area of New York would sully me or something like that. He was very big on appearances."

Nathaniel's jaw clenched during a prolonged silence. "I had looked up to my father growing up. And my mother, of course. I understand why she took me away, but a part of me still struggles with it even today. It's shocking when you realize your parents aren't the flawless, perfect people you had always thought they were."

Her hand fell away. Should she open up to him, too? It felt right in the moment. "That's why I was crying."

Immediately, he focused on her, his dark brows pulling together. "What do you mean?"

"I thought it was odd my father let me do this." She indicated around the room. "That he would let me travel across the country to tend to this mill business. This is going to sound so childish, but I was so proud of myself, which isn't something I can say very often. But the truth is, I can't do anything. I have no ownership. I can't make decisions. He did it merely to humor me."

Rivenhall crossed his arms. "Do you really think that's the reason?"

"Yes, and I feel so foolish now." To her utter surprise, he reached out and wrapped his arms around her, pulling her close.

Unable to help herself, she buried her face against his shoulder. It was so comforting. He was warm, and she felt safe in his arms like this. Emotion started rising up again, and she let out another sob. In response, he gently ran a hand up and down her back while quietly shushing her.

After a moment, he asked, "What do you want to do once we're able to leave?" His voice vibrated deep in his ribs.

"I don't know," she admitted, her ear still pressed against him. "Is there even a point to continuing? I can't do anything. My father *won't* do anything. Our entire situation is set. We won't— can't—buy the land from you even if we wanted to. And my father owns the mill, which you won't take back."

"Does this mean your father will pay to lease the land, then, as he's supposed to?"

She lifted her head in order to meet his eye. "Absolutely not."

Nathaniel laughed, and the deep, raspy sound and smile on his face, coupled with the feel of being in his arms, caused something in her to shift. This was pleasant. It was *pleasant* being this close to the Duke of Rivenhall.

Nathaniel stared down into her eyes. "I'm not ready to go back to London, if my opinion means anything."

Her heart jumped at knowing they had extra time together. Was it because he wanted to be with her, too? Or was it purely because of business reasons?

"I say we continue on. See what's there." His voice lowered with each word. "We're so close."

"Yes, we are," Julia whispered back. Were they talking about the mill—or each other?

Nathaniel's eyes softened and he gently tilted her chin with his hand, causing her heart to gallop so hard with anticipation that she could hear it roaring in her ears.

He swept his thumb over her bottom lip, as he had done before, and it caused her breath to hitch. Was something happening? More importantly, did she want something to?

Oh, yes, she did.

Nathaniel gave her a rakish, crooked smile just before leaning down to brush his lips over hers. They both let out a sharp breath, as if both were equally surprised, but the duke didn't stop or back away. He dove in.

Nathaniel surprised her by being a gentle kisser, his tongue cautious and slow when she opened her mouth in invitation, as if he weren't sure of himself.

Hoping to encourage him and needing to be as close as possible, Julia wrapped her arms back around his neck and pressed against him. This seemed to ignite something within him as he slipped his fingers up through her hair and tilted her head back further to deepen the kiss.

Almost desperately, he searched her mouth with his tongue and hers danced along. Hands explored sides and hips and shoulders and biceps. Next thing she knew, the wall slammed against her back.

All she could feel now was need; her mind could not think

about anything else. Nothing mattered right now except being devoured by this beautiful man.

Her hands flew up to the buttons on his waistcoat and they somehow worked together to fling it off of him. It was forgotten before it hit the floor. Nathaniel looked down at her with a dark, sultry look in his eyes, his hair messy from her eager fingers. He nuzzled against her temple. "Julia, oh, Julia," he said in a low voice. "I can't stay away from you any longer."

"Yes," she replied, not knowing what else to say. A warm glow unfurled in her heart upon this realization.

She needed him. Now.

Their breathing hot and fast, Julia now fumbled with the buttons of his shirt and looked up to find his eyes hooded and dark. She bit her lip and his gaze snapped to her mouth. As she reached the last button of his shirt, it fell open and he leaned down to her neck and nipped at her skin before soothing it with the tip of his tongue.

She whimpered, and he growled back.

With the wall still hard against her back, Nathaniel's chest and stomach exposed for her eyes and hands to feast upon, he swept his hand up her leg, over her hip and into the dip of her waist. All she wore was a thin, albeit matronly, nightgown and as he leaned down to kiss her neck, causing her to gasp out loud from the sharp sensation that sent waves of tingling shock through her body.

He nibbled at her ear. "You like that, don't you, my pretty Julia?"

"Yes," she breathed it back and arched into him, begging for more.

"Are you eager for me?" He practically purred into her ear, his hot breath sweeping over her neck.

"Yes." It was all she could say.

"Yes, what?"

"Yes, Your Grace."

He made a mock groan. "Not that. Never that when you're

alone with me."

She swallowed. "Yes, Nathaniel." Her heart pounded hard at saying his given name aloud for the first time while actually *meaning* it at an intimate level, in private, and during a heated moment at that. This meant something significant, this turn they had taken.

The duke responded with a deep chuckle and rewarded her by nipping at her earlobe. But then he bent down and soothed it with his hot, wet mouth.

"Nathaniel," she whispered. Her body now nothing but liquid fire, she took his hands and put them on her hips. His fingers clamped down as he moved to slam his mouth down to hers, and she grinned against him in response.

Nathaniel pressed against her, pinning her to the wall. She lifted one knee to wrap her leg around his hips, pulling her nightgown up with it. Their kissing became more frantic, louder, wetter-sounding, and she dug her fingernails into his shoulders in a communication to hurry up.

But Nathaniel didn't seem to understand what it meant. "Julia, my Julia." Nathaniel nuzzled into her hair instead of building their fire.

Something about the way he'd said it, so tenderly in such a frantic moment, caused something in her to soften despite the fact the fire had been snuffed before it could rage out of hand.

Together, they slid to the floor and he held her against his chest. Her eyes were closed to simply feel the moment, because deep down, she knew it couldn't last.

Nathaniel held her like that for a long while, and she listened to the steady rhythm of his breathing and heartbeat. His heart beat as fast as hers, so why did he want to stop?

Regardless, she knew they couldn't stay this way forever, and she grudgingly pulled away from him and went to collapse onto the bed and watch him putter about the room.

This moment was perfect. She wished it could go on.

She wondered if this meant they would sleep in the same bed

now, and she hoped he would climb in with her and hold her all night. They could do this for a few days, then return to reality when they reached the mill, right?

"Nathaniel?" She could hear the sleepiness in her voice.

"Yes?" He tucked the blanket around her tightly.

"Are you happy we did that?" She wasn't sure why she asked. Neither of them had had qualms about it in the moment; otherwise, they would have stopped before they had. But despite the fire that ignited between them, once they left the inn, they would return to being enemies. And maybe she wanted to know what he thought about everything.

Nathaniel was quiet a moment, staring off at nothing in the room, but he didn't respond how she had wanted him to. Instead, he gave her a forced smile and a quick peck on the lips. "Get some sleep, Julia."

⁂

NATHANIEL WAS IN the tavern and downing his second drink. The barman asked if he wanted another, but he shook his head.

The drink hardly dimmed the inferno that still roared within him. Julia, how beautiful and soft and lovely she was. She tasted so sweet and he wanted to lick and devour every inch of her. Kissing her and feeling her, those purrs... Christ, he'd never experienced anything like it before.

And it made him feel utterly wretched.

He had never felt such a consuming desperation before with Caroline. Caroline had very much been one who had cared about rules and following them. But Julia seemed…more uninhibited. Less afraid to be in the moment. She wasn't shy at all and had seemed to want to move further beyond kissing. Caroline, while they had shared more intimacies beyond kissing, had been terrified of him seeing her despite his reassurances that she was beautiful and would marry her no matter what.

He had loved Caroline. He didn't love Julia. So, what had happened tonight? Why was his body, his heart, his mind on fire?

Why did she take up his thoughts so much of the day?

There were a million questions to mull over, but the biggest one stared right in his face. Yes, she was beautiful and he desired her. Maybe she wasn't as silly as he had thought; she was simply uninhibited in a way the more conservative *ton* found distasteful. And he found the way she galivanted about, often chaperoneless, odd for her station. But what was he going to do about, well, them?

They were rivals. And at least one of them would return to London in dire financial straits because of the other.

He rubbed his hands over his face. Maybe this was a sign to end this silly trip. Something was blooming between them that had to be stopped. They weren't friends, and they couldn't be lovers. They were foes and always would be.

Nathaniel looked at a nearby wall clock. Julia should have been asleep by now, so he began heading back to the room, his decision made. After he helped out with the bridge tomorrow, he was going to get Julia to the nearest train station, through hell or high water—in the most literal sense—and send her back to London and far away from him.

Chapter Nineteen

WHEN NATHANIEL AWOKE the next morning, Julia remained sound asleep in the bed, exactly the way he had found her after returning the night before. Pushing himself forward, he silently grimaced from the aches caused by sleeping in a chair, but a good stretch eased most of it away.

Quickly, he changed, washed, and readied for the morning. He had thrown on clothes he wouldn't mind getting muddy and went downstairs for breakfast.

Pausing at the door, he looked back over to Julia. Watching her sleep peacefully in a comfortable bed led him to wonder how it would feel to wake at her side, his arm wrapped over her, her body tucked safely against his.

Reminding himself that if all went well, she'd be on a train back to London this afternoon, he left their room. But the thought of parting from her didn't make him feel any better.

The dining room bustled with men in work clothing. Nathaniel felt a little silly showing up in suit trousers and a white dress shirt and hoped they didn't think much of it, but it was all he had at hand: black or gray suits and waistcoats and white shirts. Every day. It was predictable, just how he preferred it.

The round-spectacled and round-bellied Joe was seated in a table nearby and Nathaniel went over to say *hello*, then sat and ordered breakfast as the waitress appeared.

"Rain's slowed down," Joe said as he sipped his coffee.

Nathaniel glanced out of the window. "So it has."

"Good news for us. You still up for joining at the bridge? The more help we get, the quicker it will go."

"That's why I'm here."

"Good." Joe took another sip, set the coffee cup to the side, and tried to covertly observe Nathaniel's clothing. "Now, erm, no one's going to need to explain how to use a hammer to you, lad, are they?"

Nathaniel chuckled. "I've helped build barns before. Nothing to worry about with me."

"Oh, excellent."

The waitress came over and set plates before them: a full English breakfast. Bacon, sausage, eggs. Toast and beans. Roasted tomatoes. Mushrooms. The perfect way to begin a chilled, wet morning.

The men dug in and for a long while, they were completely silent. Once Nathaniel had gotten his fill, though, he recalled his other point of business for the day.

"Where is the nearest train station from here?" he asked, wiping his mouth with a napkin.

Joe glanced up as he forked at a sausage. "Ignoring the bridge issue, over an hour east, maybe slightly northeast, of here. Why?"

"I'm hoping to convince my…my wife to head back to London."

Joe swallowed his bite. "Oh?"

"Traveling this far has been nothing but hazard after hazard. I'd feel better finishing off the trip by myself. Is that station on the way to Manchester?"

Joe shook his head. "Once you pass over that hill on the other side of the river, there's a fork in the road. Going straight goes to Manchester, going right goes east. One of the towns out that way has a train station. But do you think she'd abide that? Leaving you?"

"It will definitely take some convincing." A lot of convincing. Although he had been adamant that Julia not travel by train previously, it appeared to be the only way to get her home this far north from London on her own. He would simply have to push aside his deep dislike of that mode of travel for this one instance.

Joe nodded then wiped his hands on his napkin. "One of the fellows working with us today, he and his wife are heading out that direction as soon as they can; her sister lives that way and is due to have a baby any day now. She's eager to get there at once. I'm sure they'd be happy to bring your wife along." Joe picked up his fork again as something caught his attention across the room. "And speak of the devil."

Nathaniel closed his eyes and braced himself for the storm about to hit. He had been avoiding Julia since they had panted against each other, and he wasn't sure if she had realized that yet or not.

"Hello, there, Julia!" Joe called out with a friendly wave. "Did you sleep well?"

Julia returned a friendly, "Yes."

Nathaniel let out the breath he'd been holding. Maybe she wasn't in a sour mood. Risking a glance in her direction, however, proved him wrong. Julia spotted him, immediately closed her eyes, lifted her chin, and went to sit at the bar to eat her breakfast.

Joe laughed. "Trouble in paradise, I see?"

"The woman absolutely drives me mad," Nathaniel said with a glower.

But Joe just waved a dismissive hand. "That's what happens when you love them."

Nathaniel's voice darkened dangerously. "Excuse me?"

Joe continued, clearly unaware. "Women know the hold they have over men. Let me tell you the secret to a happy marriage, Mr. Honeyfield."

Nathaniel rubbed the bridge of his nose with exasperation.

"We may be the stronger sex, you especially." Joe chuckled.

"But the women hold all the power. Let me emphasize that I mean *all*. They know exactly what they do to us. We like to pretend otherwise, but we are completely wrapped around their precious little fingers. But the thing is, deep down, we like it. We're taught not to, of course. But we were made to adore and worship our women. And the sooner you accept that and give in, the sooner you'll have true bliss in your life."

Nathaniel let out a long breath. "Not helpful advice, Joe."

But Joe just grinned. "Ah, it is a hard pill to swallow. We've been raised to believe we're the natural leaders. The heads of the house. Women should be hanging off of and answering to *us*. But I hate to tell you, Nathaniel, that's not reality. It's hard to know that your sweetheart is sitting over there acting like that because she knows it will drive you mad and will get the reaction she wants. But as I said, the sooner you accept that she holds complete power over you, and not the other way around, the sooner you will both be happy."

"Agree to disagree, I suppose. She is doing that to get a rise out of me, I will agree. But she doesn't waste more thought than that on it. In fact, I guarantee she isn't even thinking about me right now."

Joe chewed, pointing his fork at Nathaniel. "Then why does she keep glancing over here?"

Surprised—and a bit disbelieving—Nathaniel glanced over to Julia, catching her in the act. Immediately, she lifted her chin and turned away again.

"Let me ask you another question," Joe said. "Does it bother you that she's cross with you right now?"

"Of course it does. Why wouldn't it?" It was the truth. She may not actually have been his wife or love in reality, but that didn't mean he was glad he'd mucked up badly enough the night before to make her this furious with him.

Joe continued. "If the roles were reversed and she was sitting here talking with me and you were eating at the bar, that cross with her, would she care?"

Nathaniel looked down at his plate as the truth washed over him. "No," he admitted. "She'd hardly think anything of it."

"Now knowing that, do you love her any less?"

Nathaniel narrowed his eyes.

Joe laughed and held up his hands. "All right, I won't pry further. But consider what you learned this morning."

"Oh, I'll consider it, all right," Nathaniel said darkly.

But Joe became only further amused by this.

⁂

JULIA LOOKED OVER at her annoying fake husband again and glared. *Look at him having a grand, old time eating a giant breakfast without a care in the world!* Did he even remember how he'd acted toward her last night? How he had kissed her passionately against a wall and then run away?

Worst of all, he'd slept in the chair when he could have slept next to her in a comfortable bed. Apparently, the spot next to her had been the least desirable option!

She *harrumphed* to herself again and when he looked over to her, she lifted her chin to show how much she absolutely, positively, most certainly did *not* care about him.

And coolly returned to her own breakfast. With a hard stab of her fork.

When she had woken up, Nathaniel hadn't been in the room. She hated to admit it, but she panicked and hurriedly washed up and dressed in order to hunt him down.

It wasn't that she was worried she had been left alone in the room. That had been a secondary thought. She'd thought he had left her behind completely!

How silly that she cared.

Because she shouldn't have. She absolutely should not have—did not—care.

She looked over at Nathaniel again and resisted the urge to

stick out her tongue.

As she finished off her breakfast, she noticed many of the men in the dining room were coming together. Maybe they were the group heading out to fix the bridge.

Deciding to find out for herself, she finished off the breakfast and pasted on a cool expression before floating over to Nathaniel and Joe.

"Hello, Julia." Joe grinned, as if positively amused. "We're just about to take your husband off of your hands. Heading to the bridge to repair it."

"Oh, I'm glad to hear," she replied airily. Nathaniel visibly tensed and she had to hold back a triumphant smile. "Any idea on how long it will take?"

Joe scratched the side of his nose. "We won't know for sure until we get there. Perhaps a few hours."

Julia glanced over to a window to find the rain had finally eased and was nothing more than a drizzle. At last! But what would she do while they were gone? "Where is Martha?" Julia glanced around.

Joe laughed. "Martha won't be awake for another three hours."

As Julia chewed her lip in thought, Nathaniel dared speak to her.

"While I'm gone," he said, "you should pack your belongings."

"Why? Are we leaving that quickly?"

His face hardened. "There's a train station a bit over an hour east from here on a road over the bridge. I've found a ride for you. You're heading back to London this afternoon."

Her nostrils flared. "And who decided this?"

"I did. And it's not up for debate."

Joe shifted as if uncomfortable.

Nathaniel thought he could tell her what to do, did he? She stepped closer to him and tilted her head. "No." She intentionally left a long pause. "We had an agreement, Nathaniel. And it's in my best interest to be there. You know this." Did he truly believe he could just toss her onto a train and continue on without her? Without a fight?

Did he not know her at all?

His jaw clenched. "Do you remember what we discussed last night, about the spot your father put you in?"

Her blood threatening to boil over, she took a deep inhale, as she couldn't respond to that in front of others. Which, of course, he knew. But he was essentially saying she held no power, even if she went to the mill. Which, of course, was also technically true.

"We will discuss this later," he added in a low voice.

Julia needed to think quick. How convenient for Nathaniel that he thought he could drop this on her right before leaving for several hours.

The group of men began to walk past her, filing out of the room. They were leaving. "Julia," Nathaniel said as he watched them walk by. "Every step of the way here has been dangerous. I'm not comfortable continuing the trip with you."

She narrowed her eyes. "I have every right to be there."

"No, you don't."

While she stared daggers at him, Joe coughed off to the side. "You don't have my best interest at heart with this," Julia said. "And you know what I'm talking about. I can't trust you to do the right thing. I'm my…" She glanced briefly at Joe and cleared her throat. "The eyes and ears. For that part of the business."

"I'm not changing my mind." Nathaniel turned away from her in dismissal and began following the men out of the dining room and out of the inn.

Julia hurried after him. How dare he dismiss her? "What are you going to do, force me to leave? You can't do that!"

Nathaniel avoided looking at her as he kept walking. "If I have to tie you up and toss you into a moving train car, then so be it."

With a scoff, Julia stopped in her tracks. "I thought you didn't want me traveling on trains!"

Nathaniel gave her a quick salute and exited the inn.

With nothing better to do, Julia stormed back up to their room. Her filthy clothing from the day before had been laundered and laid out on the freshly made bed, almost mocking her.

Pack? *Ha!*

Frustrated, she tried working on her embroidery. It passed some time, but the anger still lingered like glowing embers. Reading was impossible, and she tried a few different books the room had on hand. Pacing helped marginally. Eventually, though, she gave up.

"He wants me to *pack*, does he?" She grit her teeth together and stormed back over to the bed. As she folded her laundered undergarments and put them neatly in her trunk, she went to fetch the dress she had worn the day before. The hem was ruined, stained beyond any help. And the splatters of mud all over the skirt had faded, too, but were still clearly there.

The dress would have to be repurposed for something else. It would be a nice dress for mucking around in the garden, though, if she were allowed to do something like that.

She froze. *Muck around.*

Grinning quite widely, she laid the dress back out because a rather funny idea had crossed her mind.

Chapter Twenty

M UDDY DIDN'T BEGIN to describe the state of the outdoors after the heavy rain. *Slurry soup* was far more apt.

As Nathaniel and the other men did their best to trudge through the mud for the bridge, he was reminded of the day he and his mother had moved to upstate New York from Brooklyn. He hadn't understood at the time why they'd had to move, though it had been clear money had been a part of it. He'd soon learned they would be able to live and eat at a horse farm free of charge as long as they worked. Nathaniel's mother would help with taking care of the house. Nathaniel would help with farm work.

As soon as they'd had their meager belongings put away in their respective bedrooms, the horse farm owner—Adrian Velez, the son of their previous landlords—had put Nathaniel to work cleaning out the stables.

Nathaniel had been approaching fourteen years by then but had never experienced hard labor quite like what Adrian had put him through. Of course, Nathaniel had been familiar with horses, as the home he'd grown up in back in England had had many of them. But he had never helped care for them, nor had he known how to. As the only son of a duke, he had never been exposed to the dirty side of horse management.

Adrian had helped Nathaniel muck out the first stall. It hadn't been difficult, but it had been smelly and disgusting hard work.

The second stall, Adrian had stood back and watched.

By the fifth stall—out of ten—Nathaniel had been ready to collapse. His skinny arms and legs had felt like jelly. But Adrian had kept pushing him. "You don't do the work, you don't get to eat," he had said.

At the eighth stall, Nathaniel had broken down in angry tears. Adrian had heard and had come to see what the commotion had been. Nathaniel had dropped to his knees, begging to stop. Of course, Adrian had said *no*. "Life isn't easy and the sooner you realize you're not getting anything handed to you here, the sooner we'll all be able to get along. You think you're the first wild stallion to come here to my farm? You need to learn your place, son, and quick. I don't have time to scratch behind your ears and give you sugar cube rewards. Out there, you didn't have a care in the world, and that's great for you! But that's not how it goes here."

"I hate this place!" Nathaniel had shouted through his tears.

Adrian had smiled. "Great, go on and hate it! Go shovel some more horse manure while you hate it!"

Nathaniel had lunged at the man. Which, of course, had been stupid. Adrian may not have been tall, but he was incredibly strong. And Nathaniel had been worked down to the bone.

Adrian had gripped him by the front of his shirt and shoved him back into the stall. Nathaniel would, years later, realize Adrian had grown tired of Nathaniel's inflated and overindulged ego, but at the time he hadn't realized this.

"How are you going to fight, little man, when you have stick arms?" Adrian had asked. "You aren't going to be pampered here. You're going to work for this house, and for the food on your plate, and the bed you sleep in, and you're going to say *thank you* for all of it, too. Everyone here contributes. Do you understand?"

Nathaniel had said a particularly choice word.

Adrian had pointed a finger at him. "And watch your language."

Young Nathaniel had done the only thing he could think to do. The only thing that may have possibly riled up Adrian. Nathaniel had spit on the ground.

Evident frustration had turned Adrian's jaw to stone. "I know you're in a hard place, so I'm going to let that go one time, and one time only. And I'm going to tell you something you need to think about while you finish up these last three stalls. Why do you think your mother brought you up here?"

"To your stupid farm? I don't care."

"Not my farm, to America." Adrian had tapped at his head. "Have you once thought about why your mother would take you from a golden life? You think it was just for the fun of it? One day, she decided to leave her entire life behind for a laugh?"

Anger had felt like it had been bursting out of Nathaniel from every direction. "Because she hates my father!"

But Adrian had shaken his head. "If that were true, she would have left a long time ago, don't you think?"

Nathaniel had sniffed. "What do you care?"

Adrian had studied him for a long moment before handing the pitchfork to him. "Women are stronger than men give them credit for. Consider that, until you figure it out for yourself."

In the present day, Nathaniel walked along the muddy street in the English countryside, now nearly twenty years away from that moment. That first day with Adrian still vividly stuck with him. Oh, how he had despised the man those first few months. Adrian had been rigid with schedules. Rigid with work. Rigid from every single angle. Long before the sun had come up, Adrian had been banging pots and pans at the foot of Nathaniel's bed to get him up.

And he had always been there breathing down Nathaniel's neck.

It had taken far too long to figure out why the man had been like that. For a long time, Nathaniel had been sure the man hated him. But as it had turned out, that had been the opposite from the truth.

The crew of men came to a halt and Nathaniel spotted the derelict wooden bridge just ahead. It sagged with age, weather-worn and gray. Even the piles—the legs of the bridge—were a sorry sight.

Meanwhile, the river below it was overflowing and sputtering with anger.

One of the men at the front of the group began shouting out directions. "I'll be inspecting each wooden board that needs to be replaced! The whole thing needs to go, but unfortunately, we have to make do with what we have!"

The crowd of men murmured their agreement.

While Nathaniel went to work marking the rotten boards as asked, he looked up. Though it had stopped raining, the sky remained a sullen gray.

It didn't give him a good feeling, but then, did gray skies ever invoke positivity?

Joe appeared and they spoke with the others to determine the best way to attack the board replacements, finally deciding to divide the bridge into thirds, with men working in pairs. While Joe and Nathaniel began to gather up the new boards and nails from the stockpile, a woman's voice shouted from a distance.

Everyone stopped what they were doing and turned to see who it was.

As soon as Nathaniel found her, he let out an irritated groan.

Joe bellowed a laugh. "That one sure has a spark in her, doesn't she?"

Nathaniel grumbled something indecipherable back. What in the blazes was Julia doing?

Julia marched right up to him and crossed her arms. "You thought you could get away from me that easily, did you?"

"I'm busy," was all he replied with as he lifted a few boards, balanced them over his shoulder, and began walking with Joe toward the bridge. They were assigned the farthest end, which was a small blessing. It meant she couldn't follow him there.

"I suppose I'll simply stare at you with my arms crossed like this." Julia made a show of doing just that. "Until you go mad."

He shrugged the bundle of wood planks on his shoulder while she watched the movement. "Is that your plan here, irritate me until I change my mind about sending you back home? That makes about as much sense as swimming in the sea in the midst of winter. Why would I want to spend *more* time with the world's most irritating woman?"

She trotted after him. "No, that is *not* my plan. What would that gain me? While I *am* here to irritate you, that's merely a bonus. The real reason I'm here is to tell you I'll be continuing on to the mill, but I'll be traveling on my own."

Immediately, he spun around to face her, causing the nearest men to shout and duck under the wood, lest the bundle knock them upside the head.

Not wanting an audience for this discussion, he marched her off to the side. "Travel on your own? That's absurd! You'll get yourself killed!"

She glared. "How? I handled the highwaymen far better than you did. All I'll be doing is sitting in a nice, cushy carriage that I hire with *my money*, may I add, staying in an inn or hotel by myself, again with *my money*. Oh!" She pressed a hand to her cheek and made a mock expression of shock. "What are you going to do without my coin?"

Nathaniel inwardly cursed himself. He had forgotten all about that part. "I'll figure it out."

"There's nothing to figure out, Nathaniel. On this trip, *you* need *me*. Not the other way around."

He clenched his jaw tightly. She was right, blast it all, but he would never give her the satisfaction of him admitting that out loud.

Julia swept her hand toward the bridge. "Best get on with it. I'm already scheduled to leave as soon as the bridge is repaired. I don't want any further delays. I'm a very busy woman, you see."

Knowing it was best to end the conversation now before he

said something he'd regret, Nathaniel readjusted the bundle of wood on his shoulder, turned his back to her, and walked back to Joe.

Before they started crossing, Nathaniel couldn't help but notice how muddy the riverbank was. It didn't look stable, and he worried about the foundation.

"Do you think the piles will hold? That mud doesn't look sound to me." Nathaniel spoke over his shoulder.

But Joe only shrugged. "This bridge is over a hundred and fifty years old. It's seen plenty of rain before. It's ugly and needs frequent upkeep, but it's never collapsed."

More confident, Nathaniel began crossing the bridge to the other side, taking care to avoid the rotten boards that had been marked. If they stepped on one, their feet would surely go through. And if that happened and there was yet another rotten board or two next to it, they could fall right into the river. Glancing down at the raging river below, Nathaniel surmised they would be swept away.

As the two men approached the far end of the bridge, something out of the corner of his eye caught his attention. He turned to look and his stomach fell to find Julia following behind.

"What in the blazes are you doing?" he shouted back.

She took a step over a rotten board. "What does it look like? I'm following you!"

Oh, that infuriating woman! But there was no point in arguing with her about it now. He jutted his chin to the end of the bridge. "Get over there before you get yourself killed, for Christ's sake."

She made a show of rolling her eyes as she passed him but thankfully crossed safely onto land.

With haste, he and Joe got to work. They had many boards to replace. As they finished nailing in the second board, however, the distant sound of rolling thunder sent a stillness over the crowd of workers.

"All right, lads," a man's voice boomed. The voice came from a man with slicked-black hair and a yellowing linen work shirt.

"Let's hurry it up quick while it's still dry."

Nathaniel and Joe exchanged twin glances of furrowed brows but quickly returned to their work. Every few moments, Nathaniel checked on Julia, but she meandered about on her own, as if she didn't have a care in the world.

THE SOUND OF thunder caused Julia to look up toward the sky. The extreme amount of rain they'd received had been wonderful for wildflowers, and a field of them was bursting with color. She had been crouched next to some cornflowers to watch the bees when the thunder shook the earth beneath her feet.

It worried her that all of the men seemed to freeze when it happened.

Truthfully, the thunder concerned her as well. It was an instinctual response, though. Even if it started to storm, they could get out of here quickly.

She hoped, anyway.

Convinced she fretted over nothing, she returned to the happy flowers.

The staccato of hammers hitting nails filled the air, but the men's chatter had completely died off, their focus now solely on finishing up their work.

A gust of wind rushed past and the scent of rain tickled Julia's nose. But, surely, they couldn't get any more rain. Hadn't every single drop already fallen?

Julia lifted her gaze. The sky darkened severely to the north of them, the same direction the road went. Looking back toward the bridge, Julia watched Nathaniel work for a few moments. It was quite humid out and he was beginning to sweat as he hammered the nails, his white shirt clinging to him and the muscles of his arms and his back.

She swallowed. It didn't do any good to ogle after the man

when they would be separating soon.

It wasn't, in fact, true that she had hired a carriage for the rest of the trip to Hamwich. But he didn't need to know that. He just needed to know that she could be gone at a moment's notice on her *own* terms. Not his.

Even if his silly idea to send her home was rooted in protectiveness.

Which almost made it more annoying.

She sighed. What she would do once she returned to the inn and he discovered her lie, she didn't know.

As much as Julia hated to admit it, she didn't *want* them to go their separate ways. Even though he clearly didn't like her being nearby after what had happened between them last night, she still felt that blasted magnetic draw to the duke. But wasn't that how it always was? Wasn't it a curse of women to be attracted to that one man they absolutely should have nothing to do with in any way?

Regardless, she remained determined to see the mill for herself, so she may as well continue on with the duke as planned. How she would go about convincing him of doing this, however, remained to be seen.

Another boom of thunder, and a fat, wet raindrop splashed the bridge of her nose. The men didn't look up this time, so she decided to follow the road to the top of the hill. When she reached the top, she pursed her lips at what she saw. The distant sky was nearly black, with ribbons of rain stretching from sky to ground.

The wind kicked up again, lifting her skirts. She had to press them down.

"Julia!" a distant voice yelled. She turned to look down the hill toward the bridge. She didn't realize how far she had walked from the men. She found Nathaniel but could hardly see his face because of the distance. He was beckoning her back with a wave of his arm.

Presumably, the men were either finished or abandoning the

work for the day as they were starting to head back.

Just as she took her first step, though, the downpour hit.

She let out a sharp gasp at the shock of it. *Blast it all, not again!*

Thunder groaned, and the sound of the downpour roared in her ears. Fear thrummed through her and she began to run down the hill toward the bridge.

But the already-soaking-wet road was now even wetter than it had been before. She slipped and fell. Forced herself back up.

Nathaniel was halfway across the bridge and walking backward quickly, keeping his eyes on her. "Hurry!" he shouted.

She looked down at the bridge's deck. There was a strange pattern of dark, old wood and bright, new wood, but no gaps. It appeared they had completed their work.

Which was good for her. Because she wasn't about to walk daintily across like last time.

"I'm coming!" she shouted out to Nathaniel, water streaming down her face. As she began crossing, she noticed how violent the river had turned.

With a gulp, she put one foot in front of the other while the men made it to the other side of the bridge. Relief hit her when Nathaniel had made it safely to land as well. He waited for her, every inch of him now soaking wet, his black hair plastered to his forehead in strings, his shirt see-through.

As she reached the middle of the bridge, though, it felt like the ground began shaking.

An earthquake? Did England even *have* earthquakes?

She clung to the rail as a fear she had never experienced before in her life took over all of her senses.

And screamed as the bridge collapsed.

Chapter Twenty-One

THE DAY CAROLINE had died, Nathaniel had no memory of.

Well, that wasn't fully true.

He remembered everything up until the moment it had happened.

He distinctly remembered the sound of metal scraping against metal. The way it had screamed like a banshee foretelling death.

But the moment the accident had occurred had been erased from his memory. Forever.

As well as the aftermath.

And a few days after.

Apparently, he had wandered around looking for her, covered in blood from an injury on his side. But he didn't remember any of that, even to this day.

One moment, they had been sitting next to each other on the train holding hands. The next, he'd been waking up in a hospital bed.

Three days had passed.

And all he could remember was the sound of the train derailing, as it had jumped off the tracks to crash in a textile mill.

There'd been something haunting about noise. Something about the sound of impending death that imprinted upon one's soul.

Sixty people had lost their lives in the derailment that day. And now, ten years later, it was the sound of the bridge collapsing that stabbed him through the heart and ripped its old scar in half.

It all seemed to happen slowly.

Julia rushed across the bridge, pale and concentrating, the pouring rain and angry river framing the moment.

The bridge jolted strangely, dropped a bit, and tilted.

She froze. And so did he.

The bridge began to sway. It shook. And the rumble it made as it buckled into itself, wood snapping, nails groaning, as the muddy banks shifted and slid down into the river, bringing the bridge with it…

And Julia.

Everything seemed to move impossibly slow.

But in reality, it all happened so quickly, his mind didn't comprehend what was happening.

That was, until the deep and guttural splash the bridge made, like an enormous wave crashing against a stone cliff.

And all that was left behind was…nothing.

No bridge.

No Julia.

Nathaniel didn't even think. He acted. He may have yelled out her name, or maybe that was just his mind screaming it.

It was the fastest he had ever run. Men behind him shouted, but he didn't know what they said. Or if they followed.

He searched the water's surface quickly to see if Julia had surfaced, but there was no sign of her anywhere. The bridge was tumbling in the water, breaking up with the swift movement of the river.

Rain poured harder. Thunder boomed.

"Julia!" he shouted.

And then he saw her pale hand. It was so brief, he wasn't even sure he had truly seen it.

But if he had, that meant she was pinned and couldn't get to the surface.

The bridge had broken up, yes, but it was heavy enough and large enough to wedge itself into the muddy bottom and against large, submerged rocks that kept it from moving farther downstream.

Breathing was as quick as his heart, which raced like a train at full speed.

What would he do if he couldn't save her? What if he failed again to save the woman he cared for?

This thought hit him like a full-forced punch to the face. No time to think about it, though.

But then he remembered something. This was why he lifted hay bales. This was why he lifted boulders. This was why he moved dead trees on his own, dragged them through the forest without anyone's knowledge, lifted enormous logs in the privacy of his own home.

It was why he was so obsessive about strength, about being as big and strong as he could be.

After Caroline had died, he'd vowed to be able to save the next life in danger in front of him. God forbid his help would ever be needed, but it appeared it was needed now.

He dove into the furious water, but the current was stronger than he'd expected. Immediately, he was pushed under and didn't know which way was up.

Don't panic. Don't ever panic.

His back slammed into something hard and he reached out to feel it. A boulder. He pulled himself along it and gasped for air once he'd surfaced.

The bridge was right there.

Climbing atop the boulder, he realized there was a line of them that the bridge was wedged against. Or at least, part of the bridge. Much of it had broken apart and was rushing away with the water. With water spraying his face, Nathaniel scrambled over to the part of the bridge that remained. He only hoped Julia was here somewhere, because if she was downstream, there was no hope for her.

She would be... No. His throat tightened and he fought against the despair starting to rise. This wasn't the time to think. This was the time to act.

"Julia!" he shouted above the roaring water. But there was no response.

He found a narrow opening and shoved his arms down between the bridge and the boulders. Found a place to grip the bridge. He tried to lift it, but it didn't budge.

A sob threatened to rise.

He tried again, clenching his teeth. But failed.

Julia Honeyfield was going to die, and it was all because of him.

Angry tears mixed with the rain pummeling his face like tiny needles. Every flash of irritation and anger he had ever felt toward her, he regretted. Every time he'd wished she hadn't been around, he regretted it. He regretted that her blueberry had landed in his drink, and he hadn't taken the opportunity to begin a friendship. Instead, he'd immediately labeled her as an irritation.

But she wasn't an irritation.

These last several days with her had been the best days of his life in a very long time.

She made him laugh. Him! His last memory with Caroline included laughter. And laughter had evaded him ever since.

But Julia inspired it once again.

Julia Honeyfield was wonderful, not irritating.

She was funny. Smart. Strong. Confident. Beautiful. Charming. She glowed everywhere she went. It didn't matter if she had just woken up with the after-effects of drinking, or if she sparkled in her finest evening gown. Julia embodied all that made life amazing and worth living.

He was the irritating one, not her. He was darkness, despair. And somehow, beyond all expectation, beyond all comprehension, he had fallen in love with her and the light she exuded.

But her light was going to be snuffed out because of him.

"No," he said between rapid breaths. "No, not this time!"

Nathaniel gripped tight enough, it felt as if the bones in his fingers would snap. This wasn't going to be the end of it. And with a roar, he pulled as hard as he could, pushing against the boulders with his legs with the strength of giants.

And the bridge moved.

Every fiber in every muscle threatened to rupture like a rope pulled too tight.

But still he pulled.

And he lifted.

He yelled out again as he managed to free the bridge from the mud that tried to suck it back down and threw the mass of wood off to the side.

It made a loud sound as it tumbled through the roaring water.

But he hardly noticed.

Immediately, he looked down, and there Julia was, pressed up against the boulder by the rushing water.

Still.

Pale.

He went in after her and draped her carefully over his shoulder as if she were the most precious thing in the world. Because she was.

He swam to shore with her.

No thoughts filled his mind except to get her to shore.

The crowd of men were anxious and full of energy. They pulled him out and laid her on the ground.

But she wasn't moving.

Or breathing.

He was tired. So tired. And so cold from the water, his entire body was numb.

But he crawled to her, anyway. Breathed air into her lungs.

Not so long ago, his mouth had pressed against hers. Seeking feeling. And he'd found more of it than he ever would have expected.

But he'd shoved it away, like the coward he was.

Now, he was trying to give her back her life.

What if he failed?

He pressed hard on her sternum. Breathed in her mouth again. Pressed. Breathed.

Her eyes flew open and she spewed water all over him.

The tension that gripped every muscle in his body released like steam from a kettle, leaving nothing but relief behind.

Chapter Twenty-Two

NATHANIEL CRADLED JULIA'S limp body in his arms as he ran back to the inn, and news of what had happened spread before he reached the stairwell that led to the second floor and their room.

Shouts of surprise and fear rang in his ears when he shouldered his way through the crowd of onlookers. It irritated him, but he understood they were only concerned for her.

He glanced down at her limp form. She felt so light and small in his arms. And she was so quiet.

After Julia had thrown up all the water, she'd collapsed back to the ground, unconscious.

But by a miracle, she was alive.

Up in their room, he crossed the floor toward the bed. Someone had located a physician staying at the inn and alerted the man. Who had summoned him, Nathaniel had no idea. He was just glad the man was there.

"Lay her out on the bed," the physician said, running after Nathaniel. The physician had thick, white hair and a thick, white mustache. "Right now, the most pressing issue is to get her warm and dry. Hypothermia is a concern, even though it's not winter. You need to remove her wet clothing."

Nathaniel hesitated. Everyone thought she was his wife, and

so did this physician. But she wasn't in reality. He couldn't undress her!

"Sir, this isn't the time to panic!"

Nathaniel didn't respond and pushed past the mounting tension in his body. Hoping Julia wouldn't murder him once she awoke and realized what he had done, he peeled off the wet layers while the physician dug around her trunk for a clean nightgown, handing it over with his back turned respectfully.

The wet clothes discarded, Nathaniel dressed her despite his reservations and got her under the covers while the physician threw logs into the fire to lift the heat.

Dr. Redfern introduced himself quickly, went through his bag, then checked her vitals. He made a point to mention that her lungs sounded good for what she had been through.

As the physician checked for any swelling indicating broken bones, he talked. "Sir, I assure you that hovering is not necessary."

Nathaniel cleared his throat and took a regretful step back.

The physician returned to his examination. "Can you tell me what happened?"

Nathaniel told him in as few words as possible.

"My word, it's amazing you were able to pull her out alive," Dr. Redfern said over his shoulder.

Nathaniel swallowed and nodded.

Finishing up his task, Dr. Redfern pulled the blanket back up to her chin. "The good news is, I don't believe she has broken anything. The bad news is, she *is* hypothermic."

Worry flooded him. "Will she be all right?"

"Most likely, yes, but her temperature needs to come back up. The fire needs to be hot and she needs to stay under the covers. Also..." The physician looked him over. "You are shivering violently. I'm worried about you as well since you're still in your wet clothes. If she's hypothermic, then you're at risk, too, if you're not already there."

"I'll be fine," Nathaniel ground out, but he was now very

aware of the shivering. "I'm only worried about her right now."

The physician gave him a small smile. "And what happens to her if you can't take care of her?"

He resigned himself to that fact. "Fine. What do I need to do?"

"Body heat is best. Keep that fire roaring and go lie with your wife so you both warm quickly. Being unconscious is a normal sign of hypothermia, and that is why she is out. I don't know how long it will last."

Dr. Redfern then directed Nathaniel again to get into dry clothes. "I will check on you later," he said. "But fetch me if you need me before then for any reason at all." He then informed Nathaniel the room he was staying in on the first floor.

Once the physician had gone, Nathaniel changed into dry clothing and stood at the side of the bed. He watched Julia for a few moments in utter disbelief that she was somehow still alive. His shivering was now unbearable, though, so he climbed into bed next to her despite his uncertainty.

He thought it would be strange to do this, but he found his worry for her had tempered now that she was close. Hoping she wouldn't be angry with him once she awakened, as he would of course tell her everything despite his discomfort, he moved to lie beside her, with her on her back and him on his side. Every few seconds, he placed the side of his finger under her nose to ensure that she was still breathing.

And then he watched her.

As she lay there, still, he wondered… Would she really be all right? Had he really saved her life?

Tears stung at his eyes and he wiped them away with the heel of his hand.

What would have happened if he hadn't been able to move the bridge away? What would have happened if the bridge had fallen directly on her? What would have happened if…

Don't do this to yourself. Not again.

He remembered the years of questions he had obsessed over

after Caroline had died. Why her and not him? They'd been sitting right next to each other. How was it that she had died, and he had been able to walk away with nothing more than some scars?

But asking that did nothing. It didn't change the situation. It didn't bring her back from the dead. All it did was torture his mind and his heart every day, month, year.

After a few years, he'd had to let Caroline go and move on. He'd taken her favorite book to keep her memory alive, and it sat on his mantel back in London right now. But he knew he couldn't dwell on Caroline any longer. She was gone. Forever. And she would never have wanted him to drown from grief.

But Julia was still here.

Guilt threatened to rush him. He cared for Julia—it was impossible to deny it now. Here he was lying beside her, watching her breathe. Worry and fear crawled through him like a swarm of ants. He shifted to be directly beside her and pressed his face against her shoulder to breathe in her scent. She mostly smelled like a river, but there was a faint sweetness, too. He relished in it, put his arm around her, and held her close. He didn't want to let go, but he promised to only hold her for a minute.

❦

A HEAVY BLANKET of warmth surrounded Julia.

What it was, she didn't know. But it was comforting. And it caused a leap of happiness somewhere within her.

What was going on? It was almost like she was navigating while blindfolded, but she knew she wasn't walking. She hazily focused on her senses, but she couldn't see anything. Didn't hear anything. She did smell something familiar, though.

Balsam and lemon.

She moved toward it, and that comforting warmth increased. *This is the safe place*, her mind told her. And she succumbed to dark slumber once more.

"SHE'S STILL NOT awake?" Dr. Redfern asked from the side of the bed while frowning down at Julia.

Nathaniel stood by the fire drinking water, doing his best to eat some of the dinner Dr. Redfern had brought. But Nathaniel's worry for Julia had only increased since the physician's first visit earlier in the day.

The physician checked her pulse again. Sighed. "Well, I guess we just have to wait until she's ready, then."

"There's no way to wake her?"

But Dr. Redfern just shook his head.

"Is there a chance that…" Nathaniel paused as a sick feeling clawed at his stomach. "Maybe she won't wake?"

The physician hesitated before pulling the blanket back up over her and returned to Nathaniel. "Don't worry yourself over that yet, Mr. Honeyfield. We aren't there yet. But… try coaxing her awake. Try talking to her. If she isn't alert by morning, we will worry about it then. And only then."

Nathaniel nodded as he watched Julia's small form beneath the blankets.

"I'm going to return to my room now. I'll be back in the morning. You need to get yourself back to bed, too. It's been a hard day for you as well." The physician walked over to the door. "Make sure you don't neglect yourself." He then shot an arched eyebrow at Nathaniel before shutting the door behind him.

Nathaniel turned to watch Julia from across the room, hoping she would stir with the sound of Dr. Redfern's departure.

But she lay there, still asleep.

Recalling the man's parting words, he forced himself to eat more of his dinner before setting the dishware outside of the door to be collected. He then readied for bed, though he doubted he would be able to sleep despite the fact that his entire body ached with overuse and strain.

Standing at the side of the bed where the physician had been only moments ago, Nathaniel stared down at Julia. Her mouth was partially open, her long eyelashes swept down along her cheeks. The color had returned to her face. She would have looked rather peaceful, if he hadn't known any better.

He placed his fingertips on the top of the bed and went to climb in but paused. The physician hadn't said anything about her temperature, and he hadn't thought to ask. She looked better, so she likely had warmed up to her normal temperature.

Should he sleep in the chair like he had done the night before, or should he return to her side?

What if she did wake up and he was right beside her?

What if she woke up and she was all alone?

That final question was the one that decided for him. He remembered waking up in the hospital after the train derailment. There'd been no one in the room at the time, and he had never felt such confusion or fear waking up somewhere so unexpected.

He hadn't known how he'd gotten there, he hadn't remembered why he'd been there, and there'd been no one to ask.

The decision made, Nathaniel climbed in beside Julia and watched her again. He should try talking to her, like Dr. Redfern had asked. He considered for a moment on what to say.

"Julia, can you wake up?" he asked, feeling foolish.

Of course, she didn't stir.

Recalling his stay in the hospital and the confusion that had enveloped him, he decided to tell her what had happened with the bridge, even if she couldn't hear him.

"You got hurt," he said, his voice cracking at that last word. "And somehow, I was able to get to you. I don't know how, but I did."

Julia remained motionless.

A loose strand of hair hung against her forehead, and he gently brushed it aside. "I'm sorry you got hurt, sweetheart. I'm sorry you were there because I was being a pigheaded fool. You shouldn't have been there. You should have been safe, warm, and dry in here." He studied her profile, the faint freckles that sprinkled her cheek, her little nose that turned up just a bit at the end. "I told you that you had to go home to be safe, that there was no point in you going to the mill. But the real reason I wanted you to go was, you're affecting me in a way I never thought would happen again. I've been floating around empty for so many years and finally accepted the life I was given. And then you came roaring into it." He paused and gently brushed a knuckle along her cheek. "I know you despise me. And after today especially, you really should go home. But it's funny. Now I don't want you to leave my side. I can't let you go, even though soon enough, I'll have to."

He stopped, listening to the logs pop in the fireplace.

"I don't know how you did it, Julia, but I've fallen over the edge of a cliff for you. And this is the only time I'm able to talk about it. How would that even work?" Nathaniel let out a small chuckle. "We're against each other here. We are enemies, I guess you could say. One of us will become destitute because of the other. That will only breed bad feelings and resentment."

Nathaniel sunk into the bed and watched Julia breathe some more, waiting, hoping she would wake. He wasn't sure how long it took, but he eventually succumbed to sleep just as the horizon turned a dusty purple.

Chapter Twenty-Three

I T WAS A summer soirée, and there were white dresses and parasols everywhere on the expansive, lush, green lawn.

The adults were drunk, laughing loud at frequent intervals, and there was an unofficial horse race on the lawn that the men were partaking in for the sole purpose of showing off.

While their brother went off with his friends, likely to cause boyish mischief, Julia and Helen sat on their own in the grass, their skinny legs extended, their little black shoes bouncing from side to side, back and forth. Julia wore a white dress with a large, pink bow that tied around her waist, and a little straw hat. Helen wore something quite similar, though her bow was yellow.

Julia spotted her friend Georgette surrounded by a group of girls who seemed to hang on to every word Georgette said and wondered why no one ever surrounded *her*.

"Who cares?" Helen asked when Julia had asked the question aloud.

But Julia cared, even if Helen didn't.

Cheering pulled Julia's attention back to the horse race. It had ended and the winner was climbing off his horse to the celebration of everyone. They all began surrounding him, too.

Maybe she needed to do something big and interesting like that.

Julia looked around, hoping for an idea to spring forth, and spotted a large tree. Without telling Helen her brilliant idea, she marched past the group of girls surrounding Georgette and began climbing the tree.

The girls didn't notice her yet. But they would.

Julia climbed. Up, up, up. Halfway to the top, the group of girls walked away, clearly unaware of Julia's neat trick. Julia frowned to herself. How would they see how interesting and daring she was now?

But then a commotion somewhere behind her caught her attention.

Julia clambered around the tree to see what was going on below. There was a man and a boy she didn't know.

"I'm not going to baby you any longer like your mother does," the man said. His voice scared Julia; he seemed tense and angry but was clearly trying to keep his voice low so no one could hear. He seemed angrier than Papa had ever been, even when she'd let the chickens escape from the kitchen that one time so they wouldn't be eaten. "You're old enough now to know better. It's time we treat you like a man, not a child."

"But—"

The boy was interrupted by the man gripping the boy's shirt and then shoving him. Hard. The boy faltered back several steps before plopping to the ground.

Julia gasped and immediately covered her mouth, hoping they didn't hear her.

"Don't make me do worse." The man leaned over the boy in a dire warning. And then he left.

The boy didn't say anything or make any sound. Instead, he crawled over to Julia's tree and leaned back against the trunk.

It was a strange juxtaposition, the boy sitting alone, presumably reeling from what she assumed his father had just done. Meanwhile, a happy, blue-skied summer day surrounded him.

Julia wondered if his father scared him a lot, or if that had been the first time.

After a few minutes, he started to cry.

Julia was now in a predicament. She hadn't meant to listen in; they hadn't known she'd been there. And she *definitely* wasn't supposed to be up in a tree.

But after several minutes passed and the boy didn't move, she knew she had to do something. Her family would begin looking for her soon, and that boy could sit there all day.

"You, boy!" she shouted down from the treetop.

The boy stilled and looked around.

"Up here!"

The boy looked up with wide, red eyes.

She waved. "You want to come up?"

He sniffed. "I'm not allowed to."

"So?"

He looked as if he were going to say something, his mouth slightly open, but he slammed it shut.

"I'll come down to you." Julia took a step down to a branch, and then another one. "I didn't realize how far up here I got." It hit her how far off the ground she really was. She gulped as fear started to twist in her stomach.

"Can you get down?" The boy was now standing and looking up at her, shielding his eyes from the sunlight that dappled through the lush, green leaves.

"Of course I can get down!" she boasted. But in truth, she wasn't so sure.

But with careful footstep after careful footstep, she did, in fact, make her way down. The boy watched intently, as if she were the most interesting person he'd ever seen.

Unfortunately, as she almost reached the ground, she slid down one last large branch…and got herself stuck ten feet up in the air. It was the base of a large branch, and there was nowhere else for her to climb down to. It was also too steep to climb back up and move somewhere else in the tree.

"What do I do now?" she asked the boy. Here, she could see him better. He was rather tall and skinny and had black hair and expressive, dark eyebrows, and he was clenching his jaw as if she were stressing him. People seemed to do that a lot around her, so she knew what it meant.

"You're stuck," he said, as though she didn't already know. "You're going to get yourself killed. Should I find your parents?"

"No!" she shouted back immediately. "Maybe I'll just stay here for a while." She kicked her feet. "How old are you?"

"Twelve. How old are you?"

"I'm eight. You know, you don't look twelve."

He frowned. "What's that supposed to mean?"

"I dunno." She looked around again, still kicking her feet back and forth. "Should I jump off?"

"You'll get yourself killed if you do that!"

"Well, what else should I do? I can't live here. I'm already hungry as it is."

The boy twisted his mouth in thought. "What if I catch you?"

Julia lifted her eyebrows. "Can you do that?"

He huffed. "Of course I can!" He paused. "Well, at the very least, I won't let you die."

This satisfied her well enough. She nodded once. "All right. Catch me!"

The boy let out a shout, clearly not expecting Julia to drop down right that second, and rushed forward as she fell down from the branch. He didn't catch her, exactly, but did break her fall.

They tumbled to the ground and lay there, stunned. And when she looked over at him, he was as white as a ghost, as if he had just seen the death he had been so sure they would avoid. She burst out laughing.

"What's so funny?" he demanded, his face reddening.

"You!" She kicked her feet into the air as she giggled. "You're so serious!"

"What if something happened to you?"

She smiled from ear to ear. "You promised nothing would."

The boy gave her another frown and pushed himself up to his feet.

Then put out a hand to help her up.

After accepting his offer, she brushed the dirt and bark off her dress—there was no way she was going to look prim again—and heard her mother calling her name.

"I'm coming, Mama!" she shouted back to wherever her mother was. Julia then looked up at the boy. "Thank you."

He was still frowning. "You're a lot of trouble, you know that?"

She giggled. But then she recalled what had happened and her smile fell away. "Was that man who pushed you your papa?"

The boy immediately looked away. "You saw that?"

"Yes."

After a long moment, he nodded. "Yes. That's Father."

"Does he push you a lot?"

But he shook his head. "Never did that before."

"You should tell your mama."

He shoved his hands in his pockets. "No. She'll just get upset."

Julia felt bad. "Well, grown-ups aren't supposed to do that. That's what Mama and Papa told me. Grown-ups shouldn't lay a mean hand on children."

But the boy just set his jaw tight.

However, Mama called her name out again. As she was only eight and didn't really know what else to do, she prepared to leave. "Looks like I have to go," she said, feeling sad. "What's your name?"

He turned and started walking away. "Nathaniel."

Julia awoke with a start and sat up in bed, her head hazy and swimming. "Oh my God!" she shouted. Her sudden movement roused Nathaniel, who was, apparently, asleep right next to her. He looked up at with enormously round eyes, his black hair messy, and he kept squinting and blinking. He moved his arm off of her, but she was so excited in the moment that she didn't even realize he'd had it around her.

"You won't believe what I just remembered! I had forgotten

all about that. Oh my goodness, I don't think I've thought about that day since I was still a child!"

"You're awake." Nathaniel's eyes seemed to focus and he too flew up to a sitting position. "You're awake!"

"You told me a lie." Julia was so excited about this that she spoke as fast as a galloping horse.

"I—"

She fully turned her body to him and clasped her hands in front of her, as if she were about to begin the most fascinating gossip session. "You told me that your mother took you to America because of your father's treatment of her and his mistresses. But that wasn't the full truth, was it?"

He furrowed his brow. "No, it wasn't."

"Why didn't you tell me the truth?"

He blinked several times again and rubbed his nose. "I guess I wanted to protect you from the truth. The story I told you did happen, where she had discovered him with one of her friends, but that was a few weeks before we left. She didn't take me until my father—I'm sorry, how do you know about this?"

She was practically shaking with glee. "You were at a summer party in Bath the day before you left. Right?"

Nathaniel frowned deeply. "Yes."

"Once, a really long time ago, I got stuck up in a tree. We were at some summer party in Bath. I don't even remember whose house it was. Anyway—" And she told him the entire story, the one that had vividly roused her from her slumber, and made sure to include every little detail.

Nathaniel stared back at her, his mouth partly open. Julia thought his reaction was curious, as it wasn't *that* shocking of a story. It wasn't really so strange that they had run into each other as children but had forgotten all about it.

As she told the story, though, one corner of his mouth lifted as he seemed to recall that day, and her, too. That crooked smile, with his black, mussed bed hair and the black stubble on his face. It all warmed her heart.

Nathaniel's smile fell away and was replaced with that tight jaw he often had. "Lie back down, Julia. Get under the covers, lest you make yourself ill."

She did as he'd asked and continued the story as he ensured the blankets were snug around her. "And then I fell on you!" she said with genuine awe, turning to lie on her side. Amused, he lay down next to her on his side. "Can you believe that was me? And you?"

There was a glowing warmth in his eyes as he watched her. *Oh, my.* It struck her how handsome he looked right now. "You have a knack for climbing trees, don't you?" he asked. "And I still stand by what I said: you *are* trouble."

She laughed, but this made her realize how sore her entire body was. "Oh, I hurt all over," she said with dawning confusion as she fully realized she was in bed. With Nathaniel. Her eyes went as wide as his did moments ago. "Wait, why are you in bed with me?"

He licked his lips. "Um—"

She lowered her voice to a whisper. "Did we go to bed together?"

He turned a deep shade of red. "No, of course not!"

She frowned at his severe reaction. Would that really be so terrible to him?

He let out a sigh and rubbed a hand over his face. "Do you remember the bridge?"

Julia pursed her lips as she searched through her memory. "A bit." A memory of the bridge shaking and collapsing rushed back with a force. Her eyes widened. "Oh. The bridge collapsed."

"Yes. And it took you with it." Nathaniel then told her everything that had happened. He seemed to hesitate a bit when he got to the part where he'd saved her life but did appear to tell her everything.

"You picked up the *bridge?*" she asked, shocked that was even humanly possible.

He stammered. "W-Well, most of it was gone—"

"Nathaniel! You *picked up a bridge* and *saved my life!*" Her heart swelled and she felt tears forming. So what if he drove her mad? He'd saved her in a situation most probably wouldn't even have tried to. Maybe that was why she had remembered that long ago day after forgetting all about it.

How could she not have even a small soft spot for him now?

"Anyway," he continued, clearly uncomfortable with the attention she was giving him, "you were hypothermic and not waking up, so the doctor—oh, his name is Dr. Redfern and he's a guest here—wanted me to lie here with you. Body heat is apparently a good source of warmth."

"I see," Julia replied, taking it all in. She looked down at her nightgown. That was not what she had been wearing at the bridge. "Sorry, who undressed me?"

But the way his face reddened gave her the answer before his words did. "F-Forgive me. Everyone thinks we're married and… and it was a life-or-death situation… and—"

Her eyebrows raised high. But in the way he seemed to stutter, and his genuine embarrassment, told her there'd been nothing malicious or untoward in his action of undressing her. The embarrassment it caused him was sweet, in an odd way. She placed her hand on his cheek. It was warm and rough. "Nathaniel. Please stop worrying so much. I'm glad it was you and not a stranger."

"You are?" He sounded skeptical.

Truthfully, that surprised her too. She wasn't supposed to trust him. *Did* she trust him? She pushed the thought aside to work through later. "Yes," she decided. "And look at it this way: now we're even. Yes?"

He chuckled, and that sound put a flood of warmth through her and made her heart skip a beat.

In the moment she also recalled that, when she had woken up, hadn't he been holding her? She swore he had been, but it was all so hazy, she wasn't certain she was remembering correctly.

Against logic, the thought appealed to her.

Yesterday, she had gone to the bridge sure Nathaniel was the most awful man she had ever known. But now in a short amount of time, she thought he was wonderful.

He couldn't have been wonderful, though. He was trying to ruin her family!

Her head started to hurt. There were too many different thoughts and feelings swirling around in her right now to sort through. Even though they were enemies in terms of business, there was clearly a thread of fondness growing between them.

After all, he hadn't let her die and he easily could have. And then he'd stayed up all night with her while she'd been unconscious to make sure she was safe.

Plus, there was obviously something igniting between them based on the fact that he had kissed her two nights ago and she hadn't minded a single whit at the time. Though he hadn't been very happy about it afterward.

Laying the side of her head back down to the pillow, Julia watched Nathaniel as he moved to lie on his back and closed his eyes. He had one arm up over his head, and she admired the large bicep his pajama sleeve pulled taut over. The urge to put her hand on it was strong, but she resisted.

She did, however, make one daring decision. It was a terrible idea, she knew well enough. But she was also very good at making bad decisions.

"Nathaniel?" she asked to test if he was still awake.

He didn't stir.

Doing the exact opposite of what she should have, she slid over to be against him. The urge to be close was simply too strong to resist. And she figured she could claim it was an accident. After all, that had happened when she'd taken naps in the carriage. Half the time, she'd woken up sleeping on him and *those* moments had been truly accidental.

As she gently settled her head against him, pressed against his side and in the crook of the raised arm, he stirred.

Blast it. Her body tensed.

"What are you doing?" he asked in a voice raspy with sleep.

"Erm, nothing?"

He turned his head down to see what she was doing.

While looking back up at him, she let out a nervous chuckle, figuring he would say something like, *"Get off of me"* or *"What in the blazes do you want?"*

But he surprised her.

He closed his eyes again but moved his arm down to pull her close against him, causing something within her to leap with joy.

Oh, this *was* heaven. Julia allowed herself to sink into him and even moved her face close to his neck, relishing in his heat, and the scent of him.

His hand twitched. But he didn't ask her to move. "Go back to sleep, Julia," was all he said.

But he did run his thumb along her arm a few times before sleep took him over and his thumb slowly stopped.

Julia followed.

❧❧❧

Chapter Twenty-Four

"I REALLY AM fine, Dr. Redfern." Julia shot Nathaniel a flash of a squinty smile from across the room as the doctor pressed his stethoscope to her back to listen to her lungs.

The physician mumbled something to himself as he timed her pulse. Then, "Are you coughing at all?"

"Not too terribly. A little here and there. I'm mostly just sore. But otherwise, I'm fine."

Nathaniel shoved his hands into his pockets and returned his attention to the fire. How could she be so chipper? He was still reeling from yesterday, and those feelings of panic still lingered, like a sheen of oil on water.

A hand upon his shoulder caused him to turn. "Your wife is in excellent health, which is, to be unscientific for a moment, nothing short of miraculous."

Nathaniel nodded, but he could feel his face was tight.

"I suggest she try to get out for a bit today. Perhaps a short walk could be in order." Dr. Redfern studied Nathaniel for a long moment. "And I would suggest that for you as well."

"I'm fine."

"You both went through a lot yesterday."

Nathaniel only nodded, as it was true.

"I imagine you are still coming down from the intensity of the situation?"

He swallowed. "Yes."

Dr. Redfern looked past Nathaniel for a moment. At the door, he assumed. "Before I go, do you have any questions for me?"

Nathaniel hesitated. Something had been on his mind, but it wasn't anything related to physical health. Well, not exactly. "Yes…" He trailed off. "But it's more of a philosophical sort."

Dr. Redfern immediately put his attention back on Nathaniel. "Oh?"

This was idiotic. But still, he was curious what the physician would think. Nathaniel made sure to ask quietly, "Why are some people spared, and others are not?"

Dr. Redfern seemed to be searching for a response with the way he stared through Nathaniel, when he finally said, "Let's talk in the hallway," and led Nathaniel out of the door.

The hallway was empty and quiet as the door shut behind them.

Dr. Redfern studied his face. "You've experienced loss before, Mr. Honeyfield."

Nathaniel privately noted it wasn't a question. "Yes, I have."

"Would you like to tell me about it?"

"I—" What in the blazes was he doing? Why would he tell this practical stranger about the most horrific moment of his life? He'd never talked about it before, to his mother's and Adrian's constant irritation.

Adrian would always say, *"If you don't talk to your family, your heart will rot."*

To which Nathaniel would reply, *"What family?"*

Though in a moment of sheer weakness, he had written his father. He hadn't even cared that the man would then be able to track him down if he had wanted to. Nathaniel had been desperate, had felt lost and meaningless. Why he had wanted comfort from his blasted father and not his mother, who had protected him and cared for him all those years, he still didn't understand. But his father had been the only person he had reached out to back then. He'd told the old duke, factually, what had happened, knowing the man wasn't one for emotion, knowing he would be furious his son had been in love with a working-class American, and hoped beyond hope there would be a response. Even if it was negative, even if he berated him.

Probably aware of this, Nathaniel had never heard anything from his father.

So why was he talking now, after all this time, to a practical stranger? The words tumbled out before he could stop them. "I was engaged once before, before I knew Julia. She was killed in a train derailment. I had been with her but walked away unscathed, much like Julia will." He paused in thought. "And I've always wondered, why? Why did I live, and my fiancée died?"

Concern pulled on the physician's face. "Does your wife know about this?"

Nathaniel's mind still stuttered when someone referred to Julia as his wife. He shook his head. "No, it happened long before I knew her."

The physician shook his head, as if not understanding. "Forgive me, Mr. Honeyfield, but I don't understand what that has to do with it." But then his eyes became clearer. "You are still in love with the woman."

A sick feeling swirled through Nathaniel, guilt and grief blending together into an indecipherable gray mush. His eyes began to tear up as he realized he had to admit out loud what a horrid person he was. "If I do, it doesn't feel the same. It feels distant, almost like it had never happened. Like being unsure if a faint memory were true."

Dr. Redfern let out a sigh. "Death will always have a profound effect on our lives, my friend. And none of us can escape it. As you might imagine, I've seen my fair share of it. Death is supposed to reach us in old age, but sometimes it comes far too early and it isn't fair when that happens. There is never a good reason for it, either." The doctor glanced at the door. "Your wife is very worried about you, however."

Nathaniel blinked away the tears before they fully formed. "She is?"

"Yes. She said so in such plain words. It isn't good to keep something like that locked away, Mr. Honeyfield. It festers in our hearts and poisons us. I strongly suggest you tell your wife what happened. You may have faint or distant love for that woman, but she still has a hold on you in a way that will one day wedge itself between you and your wife once she learns the truth. And how long you kept it from her."

Nathaniel swallowed and nodded.

"Your wife cares deeply for you. And *she* is whom you owe yourself to. Forgive these harsh words, but that other woman is gone. She doesn't know you still suffer, and she doesn't care. But the woman inside the room behind us very much does. And that one deserves your full heart, not just a piece of it."

The simple words struck Nathaniel in a way nothing else ever had. And even though Julia wasn't truly his wife, the words still rung true. Nathaniel had long ago moved past Caroline's tragic death, but guilt of his survival had him holding on to her. It was time to hold on to the memories for what they were—snippets of his past—but to finally let her go.

⁂

"Oh, I am *so* glad to get out of that stuffy room," Julia said with a renewed brightness as she stepped out onto the walking path in front of the inn. For the first time in days, the sun was shining, the birds were chirping, and flowers everywhere were bursting with color. And she was happy to be alive. "How has your coachman been faring?"

"Very well," Nathaniel responded. "Apparently, Mr. Moss was stuck with the bridal suite and has been enjoying himself immensely because of it. He sent a note earlier. He'd heard about the bridge, but not that you were the woman who fell, so I let him know."

She turned around to wait for Nathaniel to catch up to her through the door—he still looked so sullen and worried—and they headed down the path side by side. The village was small, with a row of small shops on their side of the road. Across the dirt road was the river. Julia watched it for a moment, recalling the events that had occurred. The water still moved swiftly thanks to all the rain, but supposedly, it was normally quite calm.

Julia shook away her focus on the river. It was best not to dwell.

Trying to return to the moment, she took in a deep inhale of the fresh air, forgetting her soreness. The shock of the pain caused by the deep breath led to a small whimper.

Nathaniel immediately put his hands on her shoulders and looked down directly into her face. "Maybe we should get you back in bed."

"No!" she shouted, but it sounded too defensive, and she lowered her voice. "I mean, no, I don't want to go back. Please. I simply need to get out for a little bit or I'll go mad."

Judging by the worry that sat upon his furrowed brow, Nathaniel was clearly unconvinced, but he nodded slightly anyway. He did, however, take her arm in his as they began walking. "Last thing we need is for you to fall," he explained, staring straight ahead.

As she looked up at him, she wondered how true that was or if it was just an excuse to hold her. She wanted it to be an excuse. She did like being on the arm of the Duke of Rivenhall. But he had also been so worried about her all day that he had hardly left her side, so it seemed obvious this was only him being cautious.

A bit regretful, she decided that this was merely him worrying that she was going to fall, and not because he wished to hold her.

They walked at a leisurely pace, and she noted they were about to pass a tavern. "What did you and Dr. Redfern talk about in the hallway?" She had been dying to ask all morning, and now that it was afternoon, she thought enough time had passed where asking wouldn't make her look too eager.

But she was incredibly curious, even more so when his arm stiffened upon the question.

"Nothing," he decided on after a moment. "He told me you were worried about me, that's all."

"I am," Julia said and Nathaniel looked down at her. Their eyes met and her insides did a little flip.

"I'm fine."

"All right." Of course, she didn't believe him. Something was on his mind. Why wouldn't he tell her, though?

As they passed the tavern, they overheard shouting. "Oi!" a man called after them. They turned around to find a group of drunk men, none of whom looked to be the friendly sort, stumbling out of the tavern. They were frightening, with scars and missing teeth and deep scowls, and they took a few steps toward Julia and Nathaniel.

Nathaniel stepped in front of Julia. "What seems to be the matter, gentlemen?"

One of the men stumbled forward, shoved by another. He turned around and there was low, excitable whispering between the men before he turned back. He was shorter than Julia, but quite stocky. "You're not from around here, are you?" the stranger asked.

"No, we're just passing through town. Had to stop because of the storm."

"Are you that lad from the bridge?"

Nathaniel paused. "Sorry?"

The stocky man crossed his arms and narrowed his eyes. "Who would win in a fight? You? Or me?"

"Me," Nathaniel responded without hesitation.

Julia braced herself, expecting a brawl to begin. But to her surprise, the stocky man turned to his apparent friends and put his palms on his cheeks. "He talked to me! He talked to me!" The man giggled and his friends surrounded him, jumping and giggling along as well before they ran back inside the tavern, laughing.

Julia blinked. "That was…strange."

Nathaniel was of course just as confused as she was. "I'm going to blame it on the rain making everyone a bit mad," he decided on.

Julia agreed and took back Nathaniel's arm, secretly enjoying the feel of his muscles beneath, and walked just a bit closer to him. Hopefully, he didn't notice. "Oh, look, there's a sewing shop up ahead. I wonder if they carry embroidery supplies?"

"Why wouldn't they? Aren't they the same thing?"

Julia gasped. "Foolish Nathaniel! They are as much the same as a donkey and a horse."

Nathaniel chuckled as they reached the blue door and he opened it for her.

The shop was quite busy and full of everything a home seamstress could ever want. There was dress fabric, upholstery fabric, batting for quilts, needles of every material and size, silk thread, cotton thread, metallic thread. "Oh, my, what a lovely store," she said aloud.

"Why, thank you!" The shop owner, a lithe woman with white hair in a tight bun, had apparently overheard from behind the counter. As she wrote a receipt for a customer, she looked Nathaniel over and whispered something to a short, blonde woman folding fabric beside her. That woman looked the duke over, too. And so did all of the women in line to buy their sewing supplies.

A jolt of jealousy shot through Julia as she watched these women stare at him and whisper to each other. Which of course was ridiculous. Nathaniel wasn't hers, not in reality. She had no business feeling any jealousy.

Pretending that she didn't notice, she began to browse the shop.

"I don't even know where to begin with all of this," Nathaniel said, lifting up a pair of shears and turning it in his hands as if he'd never seen anything like it before. "So many different sizes of scissors. I don't understand why."

Julia laughed. "Women are quite particular about their shears, I will give you that. There're different types too, for different applications."

He frowned as he set it back while studying the large display. "I'll take your word for it."

She laughed again, and this time, his attention focused on her. There was a warmth in his eyes and it made her feel as if she were starting to glow.

And then she realized how daft that was. He was merely handsome enough that the smallest smile or tiniest bit of praise made her brain go all silly-like. He could quite literally have his pick of any of the women in this shop—no, the entire country— some of whom were far prettier than Julia.

That realization tempered her cheer.

As they walked through the shop, though, she found herself constantly looking over to the other women. They wouldn't stop staring at Nathaniel and whispering! Honestly, it was out of hand.

He probably enjoyed the attention, too.

Now feeling truly awful, Julia hastily snipped off a yard of stiff fabric and some cotton pillow filling. She had come here hoping to decide what to do with her embroidery project and in the moment decided to keep with her original plan of making it a pillow just so she could get out of the store.

In line at the counter, she could hardly look at the women and instead kept her focus on her feet. She could feel their stares, and when she finally looked up saw they were still staring at her husband.

She froze. *Not* her husband. How could she make such an idiotic mistake?

A squeeze on her shoulder pulled her from that thought. Nathaniel was trying to nudge her forward in line as she was next but was standing too far back. "I'm sorry," she said. "I wasn't paying attention." As she looked up, she found him frowning and looking her over. "I'm fine, Nathaniel. Really."

"I insist we head back after this."

Feeling defeated, she nodded and handed her items over to the white-haired shop owner.

"How are you feeling, Mrs. Honeyfield?" the thin woman asked with a pitying smile.

Julia blinked. How did they know who she was? Who she was pretending to be, anyway? "Erm, I'm fine, thank you."

"Glad to hear. What a fright that must have been! The whole town cannot stop talking about how your husband lifted an entire bridge off of you to save your life. Forgive me, but now that I can see with my own eyes that you're truly fine, I really hope that darn bridge will be replaced with a stone one."

The woman continued small talk, finished writing Julia's receipt up, and Julia handed over the coin owed. Julia found the woman staring at Nathaniel again and when she realized Julia had caught her, the woman turned bright red and hastily took the coin and gave back the owed change, retrieved from a wooden box.

Outside, Julia fumed. She didn't feel like talking and instead lambasted herself for being so obviously jealous.

Nathaniel was nothing to her. They were only here together because they had to be. They weren't friends. They certainly weren't lovers despite that one regretful kiss. The only reason he was being kind to her now was because it would have been quite rude to be snippy with a woman who had almost died.

She was mixing up politeness with fondness. Nathaniel wasn't fond of her; he just didn't want her to die on the trip while she was his responsibility.

"Why are you so quiet?" Nathaniel interrupted her thoughts. "It's unlike you."

She looked up to him and he looked almost amused with the way the corner of his mouth twitched. "I'm not quiet." Julia then made a point to not take his arm when he extended it.

Infuriatingly, this only made him grin larger.

"I want to head back, that's all," she said.

"If that's what you want."

"It is."

As they began making their way back to the inn, she noticed a small stone path between two buildings that she hadn't spotted before. The entire length of it that she could see was lined by rosebushes with pink blooms just starting to open. "Oh. What's this?" Curiosity beckoned her forward, but she stayed in place, biting her lip. Anger had made her want to go back to the inn, but this path was far too interesting to ignore.

Julia always went after curiosity. And Nathaniel followed her down the path, surprisingly without comment.

The stone path went beyond the back of the shops. Eventually, they came to what appeared to be another road, but it was lined in stone walls too high to see over. The damp air and ground, plus mossy, old stones and the rosebushes, made the scene like a living painting.

Eventually, the path ended at a lone, little house.

It was an old cottage, one with a thatched roof. Smoke curled out of the chimney, and it had the most luscious cottage garden she had ever seen. Sprays of purple, white, and yellow spread over the garden.

"What an adorable, little house," Julia said out loud as she looked up to Nathaniel. "Could you imagine living here? Oh, let's go see the flowers, please?"

"When have you ever *asked* permission to do anything?" Nathaniel smiled widely at this and it caused her idiotic heart to palpitate.

"You're right. I don't want to bother whoever lives here, but their garden is darling. I must see it." Julia marched forward clutching her paper bag with fabric and pillow filling to admire the blooms spilling over and through a white fence. There were thick masses of hollyhock and daisies, lavender and roses, bursts of color and fragrance everywhere. Butterflies and bees danced.

"This must be the happiest spot in England right now." She crouched down to smell a red rose. It smelled like cinnamon.

Standing back up, however, her head started to feel funny. Light. "Oh," she said with surprise as she put her hand to her head. Her vision started to turn gray and fuzzy.

Nathaniel immediately rushed to her side. "What's wrong, Julia?"

"I think I'm going to faint," she said, her voice weak.

"Sit down." Nathaniel gently helped her to the ground and grabbed her parcel. "Put your head between your knees."

"What?"

"Just do it. You need to get blood back to your head."

Julia did as told and realized Nathaniel crouched beside her, holding her hand and running his thumb back and forth over the top of it. But it was merely him being concerned. Anyone would be in the moment.

She tried reassuring him. "Just give me a moment and I'll be fine."

"I don't think you've eaten enough in the last twenty-four hours. The first thing we do once we get back is get you in bed again. And I'm bringing you more food."

Julia's eyes closed and she merely nodded in response. Off in the distance, she heard a door open and feet shuffling. Too weak to move, she let Nathaniel figure out what was happening.

"Heavens, what's going on?" a woman's voice asked. "I saw this young lady nearly collapse from my window!"

"She'll be fine in a moment," Nathaniel replied. His voice was so comforting and Julia was glad to have his hand to ground her spinning head. Feeling a bit vulnerable and embarrassed, though, she leaned slightly against him. He put his arm around her.

Nathaniel and the woman continued talking, but Julia focused on feeling better again. When the gray fuzziness dissipated and she felt sure she could safely stand up, she said, "I'm ready to stand."

Nathaniel carefully helped her to her feet, standing up again himself, still clutching the parcel close.

"I'm so sorry," Julia said to no one in particular. "I don't know what came over me."

"You need tea and biscuits, my dear." The voice Julia had heard belonged to a short, plump, elderly woman in a brown dress. "Come inside, then." The woman indicated that they follow her and she walked back to the little cottage.

"Do you want to go in? Or head back?" Nathaniel lowered his head to ask.

Julia came to the unexpected realization that Nathaniel almost always asked what she wanted. He didn't dictate—unless he felt she was in danger. But on everything else? He never told her what to do.

This was a rare quality in a man. Of the few men of the *ton* who had paid her any attention since she'd come out, they'd always made statements *at* her.

"We should go get refreshments." Not *"Would you like a refreshment or are you all right for now?"*

"You should go back to your mother." Not *"Would you like to continue conversing, or would you like to go back to your family?"*

And instead of laughing at a funny story or joke she told, it was always, *"That is not an appropriate joke to tell."*

Nathaniel could be Sir Crabby, that was certain. But he never treated her like a lesser, even if she technically was.

"She looks harmless enough," Julia said up to Nathaniel with a small chuckle, flushing from this realization about her rival. "I think we can go inside for a few minutes."

Chapter Twenty-Five

NATHANIEL GLANCED ABOUT the room when they entered the cottage. It was a rather old home—thatched roofs were becoming more and more uncommon—but it felt warm with the fire, faded rug, and well-loved mismatched furniture that defined the small living area. An orange cat also curled up in the window soaking up the sunshine, and the air smelled like chicken soup.

He noted a worn leather chair and, with his hand on the small of Julia's back, guided her over to it, being sure to keep close just in case. She turned her face up to him as if surprised by this gesture, causing a rush of heat in him. His only concern was getting her comfortable, and he had let himself be far too familiar with her. He expected her to make some kind of wry comment about the way he'd touched her but instead was met with a smile.

Figuring that wasn't a negative reaction, and his concern for her remained high, he crouched down beside her and set her parcel down while the elderly woman went to the back of the house, where, presumably, the kitchen was located.

Nathaniel moved his hand to the arm of the chair for balance. "Are you feeling better now?"

Julia gave a small nod. "I was just lightheaded. Sitting for a few minutes is all I need."

He was about to stand when she surprised him and put her

hand over his. Taken aback, he met her eye to see if she was in a humor and jesting with him, but he instead discovered a strange expression.

Julia seemed unsure.

A flush of pink bloomed on her cheeks as caution shone from her eyes. Neither of them said anything, instead staring at each other while the moment stretched on. Amongst the busy sounds of the clattering kitchen, Nathaniel held his breath and waited to see what she would do next.

But she didn't do anything further. She merely stared at him with those doe eyes of hers, causing an odd warmth to sputter to life and slowly begin to churn in his heart.

Before logic could talk him out of it, Nathaniel decided to make the next move. He turned her hand over and weaved their fingers together. Color rose higher in her cheeks, but her eyes glittered as a shy smile crossed her face.

Nothing about this beautiful woman seemed shy. Julia was overtly sociable. And loud. The opposite of shy and demure. But here she sat before him appearing quite vulnerable, a word he would normally never associate with her.

He had, somewhat against his will, uncovered the true feelings he held for Julia, though he admittedly still struggled to believe it. Could it be possible she had feelings growing for him, too?

He silently cursed himself for lacking the ability to know her inner thoughts. For being too scared to allow hope to shine through.

Emboldened to take it another cautious step further, however, Nathaniel decided to at least make the daring move to lift the back of her hand to his lips. While holding her gaze, he pressed a long but gentle kiss upon it. Her eyes held his, unblinking, and she swallowed.

Then leaned toward him, ever so slightly.

His stomach flipped and his pulse quickened. After that kiss they had shared, the one he'd thought he'd regretted, he'd been sure that it had been a fluke and would never happen again. Perhaps emotions had been high, or they had simply been lonely at the same time while on their travels.

But maybe, he had been wrong about that.

"Nathaniel?" Julia spoke his name on a gentle whisper.

Tingles ran down his body in response.

"I was wondering…" Julia paused, then stammered. "I-I—" Her mouth shut.

What? What was she wondering?

But the moment she opened her mouth to continue, the elderly woman came bounding back into the room. Not realizing she had interrupted something—whatever that something was, Nathaniel was sure he would never know—the friendly woman set a tray down on a table near Julia.

While his nerves rankled at the interruption, Julia's face held no emotion. She appeared calm, collected, and Nathaniel wondered if maybe he had misread whatever had just happened.

Disappointment and humiliation sunk within him like a leaded weight.

"Tea, biscuits, and some fruit." Their elderly hostess pointed to each. "Something here should help settle your nerves." The woman then placed fists on her hips as she looked down at Julia with a furrowed brow.

The urge to care for Julia in response to the older woman's concern overwhelmed the embarrassment Nathaniel felt. He cleared his throat and began to prepare a plate for her and pour her tea. It didn't escape him that he was a duke doing work a woman or servant normally would. And yet he found he didn't think anything of it.

"First-class service," Julia mused as she took the plate from Nathaniel. Her eyes were glowing. She held his gaze before flushing and turning to their hostess. "Thank you for doing this for me and allowing us into your home."

"Think nothing of it," the white-haired woman said with a nod. "It's nice to have other people in here. I'm a widow, and it's been quiet for a very long time. My name is Mrs. Potts," she said as she sat in a chair across from Julia. "You can sit as well, if you'd like." Mrs. Potts indicated another open seat.

But Nathaniel shook his head. "I'm fine, thank you." He preferred to stay by Julia's side in case she fainted again. But Mrs. Potts insisted once more.

Julia agreed, apparently. "You should sit. I promise I'm feeling much better."

With some hesitation, he took a seat nearby without further argument. He knew there wasn't a chance he could change their minds.

"So." Mrs. Potts slapped her hands down on her knees. "You are the Honeyfields, I presume?"

Julia stilled just as she was about to take a bite from a biscuit. "How did you know that?"

"The whole town knows who you are! They call you"—Mrs. Potts met Nathaniel's eye—"'the Big, Broody Bloke.' And how accurate! You're quite easy to pick out with that nickname."

Nathaniel frowned deeply at that description and looked over to Julia to see if she thought it odd as well, but instead of finding her surprised as expected, it appeared she was trying to hold back laughter.

"That explains our entire walk into town," Julia said, the corners of her mouth twitching just before taking a sip of tea. She set the teacup back down. "Everyone was staring. At him." A flash of something then crossed Julia's face, but it was so brief that Nathaniel couldn't place it.

"Well, it's good to see you unharmed and up on your feet, Mrs. Honeyfield," replied Mrs. Potts. "It really is quite miraculous what your husband did. Not only did he save your life in such a dramatic way, but after what had happened, the town finally decided to build a stone bridge, putting up a temporary wood one for now. We can all hardly believe it." She now looked directly at Nathaniel. "You must love her very much."

"I—" Nathaniel scrambled for how to respond. Even though

yes, he had fallen for Julia, he knew well enough that he couldn't tell her that. "She is my wife." He added an awkward chuckle. That seemed a safe response.

"I'm quite curious to hear the true story of what happened," Mrs. Potts said. "I've heard so many different versions."

"'Different versions'?" Julia asked just before nibbling on a biscuit.

Mrs. Potts leaned forward, evidently eager to gossip. "Oh, yes. My favorite so far is the bridge gave you a splinter and your husband was so upset you were hurt, he ripped it out of the ground and threw it into the river."

"That seems like a totally reasonable response," Nathaniel chimed in dryly.

Julia laughed brightly. "You are rather protective of me, though, aren't you?"

Without thinking, he replied, "Of course I am."

Julia gave him a sheepish look before grinning down at her biscuit. She was probably trying not to laugh at him.

"What brings you out this way?" Mrs. Potts asked.

Nathaniel shifted in his seat, as he was generally one to keep his life private. But they had already talked about their purpose with people here in Cloverly, and that may have traveled with the gossip already circling about them. "We're on our way to Hamwich. I've been tied up a bit with business regarding the textile mill there."

"Oh, the textile mill?" Mrs. Potts replied. "You don't mean Brumstock Mill?"

Nathaniel nodded, hoping he was able to keep his surprise and eagerness off of his face. Any information he could get about the mill before his arrival was more than welcome.

"That's bad business, that." She shook her head.

"You're familiar with it?"

Mrs. Potts had her lips pressed tightly together as she seemingly considered whether or not to divulge. "I used to work there about twenty years ago. Once my husband and I became too old to continue working, we ended up here." She glanced around the living room fondly. "Best years of my life, they were."

Feeling uncomfortable—what was he supposed to say to that?—Nathaniel decided to go back to the mill. "What was it like working there? We've not heard good things, and I had no idea it had such a bad reputation."

"There is no such thing as good factory work. It's grueling. Long hours, physically taxing. Dangerous equipment can maim you if you're not paying attention. You know, the usual."

He nodded, as he was aware of the danger. Most people were.

"It was entirely women who worked there when I did—I don't know if that's changed or not; I doubt it has—but it was difficult especially for those with little ones. What do you do when both you and your spouse have to work, but you have a child home sick? Which one of you stays home?" She looked over at Julia and gave her a knowing look. "Or what if you're feeling poorly yourself? Because you'll likely get fired if you stay home ill."

"Why did you end up leaving?" Julia asked.

"It got too dangerous. My husband made me quit. Like your husband, mine was quite protective of me."

Nathaniel fought the urge to shift or clear his throat.

"I used to…" Mrs. Potts took a moment to consider her next words. "I used to get quite ill every month. I wouldn't be able to get out of bed sometimes."

"Ah," Julia said as if understanding. Though Nathaniel hadn't the faintest notion.

"I collapsed from the pain one day while working there and narrowly missed getting tangled up in machinery." Mrs. Potts shuddered at the memory. "The foreman at the time was quite irate when it happened, even after I explained why I had fallen."

Julia finished off her first biscuit and was reaching for another one. "He was mad at you? You couldn't help what had happened."

"You and I know that, of course. But he didn't believe *it* could be that bad. Insisted I was faking it or using it as an excuse to get out of working. As if I wanted to miss a day's pay!" Mrs. Potts let out a bark of laughter and shook her head. "No. We needed that money. But when I went home that day, I did tell my husband what had happened."

"What did he do?"

Mrs. Potts smoothed her hands over her lap. "I never asked, but I know he went to talk to the foreman. He had left the house shaking with anger and came home with a pocket-full of coin and told me I never had to go back there. I assumed he'd threatened the boss and gotten paid to leave. We moved into Manchester after that, but I was forbidden from any more factory work, not that I was going to argue with that. So, I worked at a dress shop. I can't create an even stitch to save my life, but it turns out I'm very good at convincing wealthy women to buy expensive dresses with all of the trimmings."

Julia laughed.

"The foreman when you worked there." Nathaniel furrowed his brow in concentration. "It didn't happen to be a Mr. Fitzhugh, did it?"

Mrs. Potts went still at hearing the name. "I do believe that was it."

He exchanged a look with Julia, but neither said a word.

"He was quite young when I was there, in his twenties. A man that young bossing around a woman twice his age, ha! He wasn't present much, not that we complained. He often missed work or came in late and left early. None of us questioned it because he was otherwise difficult."

"How so?" Julia asked.

"Some days, he would have no direction for us. No goals or quotas for the day. Then, I assume, that would catch up to him and he would set impossible expectations and yell and scream, not to mention his usual handsy- and lewd-remarking self. Basically, he made everyone unhappy until he lost his voice or became tired. Before I left, I swore there were a few times I smelled liquor on him."

So the fellow often exhibited lewd behavior, shouted, and overall made everyone miserable. But he often drank on the job as well? The man sounded impossible to deal with. Nathaniel rubbed his hands over his face.

There was a gentle touch upon his knee. "I'm feeling much better," Julia said, not moving her hand. "If you want to go back?"

Could she read his mind? All this talk about the mill's foreman had Nathaniel's thoughts whirling. He needed to write to his solicitor and update the man on their stalled trip in case anything important had come through. He also needed to figure out what, exactly, they were going to do once they got to the mill. Though they had no idea what they were walking into, it was clear it would not be paradise.

All he knew so far was that they had met two women who knew about the mill, and both had shared stories about it that he noted had affected Julia quite deeply.

Agreeing that it was time to depart, they thanked the kind woman for her generosity and care and departed for the inn.

As soon as they'd emerged onto the stone path in the cottage garden, Nathaniel offered his arm to Julia without thinking twice about it. Perhaps a bit surprised, her face turned up to his and he noticed a curious look in her eyes. A ghost of a smile crossed her lips before she took his offered arm and moved to be as close to him as she could.

Never one to faff about, Nathaniel knew he needed to put a plan together for how to approach the mill now that he had some insight into its inner workings.

He also couldn't tell Julia how he truly felt about her. Not only because one of them would end up hurt by the other because of the mill, so it was fruitless. But also because, though her view of him had clearly softened, he knew he felt far stronger for her than she did for him.

At least he could attempt to find a way to minimize the pain in both regards.

Chapter Twenty-Six

As soon as the pair had returned to the inn, Nathaniel walked Julia to their room before fetching her some food, though she hardly could eat another morsel after meeting Mrs. Potts. Julia had noticed a change in Nathaniel after their departure and could only describe it as *an impenetrable wall of seriousness.*

A small desk sat in the room that neither of them had used much since their arrival, but he parked himself in its chair and for the next several hours quietly wrote letters and looked through the mill documents she had brought along.

Several times, she considered asking what he was doing, but he seemed so focused on his tasks, she was afraid to interrupt.

Julia took a nap, and when she woke, the sun had gone down. She went down to dinner, ate on her own, though several people stopped to check on her, and came back up with a plate for Nathaniel. He remained at the desk just as she had left him.

Her returning presence seemed to pull him out of his concentration because he suddenly stopped, set the pen down, and put his attention on her.

"You have to eat at some point," she mused, noting the studious crease in his forehead and finding it a bit endearing.

Nathaniel rubbed at his eyes. "I'm sorry. I should have brought that up. I didn't realize what time it was. How long have

I been sitting here?"

"Several hours now. I'm not sure exactly how many." There was a stamped envelope set to the side.

Nathaniel must have noticed it had caught her eye. "I'm sending a rushed letter to my solicitor to let him know about our delay. If you'd like to write your family, I can send mail for you as well."

"How long would it take to get to them from here, do you think?"

"It will arrive late tonight or tomorrow. There are mail carriers for critical mail who travel with armed guards and through the night. Even though the road is impassible for this town from the north, they still come by through the south and send it off on a train station a few hours away from here. Unlike me, mail goes on trains." He looked up at her with a humored glint in his dark eyes.

Julia wondered if now would be a good time to ask about his aversion to trains, but the nervousness she felt made her decide against it for the moment. The thought of writing to her family, however, invigorated her. "Actually, I would like to send a letter to them, if you don't mind."

"Of course not. I'm sure they're eager to hear from you." And with that, he dove back into work.

She placed a hand on his shoulder. "Don't forget to eat," she reminded him. He made a grunting response and placed a hand over hers in a promise.

His touch sent a jolt through her. She had noticed these small, familiar touches happening between them frequently that day. What it meant, exactly, she had a hard time determining.

Finding paper and a sharpened pencil, as well as an almanac to use as a writing surface, Julia curled up in a chair by the fireplace. In the silence of their room, she proceeded to write several pages to her family about the excitement they had experienced since leaving London.

She told them about the robber and how she had discovered

his conspirators hidden in the forest. She told them about the rainstorm and getting stuck at the inn (though she left out the part about sharing a room with Nathaniel; she wasn't quite sure what their reaction to that would be and decided it best to be cautious by keeping that to herself). And she told them about the interesting people they had met along the way.

As Julia reached the part about Nathaniel saving her life, she paused and studied him. He hunched over the desk, his black hair sticking up in every direction as if he had raked his fingers through it while thinking.

It was one more endearing piece of the man that had crept up on her and confused her.

All day, she had been at odds with it. It was like there were two voices battling in her mind.

Nathaniel obviously cared for her wellbeing, but any person with the most basic of morals would as well. That didn't mean he held a special affection for her. He simply didn't want her to get hurt or die, especially while he was responsible for her. Just like she wouldn't want that to happen to any strangers she passed by in her day-to-day life. It didn't mean anything beyond the average concern for another human being.

Nathaniel scribbled something on a piece of paper, lost deep in his own thoughts. His large, masculine hand held the fountain pen gently and she recalled that same hand holding hers earlier.

Julia frowned to herself remembering it. A man didn't hold a woman's hand as a friendly gesture. Nor did a man kiss a woman who was only a friend.

But this was Nathaniel. And she was Julia. And they couldn't stand each other.

Perhaps they had received head injuries in the bridge incident.

Nathaniel rubbed his jaw in thought, and she noted that his dark stubble was starting to grow back. He was so utterly attractive, especially with that mysterious shadow that surrounded him perpetually. But every other woman thought so, too, as she had seen. Not just in the ballroom, but even out here in the English countryside.

The duke never would have taken notice of her if they hadn't been stuck together like they had been. He had his pick of whatever woman he could ever want. Why would he want a Honeyfield? Julia knew the entire family had a negative reputation due to the barony being newer and her mother being a commoner—and an actress, to top it all off. And that wasn't even mentioning Julia's penchant for being unchaperoned.

A lump formed in her throat.

So much confusion surrounded her. They had kissed and it had been passionate, but then he'd seemed unhappy about it. But also, Nathaniel had saved her life. He'd stood at her side. He'd held her hand.

Under the right circumstances, perhaps they could not only get along, but find a mutual attraction. And while they may have been getting along well enough now while stuck at the inn together, they would have to leave and return to real life soon enough.

A life where they were foes. Where he was trying to ruin her family, and she was trying to ruin him back. Even if they married—not that that would ever happen and why that thought had even crossed her mind, she couldn't begin to fathom—the mill would remain a financial drain to the both of them, leading to utter ruin.

The mill was an inescapable burden, an impenetrable wall standing between them.

"You said you had tried selling the mill, right?" she called across the room.

He didn't lift his head. "Yes. There were a few businessmen who were interested, but once they looked at it closely, they all lost interest."

"And why didn't you shut it down instead?"

There was a long pause. "I suppose my own history in America, as well as my friends there, made me a little more sympathetic to the workers. I hope there's a solution."

She watched him continue to read before returning to her letter, but her mind remained on him.

She couldn't keep brushing off the growing feelings she had for him, and she wasn't daft enough to think they would disappear once they reached Hamwich, where they wouldn't be able sell the mill, which would have made all of this so much easier.

Her affection for the duke strengthened every day. When she had first recognized it, she'd been sure it had been something that would fade quickly. Handsome men often become quite boring and lackluster after one spent time with them. But the affection hadn't weakened as she had expected it to. It had grown stronger. And not just little by little—it had seemed to fly straight up.

Anything between them would be impossible, she knew this, but her heart kept pushing back against that negativity and fighting against logic.

Normally, a particularly difficult conundrum would be solved by spending an evening talking it out with Helen. They would stay up all night together and Helen would help her figure out a solution.

But Helen wasn't here. Julia was all on her own and had to figure out what to do without the help or input of her family.

She had to be independent for this one.

Julia looked down at the pieces of blank paper she still had.

While she had to face this one on her own, she could write Helen her own letter. Julia could work through it that way, by pretending to talk to Helen about it. That seemed like a good solution.

Julia pulled a new piece of paper over and put her pencil to it.

Dearest Helen,

How I miss you so! Every day, I find myself wishing I could turn to you and talk, but obviously, you aren't here.

First, if you haven't read the letter I sent to Papa and Ma-

ma, read it at once! I have been on quite the adventure as of late and the events disclosed in the letter will be pertinent to the rest of this one. Now, go read that letter.

Have you returned? Excellent.

I am working through a conundrum that would probably be solved if you were here and I could talk to you. Unfortunately, you are not here, so I will write this letter to you instead and work through it on my own that way.

I am utterly despaired to report to you that I am finding myself quite attracted to Nathaniel.

Sorry—the Duke of Rivenhall.

I can already see the look on your face. Yes, I know he despises me and the family. And we may be months away from ruin because of him, also. I'm aware of it all.

Because of the above, and I'm sure more I am not thinking of in the moment, I have enjoyed annoying him every chance I get. I find great joy in the unamused expressions he gives me in return.

However, recently we seem to be warming up to each other. I will admit to you that we kissed one night and it was something I will never be able to forget for the rest of my life. Figuring that had to have been some sort of fluke, though, I did my best to move past it, especially as the duke had seemed displeased that it had happened. But everything changed when he saved my life yesterday.

Helen—the man dove into dangerous water and lifted a bridge to save me. He pulled me out, carried me to land, and breathed life back into my lungs! He was my brave knight, rescuing me from the threatening dragon like in a fairy tale.

Have you ever before heard of something so brave and romantic ever in your life?

And he has been stuck to my side like my own shadow ever since, watching me with ever-present worry. He constantly asks me how I am feeling. Or if I need anything. Insists that I rest and eat enough food.

And the funny thing? In a strange way, I enjoy the attention. Writing it out, it sounds like it would be most irritating and suffocating, but for some reason, with him, it isn't.

It's endearing. I never would have expected to discover that the duke is a kind and caring man.

Don't tell Mama and Papa this next part. I know they're often unaware or uncaring of what I do, but even they may put their foot down about this. Last night, he slept beside me in bed because I was hypothermic and the physician told him body heat would help me. We pretended to be married when we learned only one room remained at the last inn we could find, so the physician of course thought nothing of prescribing this.

All night, Nathaniel lay next to me in the bed, making sure I was breathing and warm. He held me close to give me the best chance to recover. I know he did that only because it was the best chance of recovery, however.

It's a miracle I escaped all of that with nothing but a few minor scratches and some soreness.

But, dear Helen, my heart doesn't seem to be escaping unscathed.

You and I both know I'm secretly a deep romantic. Logically, I know Nathaniel did all of that just to keep me alive, for the general care of another human. Anyone else would do the same, or at least try to. But my heart won't accept that logic. It wants to believe there is more to it!

We went for a walk today to get me out of the inn, and the simple outing was one of the best of my life. Feeling weak, I hung on to his arm the entire time and oh, the leaps that tickled inside my belly from the simple touch! And then he held my hand after I had felt faint, and while my heart wants to find romance in that, I wonder if he had merely been trying to comfort me.

I don't know what to do. Here at the inn, we're in our own little world. We aren't enemies. I enjoy his company and, believe it or not, I think he enjoys mine. Oh, Helen, how do I clear my mind of him before we leave and become foes once again? After my bridge incident, the town has agreed to finally build a stone bridge and a temporary wood bridge will be accessible tomorrow. I will likely be at Brumstock Mill tomorrow, and I am finding myself hoping he sleeps by my side again tonight because I want to be aware of his closeness, to be held by him. Perhaps it will soften the heartache I am destined to feel at journey's end.

Julia paused her writing to glance up once more and found Nathaniel stretching his muscular arms high above his head. At some point, he had rolled his shirtsleeves up to his elbows and his corded forearms flexed with the movement. As he did this, he seemed to fully notice his plate for the first time. He looked back over his shoulder and caught her watching him.

"Did you get this for me?" he asked, nodding toward the plate.

Julia tucked an invisible tuft of hair behind her ear. She knew he didn't care for her in any significant or lasting way, but they were obviously beyond friendship. She wanted to sleep beside him again, to be held by him again, but this time be aware of it. It was a strange request, one that was unbelievably and ashamedly inappropriate. Would he laugh at it? At her? Perhaps he would balk at her.

"Yes, I told you about it, too," she replied while trying to work up her courage.

"I'm sorry. I've buried myself far too deep into this." The duke tapped at the desk. "I won't be much longer. I promise."

"It's not a problem, I'm just writing to Helen. What are you doing, exactly? I've been wondering but didn't want to interrupt."

He let out a sigh and rubbed a large hand over his dark, stubbled cheek. His shoulders were starting to sag, and there were shadows under his eyes. "I'm trying to figure out what our plan is once we arrive."

Our plan? Julia decided to keep that comment to herself and clamped her mouth shut.

He continued. "I'm not one to head out on a multi-day trip to arrive somewhere without a plan, no matter how small it may be. What time would be ideal for us to arrive at the mill? Should we give advance notice? Should we be nice and give Mr. Fitzhugh time to explain himself, or should we go in demanding answers at the utter failure of the mill?"

"I'm not sure what's best for *you*, but I plan on arriving at my earliest convenience, not a set time, and going from there. And what exactly would we plan for? For all we know, the foreman might be in his cups or still at home nursing a headache. And from what we've learned about him, Mr. Fitzhugh seems a combative man. Are you going to arrive planning on an amiable and nice conversation but then realize he's ready to argue to the death, or worse, fight?"

"It's always best to go somewhere with a plan set in place, even if it has to change." Nathaniel took a bite of his food and returned his attention to the papers before him.

Resisting the urge to roll her eyes, Julia said, "Then our plan is we arrive defensive. Not offensive. On our guard, not jumping out of a carriage to immediately antagonize a hotheaded man who enjoys bullying women. And that's that." And she promptly returned to Helen's letter, receiving no further argument from him.

> *As I write to you, I have discovered he can still irritate me as much as he ever did before. But it's almost amusing now, if anything. It isn't a true bother like it once had been. Not so many days ago, I utterly despised the man. Now, I can't imagine him not being there.*
>
> *I hope I can handle it when we separate.*

Upon her throat tightening, Julia stopped again to watch Nathaniel some more. Soon, he would be gone and would no longer be a daily presence. They would likely see each other at dinner parties and balls, perhaps even summer house parties, but it would never be like this ever again. In fact, they would likely do everything possible to avoid each other once one ruined the other.

She may see him on occasion, but they would never skirt

friendliness again. In fact, they probably wouldn't even speak to each other. It would be too hard.

Uncharacteristically distressed, she did something rather daring. Nervous, she stood and crossed over to him. Her pulse racing, she stopped behind him, unnoticed. Then she placed her hands on his shoulders and, without uttering a word, began to rub his shoulders slowly. For a long moment, he sat there, probably surprised, but didn't say anything. She massaged his shoulders for a few minutes, then moved up to the base of his skull, where she often felt tension on herself, but then she decided to try to test something a little more intimate: running her fingers through his black hair.

His hair was thick and there was a lot of it, but it was silky too. She enjoyed the feel of it sliding between her fingers.

"Thank you," he whispered as he let out a contented sigh.

Satisfied by his reaction and taking it as a sign that he wouldn't balk at her request later on, she went to return to her task and leave him to his work.

But instead of doing what she had expected, the duke spun his desk chair around and pulled her onto his lap, causing her to yelp. Her hands resting on his chest for balance, she stared down at him with wide eyes to discover a tension in his face that she had never seen before.

And she could feel his heart racing as quick as her own.

Nathaniel's arms wrapped around her waist, tight with possession, holding her close, as if he didn't want her to move away. She fit perfectly in his embrace, and his body felt hot and hard against hers. Their faces were close enough that if she tilted her face even a little, their lips would touch.

He held her gaze for a long moment, as if coming to terms with what he had done, before searching her face.

If only she could read minds and know what his thoughts were.

Not one word was uttered by either of them, but she wasn't sure there were any good words for the moment. They sat like this for a long while, and it seemed to be a moment for feeling, not speaking. She wasn't even quite sure what, exactly, was happening or what this was. He held her in an intimate embrace but didn't kiss her like he had before. He didn't do anything beyond holding her.

It was entirely possible he didn't know what he was doing, either.

She gave him a small smile. "Nathaniel."

His breath hitched upon hearing his name, as if she had broken a spell, and he grabbed her face with both hands, palms rough and warm. His eyelids lowered as their breathing quickened, and then he slammed his mouth to hers. She couldn't help but whimper into the kiss, run her hands through his hair again. The duke, a man whom she had thought emotionless and severe, gave her the most impassioned, heartfelt kiss she had ever experienced in her life.

They pulled apart a minute later, breathing labored, staring wide-eyed at the other. He gave her a lazy, crooked grin that absolutely destroyed her.

"That was a nice distraction," he said finally.

She couldn't help but grin back, feeling almost foxed. "I thought you could use a little break."

"I definitely needed a break for that."

"You aren't mad?"

He gave her that crooked smile again. "For that? Never."

Unable to help herself, she gave him a lip-biting smile in return. Courage now renewed, she asked, "Will you be sleeping with me again tonight?"

The grin melted away as he studied her face, his eyes guarded. "Do you wish me to?"

Instead of responding verbally, she gripped his loosened cravat with one hand, pulled him forward to brush her lips over his, and this time kissed slow and gentle. When she broke away, she said, "I hope that answers your question."

Nathaniel cleared his throat. "I think so."

Julia climbed off of his lap and gave him a coy grin. "Don't work all night," she said in a singsong voice as she returned to her chair and her letter.

She allowed herself one final quick glance of the duke and discovered he was watching her slouched in his chair, his knees wide, eyes dark beneath lowered eyelids. He didn't say anything for a long while as they watched each other in the dim light of the room, but eventually, and with a sigh, he returned to his work.

Satisfied, Julia returned to her letter as well, feeling much more confident in herself.

Chapter Twenty-Seven

THE REASON NATHANIEL sometimes had a nightcap before bed was it helped his mind slow down from the day. His mind often felt like a room of circulating air full of feathers. Each feather represented a different thought and they swirled and flew chaotically in the daytime. But once he sat down for the evening with his glass and a book, the feathers fluttered down to the ground and all became calm.

Once that happened, he could sort through his thoughts more clearly.

Right now, as he read his book, his mind began organizing the day's events and thoughts into categories. Work-related feathers regarding the dukedom or mill became tied together neatly. That evening, he had gone through all of the mill documents brought on the trip as if he were a detective hunting for clues that would guide him on how to shed the land, or how to help her shed the mill.

Unfortunately, he didn't find anything useful. But he wouldn't give up so easily, either.

There *was* a conclusion he was able to come to regarding their arrival at the mill: they were planning on leaving tomorrow if the temporary bridge was ready as planned. They would arrive during the first half of the workday. This way, the workers would be settled in for the day but not yet checking the clock every few minutes eager to go home. He knew from experience the first half of the day was when people were in their best mood while at work.

Additionally, he decided not to give advance warning to Mr. Fitzhugh, as he suspected many of the mill's issues stemmed from the foreman. The mill's books, for example, didn't make sense once he'd really sat with them and finally figured out why. The hours from the workers clocking in and out seemed to be recorded correctly. There weren't any glaring differences week to week that raised any red flags. Additionally, their recorded wages matched their hours worked.

What *did* stand out, however, was that the income from selling the textiles didn't make sense. Similar types of textiles shipped out in similar ways—for example, tweed by train to London or linen by hand delivery to local businesses—often had very different earnings from orders that were the exact same but on different days.

Something about this didn't sit right within Nathaniel.

But it was also possible he simply didn't know much about selling textiles. Different fiber qualities, whether it was woven (done by machine) or knit (done by hand), different dyes, if there were patterns or not—all of it must have affected the cost. And it made his head jumbled.

What he did conclude was that his father must have been absolutely mad to think he could run a business he'd known nothing about.

Unfortunately, Nathaniel had also come to accept that he wouldn't be able to identify the true cause behind the mill's money drain until he went there in person to see everything for himself and talk to those familiar with the inner workings of the mill.

The books could have been manipulated, or the workers might not have been putting enough product out to recover costs. There was no way for him to know until he arrived on site and investigated in person.

Nathaniel had also sent out the letter to his solicitor, and Julia's letters to her family. He was reassured by the fellow who picked them up to send off that they would arrive by tomorrow morning at the absolute latest.

That had him satisfied at least.

The other feathers flying around in his mind that day were solely dedicated to Julia and his ever-deepening feelings for her. She had asked him to sleep by her side again tonight, and in the moment she had asked, the question admittedly scared him. He didn't know what she was asking for, exactly, and he felt too embarrassed to clarify.

Worse, he kept waffling back and forth on whether or not he should tell her his…inexperience.

But that wasn't all he needed to tell her, either. He had also come to the conclusion to divulge everything tonight: not just his lack of experience in regard to intimacy, but about Caroline, as well as his mother and Adrian.

And he was terrified. He had never opened up to someone close to him in such a raw way. Something as minute as a slight hesitation from her would feel like a stab to the heart.

But, despite his fears, he had to tell her about all of it. He couldn't keep his past from her any longer. It had too much to do with the man he was today.

Mustering up a bit of bravery, Nathaniel watched as Julia sat by the fire drying her hair, bedecked in a nightgown covered in tiny bows. About an hour ago, he had taken a break from the mill documents to allow her to take a bath, per her own request. He had gone down to the dining room, where several people had held conversations with him. He vaguely recalled questions asking after Julia's health, and some discussions around the bridge as well. Several had insisted he stay with his wife when he'd inquired about helping them put up the temporary bridge. But otherwise, he really didn't have much detailed recollection of any of it. His mind had been too distracted. All he could think about was Julia upstairs in the bathtub, the gentle sound of dripping water, what the scent of soap upon her skin would smell like.

Unfortunately, he had a vivid imagination and could nearly experience it all as if he were in the room with her.

What would he do tonight if she offered herself to him? Would he really be able to turn her down like he had thought he could not so long ago? They wouldn't be in each other's futures, which of course they had already known.

But then would he regret not being with her when he could have? Furthermore, would he be able to live with himself if he did and didn't offer marriage?

And what if he did offer marriage despite everything with the mill?

The mill would still be their downfall, so it would be out of duty, of course. Right?

The thought gave him significant pause.

But that was assuming she even wanted that. Perhaps he was getting a bit too ahead of himself.

After some time, he returned to their room and readied for bed while Julia sat quietly by the fireplace, combing her fingers through her now mostly dry, long, chestnut hair.

Nathaniel watched her do this as he changed into pajamas, brushed his teeth, and washed his face.

"Julia," Nathaniel said when he'd finished. His heart jumped alive and started to race, nervous that it was now time. It was a cool June evening, and the light from the fire and lamp beside the bed provided a dim but warm romantic light. "Come here." He motioned to the bed before climbing in.

Julia sauntered over and climbed under the blankets with him without any hesitation.

He lay on his back while staring up at the ceiling, finally deciding that he would follow her lead in whatever happened. Or didn't happen.

But whatever the evening led to, he wanted to talk to her first.

Without saying anything, Julia snuggled right up against him and rested her head on his chest, releasing a contented sigh. There was no hesitation from her, no caution whatsoever. She seemed so sure of this, while he seemed to carry all of the worry.

Despite this, Nathaniel closed his eyes to relish the feeling of Julia snuggled up to his side, warm and safe.

"I need to tell you something," he said once he'd mustered up the courage.

"And what might that be?" Julia's voice seemed cautious yet curious.

He turned to his side in order to face her and found her frowning slightly at him.

Itching to touch her, he reached out to a piece of her hair and began gently curling it around a finger. "First, I need you to know something, in case you don't know already. I find myself incredibly attracted to you. I don't know if it's because we've been together constantly for the last several days, but you're on my mind all the time. So much so that I've been trying to reconcile why I had disliked you at first." He hesitated. "I don't think it was any secret that we didn't exactly begin as friends."

She furrowed her brow but waited for him to continue.

In response, his heart started to race faster. "I'm drawn to your beauty, Julia, make no mistake. But now that you've had a chance to know me better, and I you, you now know I'm a rather withdrawn man. I prefer it that way and always will be that way."

Though she kept quiet to allow him to talk further, her stare had become pointed.

"I just want you to know that," he added. Confidence faltered in her silence. He was really going to make a mess of this, wasn't he? Already, it felt like he fumbled around.

"I already knew that, Nathaniel," Julia finally said. Then she grinned, coy. "Do you really think I'm a beauty?"

"Surely, you already knew that."

She shook her head.

With a swallow, he nodded. "Then yes, it's true. I thought so when I first met you thanks to your, erm, misplaced blueberry. At first, I found you to be too much of one person. Too loud, too energetic. And your family has an infamous reputation."

She began to sit up. "Are you trying to—"

He gave a small chuckle. "Julia, sweetheart, give me a moment to finish my thought. Please?"

Slowly, she lowered back down to her side.

"It's no secret that many of the *ton* dislike your family. I'd heard it all from them. And I've heard your father's bawdy stories, which I admittedly find distasteful."

"You *really* do not need to tell me what, exactly, those stories entail, but you are aware those stories are about him and my mother, right? Not him and random women? He has never had a mistress or set his attentions on any other woman other than my mother."

He stammered. "I-I didn't know that, actually. And that further supports what I'm trying to get to. First, though, I want to ask you: did you grow up a happy child?"

"Nathaniel, *where* are you going with all of this?"

"I've told you small pieces about my family, but I want you to know all of it tonight."

She blinked. "You do? Why?"

"Because I—" He nearly told her the truth of his feelings for her but caught himself right in time. He wasn't a fool; he knew that once they left, everything would go back to the way it had been before. He knew she didn't feel as strong for him as he did her, but also, the blasted mill risked wedging itself between them. But they still had tonight. "Because I want you to know everything about me. I have been telling you careful snippets here and there. My family life was not happy, as you know. But I've never heard you talk about yours."

Julia looked off to the side, as if lost in thought. "My childhood was rather standard, at least in that nothing traumatic or exceptional happened. I suppose it will come as no surprise that we did things a bit different on occasion. We had our meals together when children usually eat separate from their parents. Went on holiday together, played parlor games together, which I suppose isn't so unusual. But we go everywhere together; it doesn't matter where. Balls, shopping, promenades, all of it. Well, I didn't go to balls. But when I was small, my mother brought me along with her to the modiste, which are some of my favorite memories, in fact." A pause. "None of my friends back then went to the modiste with their mothers. Or, really, many places with them in general. Not until they were much older, at least."

He reached his hand out to her cheek and ran his knuckles lightly across her soft skin. "You're right, that is unusual in the *ton*. And I admit their negative talk about you, your family, it initially affected my view of you. Then I spent time with you. I know your brother's absence affects your family and I see the way you bury your feelings about it and ignore it. But I think from what you've told me, you've all handled it the best way you can. And, yes, your father tells bawdy stories, even if they are about him and your mother. And despite how everyone judges your family's behavior, they keep you all around for humor at your expense. And you all embrace parties more than most. But you're a close family. You're happy. You get along. You love each other. You enjoy life together. That is *not* how it is in the *ton*. Most others have stories similar to mine. Abusive fathers are aplenty, so are absent or emotionally distant mothers. There are secret children from affairs, just endless trauma and drama and secrets. Julia, my pretty Julia, the ones who turn their nose up at you are *jealous*. And they are not better than you. In any way. Quite the opposite, really."

Julia pushed herself up, her eyes as round as saucers. "Do you think so?" With a shake of her head, she gave a small laugh. "You think all this time, that's what their issue with me, with us, has been?" Tears welled in her eyes.

He continued caressing her cheek. "Yes, I do. They see that you go wherever you please, when they can't. They see that your parents love each other, when their own don't. They see how unbothered you are by social constraints that may as well be law to them. And they lash out, judge you further, wag their tongues more with the hope of bringing you down to where they want you to be. There is nothing wrong with you. You're charming, beautiful, funny, smart, spirited, interesting, fashionable."

She placed her chin in her hand. The sadness in her eyes disappeared to be replaced with sparkling humor.

His heart swelled because he knew he was the one to have done that.

"What else am I?"

He laughed. "Perfect."

With a wide grin, she studied his face. "I like you very much, Nathaniel," she said before leaning forward to place a gentle kiss on his cheek.

"Now that I've established that I think you're perfect," he said, "I want to tell you about my life in New York."

"All right."

His courage was starting to falter again. Could he do this? Could he really open himself up to someone again? "As I've previously told you, my mother and I lived on a farm in upstate New York. The farm was owned by Adrian, whom I had worked for. At first I'd thought he despised me, but when I was older, I realized that was the opposite of true." Nathaniel paused, remembering those long-ago days. "As you know, getting a divorce granted in our country is near impossible. My father probably could have made a case if he had made public where my mother had gone and argued abandonment or something, but he didn't. I never found out why, exactly, but I figured it was one of two things: either he didn't want to face the humiliation, or he wanted to keep my mother looking over her shoulder with the knowledge he could reappear at any time to take me back."

Julia's eyebrows furrowed. "I don't understand."

"My mother and Adrian had fallen in love, Julia. I don't know if my father knew about Adrian, but I'm sure he at least assumed she would eventually find someone else. Anyway, my mother and Adrian have been together almost since we had arrived in America. Of course, they couldn't get married, so they had to keep it relatively quiet. They kept it quiet even from me for a long while."

"Wait, your mother is still alive?" Shock rang true in her voice.

"Oh, yes. Though when my father passed, she didn't want to return with me. That would mean leaving not just Adrian behind—he has the horse farm that he can't easily leave—but the life she had built over there as well."

"That is understandable."

Nathaniel sighed. "For so long, I thought Adrian hated me, but in truth, he treated me as if I were his son. He broke me in, helped me adjust to my new life, then helped raise me during some of the most difficult years of childhood. It took far too long for me to realize he was a good father to me when all I had to compare him to was my own father."

"Oh, Nathaniel." Julia laid her head back down on her pillow. "You must miss them so much."

He looked away. "I do. I've felt like an outsider here. The Earl of Fenwick has been my only genuine friend, and I'm grateful for his friendship. We hadn't seen each other since we were children but quickly fell back into it as if no time had passed at all. And then, well, there's you now, too."

She flushed prettily but didn't respond. Again, he was getting too close to how he felt for her. Time to move on.

He put an arm over her side and began to rub her back. How did she not see in his face, in his own eyes, the way he felt for her? "I have one last thing to tell you." His pulse began to quicken again, dread sliding through him like a snake. Though determined to tell Julia about his life in America, this next part was really what he was dreading most.

She gave a nervous chuckle. "Why does that sound like a warning?"

"I-I…" He stammered. Cleared his throat. Forced the words

out. "I was engaged. When I lived in America."

She paused so long, it hurt. "Oh."

Nathaniel closed his eyes briefly and took in a deep breath. He wasn't sure what to say next.

"I'm assuming you loved her?" Julia asked, making the correct assumption. Being away from England, he would have been free to choose who would be his wife, as the pressures and expectations that come from being the only son of a duke were nonexistent over there.

Nathaniel finally opened his eyes. "Yes, I did."

There was another long pause. "You're not about to tell me you're married, are you?"

"No," he rushed the word out. "We never married. And I never married anyone else, either."

The tension in her face softened, and he didn't dare to allow that to comfort him, as it would be short-lived. "What happened, then?"

His heart pounded hard in his ears. "She died."

Julia sat up straight, her face pale and eyes wide. "Nathaniel! How could you keep something like that to yourself?"

He fell back and covered his face with his hands. "Because it's a horrific story." After a beat, he forced himself to tell her about the train derailment. Told her, essentially, the same exact story he had told Dr. Redfern. Julia didn't move the entire time and hung on to his every word.

Once the whole sordid tale had completed, she stayed quiet. Instead, she stared off in the distance at nothing for a long while. Coming to terms with what he had said, taking it in, maybe thinking about how she wanted to escape this room, escape him.

At least, he assumed that was what she wanted to do.

Then finally, she said, "Is that why you have this?" As she spoke, she moved one side of his unbuttoned pajama shirt to the side to expose the scars the accident had left behind. She placed a gentle hand over it and, for some reason, this made emotion tighten his throat like an overstretched violin string.

"Yes," was all he could say.

"I'm so sorry." She breathed out. "I don't even know what else to say. That's so sad, so horrible."

"Yes." He swallowed the lump in his throat. "There's a reason I'm telling you about Caroline, though, Julia. While I want you to know what had happened in my past, I also want you to know she's a *part* of my past. It happened long enough ago that I'm no longer drowning in that grief. I've been able to move forward with my life, and I want to continue to move forward, where I didn't before. I want you to know I've been in love before, and while she will always hold a special place in my heart, she no longer holds it all to herself."

Julia pulled back. "What are you saying, Nathaniel?"

Blast it all, he'd gotten far too close to that again! He took a deep breath to re-center himself. "Part of why I'm telling you this is because Caroline, like most women, wanted to wait until marriage for us to lie together." Hoping that would explain it, he stopped talking and waited.

"All right…?" Julia frowned and furrowed her brow.

She didn't understand what he was telling her, and he let out a small sigh. "I've never been with a woman before, Julia."

Julia stared at him for a long time, her soft, pink lips just barely parted. She didn't say anything. She didn't move. She simply looked at him with a blank, almost guarded, expression.

"Are you lying to me?" she whispered.

The corners of his mouth pulled down. "Am I lying? You think a man would lie about something like that? Do you know, at my age, how humiliating that is for me?"

"You've never even been with anyone since she passed?"

He hadn't. And he'd never really given that much thought to it, either. "No. I suppose I could have if I'd wanted to. It never had appealed to me, really."

But Julia didn't say anything. Instead, she stared at him with that blank expression again. The room was frightfully quiet, the only sound the occasional pop from the fireplace logs.

"Blast it all. Would you say something?" He collapsed back down to his pillow and stared up at the ceiling. Shame coursed through him. "You find me a laughingstock now, don't you? I was afraid telling you this would completely turn you away from me. I took the gamble, but I should have known—"

With lightning speed, Julia bolted upright, hovered over him, and pressed a hard kiss down to his mouth, stunning him silly. When she finally broke away, her eyes welled with tears. "You stupid, ignorant, beautiful man—you don't know anything, do you?" A sob topped it off.

"What? I—"

She slammed her mouth down to his again, but this time, he was prepared. He wrapped his arms around her tightly to hold her close, and they kissed ferociously.

He had shown her the most private pieces of his life, something he had been terrified to do. And she hadn't laughed at him. She hadn't made faces or jests. She hadn't questioned him—not beyond trying to understand better—and hadn't turned her back to him like he had feared she would.

Julia accepted him and his past exactly as it was.

And in this realization, his worry melted away and everything became clear. He didn't wish to wait any longer, and there was absolutely no doubt in his mind about that. It surprised him in the moment to come to such a big realization, to make such an important decision, but it was the right one to make.

Nathaniel grabbed her face with his hands and kissed her slow, with the love he felt for her in his heart. Soon, he would tell her the truth of his feelings for her. After all, being with her meant he would have to propose marriage to her. Blast the mill and its ruination! Perhaps he was becoming harebrained by her, or perhaps he had come to realize what truly mattered in life.

But would she be receptive to marrying him? To loving him?

Doubt bloomed in his stomach. A warning he would have to examine. But tonight, he was going to willingly give this part of himself to her, though he knew he would never be the same.

Especially if she denied his offer.

Chapter Twenty-Eight

J ULIA KNEW GOING to bed with her mill nemesis would end up being a bad idea, but as was her nature, had done it anyway.

But Nathaniel Blackwell, the Duke of Rivenhall, Sir Crabby, defined temptation. How could she deny herself when he looked at her like *that*, his gaze anchored to her with those hooded eyes, his face slightly slack with wanting?

She couldn't deny herself any of it. Wouldn't, in fact. No one would ever find out what they had just done, after all. Their travel together was unknown to anyone outside of family and servants, plus his solicitor. All of whom were trusted. She trusted the duke fully, too. He was far too much of a gentleman to gossip about it or their shared intimacy. And her family would get too tired from too many questions and would come up with a convincing story of illness to explain away Julia's absence.

Julia well knew he would explain his silence on the matters as protecting her reputation, as if he didn't know hers had already been sullied by her habit of gallivanting around wherever she pleased.

By herself.

The only consequences she would suffer would be emotional and easily hidden away.

What she still couldn't fathom was that Nathaniel had never

been intimate in such a way before. She believed him, of course—there was no doubt he was being honest about that. When he'd opened up to her—not just about his lack of experience, but the raw truth about his past—there'd been the oddest feeling in her heart, like it soared high above in the sky, sparkled like the stars out of reach. She had a feeling she knew what that was, and took it as a warning.

That feeling was also probably the worst outcome that could arise from all of this.

Briefly, as they lay side by side while coming back down to earth, her eyes closed with contentedness, she wondered if he would have the gentlemanly reaction of offering marriage. For the briefest moment, the thought pleased her. Imagine her, of all people, marrying the mysterious and handsome duke!

She knew better, though. A duke would never want to marry someone like her. And in fact, she rather liked being able to gallivant about as she wished.

It was good they were leaving tomorrow. She was glad for it, in fact. There would be no shed tears, no regrets weighing on her heart. None at all.

As Nathaniel gently ran his fingers over her bare back, a small voice in her head told her that she wouldn't, in fact, escape this unscathed, but she shooed it away. Reality had no place being in bed with them at the moment.

Julia listened to his racing heart as she tried to come to terms with the fact that yes, that had truly just happened. He had given himself to her like that. And she had given herself to him.

Julia opened her eyes and lifted her head to look at him, discovering him watching her, and felt herself flush under his study. "Did you like it?"

Nathaniel chuckled deeply, and the sound sent a rush of tingles up her spine. "Did I like it?" He then nuzzled against her hair. "My pretty Julia, I don't think a word exists that does justice to how I feel right now."

She couldn't help but grin, feeling girlish and even a bit shy.

Nathaniel turned to snuff out the small flame in the lamp beside the bed. The only light now glowed from the dying embers in the stone fireplace. "Was it…" He paused, as if trying to find the right words. "Was it all right for you?"

"Darling, my entire body has melted and I'm not quite sure I'll recover."

He laughed, but it sounded like relief to her ears.

"I could get used to that, in fact," she added on without thinking. Immediately, she silently cursed herself in the dark because she felt his body go tense.

"Julia," Nathaniel said after too long of a hesitation.

"But we will be leaving," she continued, putting an end to that conversation before it could even begin. When he didn't say a word further, her throat felt tight. "Time for sleep."

WHEN JULIA AWOKE the next morning, the sun shone brightly, and blankets wrapped around her tight. With a yawn, she stretched and let her arms fall out to her sides.

And she found the bed empty and cool beside her.

Her eyes flew open. Where was Nathaniel?

Quickly, she sat up, pulling the blankets with her to keep covered. She glanced over to the spot where Nathaniel had held her overnight. But now, he was gone.

Caution snaked through her. She should calm down, use a bit of logic before she let emotion get to her. Maybe he was going through his traveling trunk?

Her eyes darted around the still, quiet room. Not only was Nathaniel not going through his trunk, his trunk had disappeared entirely!

She swore out loud, a fiery fury blasting through her.

He had *left her.*

No. No, he hadn't simply left her. He'd snuck out! How he'd

managed to wash up and dress, pack up, then leave with his trunk all without waking her, she couldn't figure out. But somehow, he had done it. He thought her a fool.

Unfortunately, he would be right!

She closed her eyes and took a deep breath. She wanted to go and destroy anything she could grab, but she wouldn't give him that satisfaction, not that he would ever know. It took some prolonged deep breathing, but she was able to calm herself down enough to function at the very least.

Julia quickly washed up and changed, then threw her belongings together in her trunks. She was relieved to find her coin purse, but as she hadn't been keeping track of every single coin, she couldn't tell if he had taken any of it to continue on with his travels.

But anger overtook her and she decided that he wasn't, in fact, the gentleman she had thought. Which could only lead to the conclusion that he had both left her and taken her money.

"I will *kill him.*" She growled the words to herself, as there was no one else to hear.

Once her chore was completed, she stormed downstairs and marched up to their redheaded innkeeper, Mr. Baker, who had just checked in a visitor.

He looked her over as he set his pen down. "Good morning, Mrs. Honeyfield! Did you sleep well?"

She could feel heat creeping over her face at that question. "I shall need to hire a hack to the Manchester area. How long does it take to get there from here?"

He scratched the side of his nose. "Oh, about two hours, maybe a tad more."

Since Nathaniel had a head start, he would get to the mill first. Blast it all!

"And the temporary bridge, is it in working order?" Maybe it was still out of service and the duke had been delayed.

"Yes, it is, it re-opened at sunrise. Many people are quite happy about that!"

The man's cheeriness did not help her mood at all. In fact, it might have made it worse.

Clenching her fists, she thanked him before going into the dining room. Her eye twitched while she tried to keep her anger below the surface.

She couldn't believe they had shared last night together and the blasted duke had run off like a coward before she'd woken up.

"Julia!" someone shouted.

Her gaze darted around the crowded dining room until it landed upon Martha White waving her hand high in the air. Martha smiled widely, her eyes crinkling with it. Julia was jealous of her cheerfulness—everyone seemed so happy this morning— but went in the direction of the woman, anyway.

Julia sat at Martha's table with a huff. Martha, whose brown- and gray-streaked hair was in her usual low bun, furrowed her brow.

"Stressed about your travels?" the woman asked.

"Something like that." The waitress came by and despite Julia's fury, she still managed to have an appetite and ordered warm oats with fruit. Once the waitress had left, Julia put her attention back on her friend. "I'm glad, though, that I'm almost at my destination. I'm surprised to see you eating alone this morning." Julia had seen Martha and her husband, Joe, together at all times during their stay here.

Martha was in the midst of taking a sip of coffee and raised her eyebrows at Julia. "You are? My husband is with yours; I thought you knew that."

Julia furrowed her brow. "Your husband went to Manchester with mine?"

Martha's eyes went wide and she belted out a laugh. "Goodness, no! The men had breakfast early this morning, went to make sure the bridge was operating, and now they're fetching your driver at the other inn."

Julia frowned. She had noted before that at the front entrance of the inn there were always several travel trunks waiting for departure, but it didn't occur to her to check if Nathaniel's was there.

"You thought your husband had left without you?" Martha asked.

Julia forced a smile. "It does seem silly now."

Martha set her coffee cup down as the waitress returned and set out Julia's breakfast. The older woman studied her for a moment, as if at odds with herself over something. Finally, she leaned forward and spoke in a low voice. "Forgive me for prying, but your husband did seem in a rather sour mood this morning. I figured it was simply stress from travel, but now I wonder if everything is not all well with you two?"

At first, Julia felt surprised to receive such a personal question. But it wasn't as if she would see Martha again after they left. And the woman did seem to genuinely care. Maybe she would offer a word of advice. If only Julia could tell her the full truth of everything. "I do think travel adds stress, but I don't know. We seem to be at odds with each other." It was the best way to describe it to a sympathetic ear. She thought back to the night before, how he had stiffened and gone silent after her comment about "getting used to that."

"Over what?"

Julia stirred her spoon in her food a bit. The reason Nathaniel had acted odd after her comment, at least partly, seemed obvious now after the clarity of a full night's sleep. He regretted their intimacy because he incorrectly assumed she would become emotionally clasped to him now, thanks to her offhand comment. Their affection for each other came easy in Cloverly because it was a temporary escape. Once they left, they would return to reality. And in that reality, Julia was a scandalous Honeyfield and he was the crabby duke who was verbal about the fact he didn't wish to marry right now.

Plus, they remained at odds with what to do with the mill.

However, she couldn't very well tell most of that to Martha. She could, however, bring up the mill.

"As you know," Julia began, "we're going to be looking at that textile mill in Hamwich for business reasons. I'm not sure what he thinks he's going to find, but…" She decided she had to fib a bit. "He seems to hope to buy it for a low price."

Martha nodded as if understanding. "I *have* heard rumors the owner has been trying to sell it, but no one wants it. Not that I blame them, of course. It isn't doing well. Though perhaps the owner would be willing to sell it for a very low price at this point."

"But it would cost some coin to bring it up to current standards, don't you think?" Julia asked. "I haven't seen it, but it sounds like it's been in disrepair for a while now."

"To be honest with you, I think the factory itself is fine enough. I mean, everything always needs upkeep. But the problem seems to be with the workers."

Julia was taken aback. "Really? That surprises me. I figured the mill was rundown and not working efficiently."

"It's not. Usually what happens is the workers become unhappy. The women who work there certainly are. And the foreman, if he doesn't care about the work getting done, then why would they? I wouldn't work my fingers to the bone if I didn't have to."

Julia had to agree. "Nor would I." She could not know what it was truly like working in a factory, but she knew enough to know it was grueling. "We seem to be at odds about the mill. I think it's a terrible idea. He thinks it brilliant." That was the best way to verbally explain them at odds with each other, at least.

Martha sat quiet a moment, presumably mulling this over. "I don't know the right answer, but I can tell you something that may help. Take it from me, those women need to be happy to work there. If you two are able to somehow buy it, leave the business part to him, and you can take on the women. They won't care what your husband has to say. But because you're a woman, and you know what it's like to be a woman, perhaps they will listen to you. Or at least, you would have a better chance at reaching them."

Julia considered this as she ate her breakfast. What Martha had said made sense. She wasn't quite sure just yet, but she felt like this advice would come in handy in the future. Would she tell Nathaniel about it or not? As she had yet to see him this morning, she wasn't sure where they stood after what happened last night, especially now that she knew he had not, in fact, abandoned her.

"Enough about business." Martha waved her hand dismissively. "I'm sure part of that sits on your husband's shoulders. But I've also found, despite what they claim, men are far more emotional than women. They take slights to heart more than we do, even over, erm, heated discussions over business. Or not over business."

Helen met Martha's gaze. Did she know there was more to her worry with Nathaniel, then?

"We women have to be tough in this world, don't you agree?" Martha asked.

"Yes, I do."

"I've found that when Joe and I have a disagreement, no matter how mild I perceive it, he's the one who needs his wounds soothed. I can feel better on my own, but he always needs attention from me. Now, I'm not sure if something did happen between you and your husband, and if it is about the mill or not, but I can tell you he is likely taking it to heart more than he will ever let on."

Julia had her doubts. "Perhaps. I don't know."

Martha leaned forward, gave Julia a motherly pat on the hand coupled with a wink, and then sat back. "Despite what people say, marriage is actually easy if you genuinely love each other. I think too many people marry for reasons that aren't for love, or they make themselves think they're in love when they aren't. And any reason for a marriage outside of love can always be lost. But love, true love, cannot be shaken. Everyone goes through good times and bad times—I'm not saying everything is always perfectly happy. But on those difficult days, if you are able to say to yourself, '*At least he's by my side through this*,' then all will be well."

Julia wasn't so sure about that but nodded anyway.

And then Martha's face brightened. "Ah, here they are!" She stood up as her husband approached her and they gave each other a quick kiss as a greeting. Nathaniel trailed behind and saw how they greeted each other, too. But still, when he greeted her with only a tense nod, her stupid heart still managed to hurt.

Vowing to never again let him bother her, she turned away from him gracefully as he sat beside her.

"Your silly wife thought you had left her behind!" Martha chuckled and playfully patted Nathaniel's forearm.

Nathaniel shifted in his seat and then hazarded a glance in her direction. "I didn't wish to wake you."

"It's fine," Julia said with a flat tone. She refused to look in his direction.

He let out long breath. "Will you be ready to leave after you eat?"

"Yes, my trunks are all packed."

Nathaniel jumped up from his chair suddenly. "I'll go tell Mr. Moss so they can be loaded up in the carriage, then." And he ran off.

As was his usual response when in a slightly uncomfortable situation.

Julia watched him disappear through narrowed eyes. It seems he had decided avoiding her to be the preferred reaction after last night.

Likely, that meant he regretted it. She was a Honeyfield, after all. Perhaps in his own clarity after a good night's sleep, he had realized the full depth of what a terrible choice she was as both a bed partner and a life partner.

So be it. Maybe last night meant nothing to her, too. Maybe her affections for him had faded as well!

They hadn't, of course. But he didn't need to know that.

Julia tried to reach back into the past to recapture the old feelings she used to have for the duke.

Except she couldn't muster them up. She didn't find that annoyance in her heart, and she definitely didn't despise him. Instead, she recalled vivid snippets of last night and it made her heart beat faster.

Chapter Twenty-Nine

NATHANIEL DIDN'T SEEM to breathe until they passed over the temporary bridge and were safely on the other side of the river. And then he could hardly believe they had finally managed to leave Cloverly.

His nerves had been on edge all morning anticipating their departure. He'd awoken with a start before sunrise, and when he couldn't fall back to sleep, he'd packed. Julia had still been sound asleep, so he'd snuck out with the trunk, lest the inn workers make a loud fuss doing it for him and waking her, and gone with Joe White to check on the bridge.

But the previous evening had not been far from his mind since he'd opened his eyes to the day. Nor was what he wanted in his future. But how to bring that up? Did he simply blurt the question?

No, she would think he'd asked out of duty. And he did not want that. He wanted her to believe his question to be true, and from the heart.

Nathaniel looked over to Julia seated beside him in the carriage as they bumped along the dirt road with more divots than usual thanks to the rain. Julia's attention was squarely out of the window, but she had her embroidery hoop in her lap.

He studied her creation. It was a large piece of cloth covered in flowers of different sizes and colors.

"That turned out nice," he said, wanting to compliment it but not sure how to.

Julia looked down at it with a frown. "I'm going to make it into a pillow. I was going to give it to you, but then I changed my mind. I made it, so I think I shall keep it."

Nathaniel didn't know what to say to that. Was she sour toward him? Why?

He had fallen even more in love with her after they'd shared the previous evening together. But maybe she didn't feel the same way. Maybe she had simply wanted a tumble in the sheets and that was it.

After all, ignoring him seemed far too easy for her right now to think that she felt as he did.

With a sigh, he looked back out his window, unsure how to handle her unexpected mood. A crisp, blue sky draped overhead, and the sun shined brightly. It was a beautiful late-spring day with a hint of summer in the air.

Yet he felt drab and gray.

But he wasn't having it. He forced out what needed to be said, even though it terrified him to open himself up in such a way. "Thank you. For last night. For sharing that with me."

Her eyes flew up to his and her cheeks reddened. But she put her attention back out her window as if dismissing him. For a moment, he was wrought with despair.

And then she said, "I thought you abandoned me this morning."

He frowned. Deeply. "Why would I leave without you?"

"Because you regret last night."

"I don't regret last night at all. Why would I?" He furrowed his brow, trying to understand that statement but failed to do so. "Even if I did, that doesn't mean I'd leave you stranded like that."

Her mouth opened, but she promptly slammed it shut. Then, after a moment, she turned back to face him, though her eyes remained averted. "I suppose last night was very nice."

Very nice? That was how she saw it? To him it had been life changing, soul shattering. "That's it, then? It was just a nice evening? I don't get it."

"And that's it, yes," she said. "It was your first experience. I assure you that you will find a similar experience with other women, you don't need to worry about a Honeyfield clasping on to you. As an unmarried duke, you should know by now there is an unending string of women who would be happy for your, erm, *companionship.*"

"No, I won't find something similar, actually," he replied with a dark voice. "And I don't want to experience that with other women." He nearly added that technically, he had ruined her and they would have to marry for her own sake, but that would not go over well. To say the least.

Her eyes widened and flashing with anger. "Why are you making this so blasted hard?"

"Why does it have to be hard?" Nathaniel ground his teeth with frustration. He loved her, he wanted to tell her, he wanted to show her. But for some reason, she brushed him off when he opened up the subject. "I want you, Julia, I want you for myself. I don't want anyone else, and I don't want anyone else having you. I am very selfish in that regard and don't care to share."

Julia choked on a sob of a laugh. "And you are going to do that how, exactly?"

Nathaniel clenched his jaw again. In his mind, this conversation was supposed be emotional. Maybe they would kiss, exchange pretty words and open up their hearts and minds. But instead, it felt like an explosive was about to ignite. He wanted her to know he loved her first, and he wanted to know how she felt about him.

Before he brought up the most important question of his life. This all had to be done according to plan or it wouldn't work. And yet she seemed to be unraveling that plan.

"Are you going to ask me to marry you? And are you going to ask my father for permission first?"

He cursed inwardly. "I don't have to ask for his blasted permission if I want you to be my wife. I'm a duke, aren't I?" He said the words low and could hear the danger in them.

Her face was bright red. "Actually, you do need to ask him. I don't know how it happens in America, but that's how we go about it here in England. And my family means everything to me. If you can't ask my father, if my father isn't amenable to it—and I very much doubt he would be—then there's nothing I can do to help you."

"Are you saying there's a possibility?"

She gasped with genuine outrage. "You can't be serious! Nathaniel, I'm a Honeyfield! You know my reputation! I understand you're still coming down from the events of last night, but do you fully understand what you're asking here? I have a terrible reputation. You cannot be serious right now. You're a duke and I'm an unruly Honeyfield." She flung a hand to the window and her voice climbed high with distress. "And what about the mill? What about the fact that you purposely tried to hurt my father, my family, with your mill? You would leave us destitute without a thought, and in fact we're on our way to that right now, are we not? What about the fact that we are ruined because of you? Do you really think some miraculous solution is going to emerge when we get there? No! Our reason for coming here is because we are desperate. You. Me. Neither of us knew what else to do, except go to the mill. But we keep ignoring the truth and the truth is this: no one will ever buy the mill because everyone else is smart enough to see how hopeless it is. And then, after all of that, you're going to ask my father if he would agree to a marriage between us?" She laughed, but it wasn't the sound of amusement.

He swallowed.

"My family would not accept your interest in marriage to me because of all of the above, and my family means everything to me. Please get this silly notion of marriage out of your head at once. I am simply not worth it."

Despite that it was clear she was spiraling out of control in mind and emotion, everything she'd laid out was the painful truth. He could see the defiance in her eyes as she'd said it all, daring him to lie to her and tell her she was wrong.

But she wasn't, and they both knew it.

His heart fell into a million pieces. He tried to keep his face blank, but he failed at that, too, and could feel it harden protectively. He didn't know what he looked like and didn't want to know. He probably looked rather pathetic. But her face softened ever so slightly. "I'm sorry, Nathaniel. But it is the hard and cold truth."

"Not to make things worse," he said, making sure his voice sounded as bitter as he felt, "but I fell in love with you on this nightmare of a trip and it will become one of my life's biggest regrets."

Infuriatingly, she only responded with a nod, then turned to stare out the window again. There were no words said in anger at him, no gasping, not even shouting, which he almost would have preferred. Instead, he could hear sniffles. She was crying. He had made her cry. And there was nothing he could do to make her feel better, either.

The remainder of the hours-long drive to Manchester was horrific. Neither of them talked to the other, and Julia cried on and off. He felt horrible, but just because he wasn't crying didn't mean she hadn't destroyed him as well. He probably felt as wretched as she did.

Once they'd arrived at Hamwich, they located the mill quickly. It wasn't too far off the main road they had come in on. The mill was an enormous, red brick, multi-story building. The land it sat on and the empty area around seemed to expand forever. Beside it a small canal rushed by. It was rather rural compared to the factories in London, though Manchester was only a few more minutes down the road.

As they approached the building and the carriage came to a stop, one of the factory's doors flew open and a crowd of women came filing out. They were talking all at once to each other, but the noise didn't sound like happy chatter, as one would expect to hear during break time. It sounded terse, maybe even a bit angry.

Nathaniel climbed out of the carriage with Julia following and promptly ignoring his extended hand. Neither said anything to the other, but they did exchange frowns.

There looked to be about two hundred women workers when they had all filed out and the doors shut behind them. As the last woman joined the expansive group, they gathered together to face the door they had just exited and began chanting while pumping their fists into the air:

No work for no wages!
No work for no wages!
We don't work for free!
We don't work for free!

Were they not being paid? Or were they playing with words and were simply unhappy with *what* they were being paid? That had to have been what it was. Nathaniel had seen with his own eyes that they were paid. Mr. Fitzhugh recorded their wages each week.

Then a man emerged from the door. He looked to be in his late fifties, maybe early sixties. He was mostly bald except for a few remaining thin, sporadic ribbons of hair that blew about with the wind, and he had a bulbous, red nose. His clothing was worn and messy-looking, and he was holding a bottle of liquor. He looked over the crowd of furious women and laughed before taking a swig from his bottle. Nathaniel had to stare at the man for a long moment, shocked by what he was looking at.

Was this Mr. Fitzhugh?

During their trip, they had heard nothing but negativity about this man. But was he really so bold as to walk around a factory with a bottle of liquor?

No, it couldn't have been him. This was absolutely ridiculous.

"Are you just going to stand there?" Julia asked Nathaniel.

His face pinched, but he didn't know what to say.

She scoffed and grabbed his arm. "Come on."

Nathaniel told Mr. Moss to wait for them, and the coachman nodded. Nathaniel was dragged over to the crowd of women by Julia and, together, they walked around the edge of the angry gathering when one of the women noticed the pair. This woman approached them with caution in her eyes.

"What do *you* want?" the woman asked in a heavy Manchester accent.

"What is going on here?" Nathaniel replied before Julia could speak up. Julia shot him a look but didn't say anything.

The woman, who had on a worn, cotton, gray dress, somehow seemed to be the same age as Julia but looked far more weathered, with a ruddy complexion. But of course, she likely had had a far more difficult life than Julia. "We're furious. What does it look like?" the woman finally said.

"Is that the foreman?" Nathaniel indicated the scruffy man laughing at the women.

"Yes, that's Mr. Fitzhugh. The worst boss anyone could ever have. He's been here forever and treats us worse than he does mules or street mongrels." She looked over at the man and shook her head. "If I could get a job anywhere else, I would, but I'm stuck here for now. Hoping that it will get better. Imagine my surprise when it doesn't!" Of course, that last bit was dripping with sarcasm.

Another woman had noticed them talking and approached as well. This woman was very thin and tall, and she wore spectacles on her narrow nose. "What's going on, Cynthia? Who are these people?"

The woman they had been talking to, apparently Cynthia, turned to the other woman. "Hello, Mabel. I don't know. They appeared right as we started striking. I just wanted to make sure they weren't the police." She gave Nathaniel a long look over, her mouth pursed. "Definitely not the police."

Julia stifled a laugh as the tall woman's eyes went quite wide.

"Oh, that would be quite bad if they were," Mabel said to her friend.

Nathaniel ignored their judgement of his appearance. "Why would it be bad if the police showed?"

"Because they would pummel us and arrest us, of course." As Mabel said this, she removed her glasses to polish the glass lenses, as if she were simply sharing the time of day to an inquisitive stranger.

Julia's mouth made an "O." The comment had rendered her silent, which was no small feat.

The enormous crowd of angry women continued their fist-pumping chant while Mr. Fitzhugh continued his drunken guffawing. Nathaniel wondered how often walkouts like this happened. It would be infuriating to work for someone like Mr. Fitzhugh, to have to answer to someone you didn't respect. He had struggled with working for Adrian, but at least he'd respected the man, as he had seen how well he treated the horses and the men who worked for him. Adrian would sometimes do the grueling work at Nathaniel's side, too. Hard to begrudge a boss who did that.

"What business do you have here?" Mabel asked, looking between Nathaniel and Julia.

"Yes," Cynthia asked, crossing her arms and looking the pair over with a narrowed gaze. "Why *are* you here? And, perhaps more importantly, who are you?"

Nathaniel wished they would have known the women would have been protesting upon their arrival. His plan had been to walk into the mill, get a chance to look around and see how everyone worked. And then he would go and approach Mr. Fitzhugh in private and demand answers.

It appeared that not one plan of his today would progress as he'd wished it to.

Instead of him questioning Mr. Fitzhugh, they were being questioned by the workers and there were quite a lot of them. And they looked as if they were ready to pop their corks. Likely they could throw a good punch, too. These women looked tough.

"Well…" Nathaniel cleared his throat, feeling nervous under the scrutiny of a large crowd of women. He had noticed others had started looking in their direction. One by one, heads turned, and the crowd's energy and noise died down with it as they focused on the strange man and woman. Nathaniel began to sweat as hundreds of pairs of eyes, of stranger's eyes, stared at him, waiting for him to say something.

His heart pounded in his ears and his nerves twitched. Suddenly, he forgot what they were doing here. *Oh, yes, that's right. Curse this blasted mill and how it ruined everyone who goes near it.*

Terrified by the sudden silence as every single person present now stared, some even whispering to each other, he remembered the first time he and Julia had walked into the dining room at the inn in Cloverly. Julia had been so kind about his struggles with socializing, and she'd even promised to help him if he gave her arm a gentle squeeze to let her know he needed that offered help. Even though, to both their surprise, she had been the one who'd ended up needing the excuse to depart that evening.

But Julia was the one who liked talking and sometimes, he would swear she enjoyed talking for hours on end, which seemed utterly mad to him. But what did he know?

In fact, they actually made a good team.

And you know what?

Blast the mill and its ruin of me or the Honeyfields. It seemed there would be no way to avoid it; may as well go down with the woman he loved.

Despite everything that had happened, despite everything said in fear and anger in the carriage, he was going to ask Julia to marry him as soon as they figured out how to keep these workers happy, as he had yet to do so in such explicit words. If she decided when actually faced with the question that she would still say *no*, then there was nothing he could do about that.

But back to the task at hand. He was not going to let these

workers be walked over any longer, that was for sure. He was also sure they wouldn't let him leave with his life if he did once they realized who he and Julia were.

But the fact remained that he was terrified into silence by them. Resigned to the fact that he was too nervous to do anything, he squeezed Julia's arm. And by the way she looked up at him with those doe eyes, she appeared to understand what the arm squeeze meant.

She remembered.

His heart swelled through the terror when she gave him a little nod.

And turned to the crowd of women.

"We have come here to visit today because I am the new owner of Brumstock Mill," Julia shouted out. Her voice, her demeanor—she sounded and seemed so strong, with no worry, as if she spoke to crowds of angry women on the regular.

The crowd remained quiet for no more than one additional second. And then, they erupted with conversation, throwing questions to Julia, flaming accusations against Mr. Fitzhugh.

It was impossible to sort through the noise, and he had to resist covering his ears.

Julia took Nathaniel's hand in hers and brought him to where Mr. Fitzhugh stood as the women watched on. The drunk foreman looked at them through lowered eyelids and took a deep drink from his bottle. "You must be that Honeyfield woman," the foreman said. "I got word from your father, the *actual* owner, that you might be coming. Bah! Sending a woman to talk to me!" His voice held pure hatred in it, and it made Nathaniel's skin crawl.

Nathaniel stepped forward. While he had failed at addressing the women and their concerns, he could be useful in other ways. And right now, that was to be the muscle. "Watch how you talk to her." He growled the words out at Fitzhugh.

The foreman seemed to notice him for the first time and his bloodshot eyes went quite wide as he took a hesitant step back.

The crowd of women saw this happen and murmured lowly

to each other.

Julia gifted him with a little smile before turning to face the women once more. "Ladies, as you have just heard, my family is the new owner of this mill. I am the family representative. I am also, quite unfortunately, rather in the dark about happenings about the mill, which is why I came here to speak with you. Could someone be so kind as to inform me why you are protesting?"

"He steals our wages!" someone shouted from the crowd.

The rest of the crowd shouted in unison, "Yes!"

Another woman yelled out, "He grabs our arses!"

"Yes!" the crowd shouted in agreement.

"He fires us if we miss one day of work!" another accused.

"My friend got fired as soon as her pregnancy started showing, but she was still fine to work!"

"My sister's husband got hurt at his job. Mr. Fitzhugh wouldn't let my sister leave early and fired her when she went ahead and did, anyway!"

On and on, the women aired out their grievances. Mr. Fitzhugh didn't seem to care a whit about what they said about him, though. And why would he? He'd been doing this job for decades with no repercussions. They knew the previous duke had apparently tried to fire him before, but he simply wouldn't leave and no one fought against it. Perhaps they had been unable to find a replacement.

That was, until now.

Julia pressed her mouth in a tight line as she listened to the women. This was a life foreign to her, but she also held the power here, even over him. So many took advantage of such a position and made the world worse for it. Nathaniel had seen and heard about that plenty himself, especially during the years of America's Civil War. Very few embraced their power for good. Most used it to take advantage of those with less. But the few who took their power and used it for good?

They changed the world.

And Julia, despite her ignorance to the struggles of the working class, despite her pampered upbringing, was a good person at heart thanks to her wonderful family.

Nathaniel leaned down to her ear. "You're doing very well," he said, hoping it would encourage her. She looked up at him, misty eyed, and nodded.

This seemed to invigorate her as her shoulders pulled back. "Mr. Fitzhugh." She turned to the red-eyed and drunk foreman. "My friend here"—she glanced at Nathaniel—"will take you back to the office. There, you will collect your current records of the hours these women have worked for you. You will also collect all of the cash and checks you have back there. For the rest of today, you will pay each individual worker what they are truly owed and offer an apology. Then you will leave, never to return. If you do not comply, as I know you are wont to do, my family will press charges against you for fraud. You will go to prison, and it would be rather easy to prove, too."

Nathaniel knew she was overdoing that last point. Nothing about fraud had been clear in the documents they had. He held his breath, his heart galloped, waiting for Fitzhugh's response. The man was such a blowhard, Nathaniel was sure he would scoff, laugh, perhaps even retaliate physically.

Mr. Fitzhugh clenched vibrating fists and his face twisted. One eye twitched. He only took a single step toward Julia before Nathaniel rushed forward and shoved him away from her. Hard.

But after Nathaniel had shown his strength, the foreman didn't argue, didn't raise a hand to her, didn't retaliate.

Julia's approach had worked, where no man's before her had.

"Let's go." Nathaniel dragged the liqour-stenched Fitzhugh to the entrance of the mill before the cad could change his mind. "Now."

Chapter Thirty

J ULIA'S HEART RACED. She felt like a fraud. In fact, she *was* a fraud. She didn't know what she was doing! None of this had been planned out, and they'd had no idea Fitzhugh had been stealing. She didn't know anything about business. She didn't know anything about managing people. She didn't know a blasted thing she should while standing here in front of these women and making decisions. Usually, when crowds watched her, it was because they were laughing at her, not because they looked to her for guidance.

While Nathaniel took Mr. Fitzhugh to the office, Julia addressed the crowd of tough women, her pulse racing with nervousness as she looked them over.

"Ladies," she said loud and the crowd went silent, their full attention now on her. They seemed interested in what she had to say, but did they not see what a fool she was? Surely, it was obvious to them? No one took her seriously. Not her peers, not even her family sometimes. "Mr. Fitzhugh will no longer be employed here. You will not need to deal with him any longer."

Cautious clapping scattered through the crowd.

She swallowed. "Seeing as we do need a replacement for him, I think we should put up a vote for Mr. Fitzhugh's replacement." The next foreman would have to be one of the women in the crowd. Someone who knew the jobs, the mill, the struggles the workers faced. At least, this made the most sense to her. Usually, men worked those types of roles, but she would never find one so soon. "As we do not have time to post the job for interviews, I think it would be best that you all take a vote for Mr. Fitzhugh's replacement. Someone here who knows the mill and the mill business inside and out."

She silently hoped there was such a person who would fit, and that the process would go smoothly. She didn't know any of these women. For all she knew, fists would fly over who would get the higher-paying job.

The workers surprised her, however.

It only took a few minutes for the women to vote for someone named Vera Yarde. When Miss Yarde emerged from the group by stepping forward, she surprised Julia. Upon first impression, she was exceptionally beautiful. She had clear, blue, expressive eyes and light-brown hair in a utilitarian knot. She was thin yet muscular and looked to be about the same age as Julia. Julia would have figured the workers would have picked an older woman with more experience.

But Julia understood why she was their choice almost immediately.

Miss Yarde, she came to learn, was not shy at all. She introduced herself properly, of course, insisting Julia call her "Vera," but then she showed no mercy.

"Why do you suddenly care about us?" Vera asked, lifting her chin. "We've always been apprised of any new ownership. Mr. Fitzhugh takes glee in telling us when we have a new owner because he knows it will create confusion and chaos for us by giving us false hope that perhaps, everything will finally be better under the new owner. Do you think it ever was, Miss Honeyfield?"

Julia cleared her throat and shook her head, slightly afraid of the woman.

"Two dukes have owned Brumstock Mill in recent memory,

and then we learned yesterday of a baron. Do you think any of those titled men were arsed enough to come here and toss out Mr. Fitzhugh? No, they never cared enough to. They simply sell it off to some other nob and give them the problem to deal with." She stared down her dainty nose, her sharpened eye daring Julia to be offended.

Julia merely cleared her throat.

"Your father must be the baron. Why did he send you and not come himself?"

"He didn't send me, exactly. I sort of… stepped forward to do it."

"I see." Vera's hardened face and stance softened slightly. The crowd stood behind her, silent, watching, waiting. "And why have you come here?"

Julia swallowed. It was like being a child with a strict governess looking down at her and scowling at her troublesome behavior. "I wanted to figure out why the mill is doing so poorly."

"That's an easy one," Vera immediately replied. "Because of Mr. Fitzhugh. Sometimes he pockets money from buyers. But mostly, it's because we refuse to work when he mistreats us or stops paying us. We're tired of his false stories that something came in the way of our pay. Bank issues, owner issues, what have you. If we were treated like actual human beings worthy of respect, we would do our jobs just fine."

Julia stared at the woman in disbelief. "That's the reason? Because you stop work when he does all that?"

"That's the reason."

None of this was reflected in the records Mr. Fitzhugh had sent them. Obviously, he had to have been making everything up in the records. Julia stared off to the side considering it all. The problem remained, though, that her family didn't have any business owning this place. They knew nothing about factories or mills or making textiles. Even if Vera was right that a profit could be had if the workers were happy, what if that didn't happen?

What if in the meantime, there needed to be repairs or upgrades to the machinery? And they still had to cover unpaid wages. Who knew how much that would take.

And after telling Nathaniel off the way she had, she couldn't exactly ask him for help now.

Thus, they would still need to sell it.

What was she going to do about that?

She didn't want to let Vera know this, however. Maybe, if she made the workers happy now, they would increase production enough to show a potential buyer that Brumstock Mill did, in fact, have value. And simply hope that nothing went wrong in that time.

Julia put her attention back on Vera. "What do you want?"

"We want raises," Vera said immediately. "And we want shorter days without a cut in pay."

Julia fought back a grimace as the cost to do this all added up. "You've already put thought into this, haven't you?"

Vera's tight-lipped smile was brief. "We will increase production, if these needs are met. That's all I can say about that for now."

This worried Julia. There were so many unknowns. If only she could get help or input from her family! From Helen, from Mama, from Papa, even Evander if he were here.

Or even from Nathaniel.

But she had to do this on her own. She alone had to make this major decision. She was the one who had to do this.

Julia nodded, ignoring the worry that wrenched in her stomach. "All right. I think we'll need to negotiate how many hours, and how much of a raise. But I agree to improvements." How it would happen financially, though, remained to be seen.

Vera's mouth fell and her eyes widened ever so slightly. Her hard mask had come undone. "Really? You'll do it?" she asked low so the others could not hear.

Julia nodded.

Vera closed her eyes and a few tears fell. She promptly wiped them away, returned to her previous stony face, and turned to the workers. "She said *yes!*"

The crowd of women caused an uproar with their cheering. And when Nathaniel returned with Mr. Fitzhugh, the former foreman scowled at the celebration. But Nathaniel? He looked immediately at her. And smiled. He didn't yet know what she had done, that she *may* have made things worse, but she could see the pride in his eyes.

It made her stomach flip. But it didn't make her happy.

Earlier, Nathaniel had admitted to loving her. She'd refused to let herself believe it, as for so long, she had been made to feel unlovable by her peers, someone who couldn't possibly ever marry or deserve marriage because of her reputation, and she had made herself rigid to protect herself. Worse, she'd said words she had known would push him away. Hurt him. She had hurt him on purpose.

But how could she not love this man back? He stood here with her. He celebrated with her. He supported her. They complemented each other so well. How could she honestly go back to London and never speak to him again? How could she not have him in her life?

But what would Papa say? She knew he didn't like the duke. Would he agree to the marriage if Nathaniel asked despite that? Or if she talked to him about it first? She had mostly brought that up to keep Nathaniel from breeching the subject further. But what if she was right that Papa wouldn't be fully on board? What then?

And what about bringing up the subject again? She had already turned him down, in a way.

Too many questions! Too many questions for which she did not have answers.

For the remainder of the day, the workers lined up and Mr. Fitzhugh paid them and offered his apology. It was the most pathetic apology Julia had ever heard, and it was clear he wasn't genuinely remorseful, but the women all seemed satisfied that at least he was the weaker one in the moment.

Eventually, after a long while, the line dwindled while the women trickled home for the day. Julia pulled Nathaniel to the side, as she wanted to say something.

But before she could, he spoke first.

"You did an amazing job today, my pretty Julia, I hope you realize that. You solved the problem all on your own."

"You were with me," she corrected him. "I only had a modicum of confidence, any confidence at all, because of that."

He gave her a gentle smile. "Anytime you doubt yourself or feel small because of the way other people treat you, I hope you remember what you did today. No one else could have done it but you. Of that, I am sure."

Emotion rose in her throat and she spewed those emotions all over with barely any control. "Oh, Nathaniel, you told me you loved me and I got so mad at you, but it wasn't because I was upset you said that. I mean, I *was* upset you said it and then brought up marriage. I was convinced you weren't thinking clearly and would rescind it all once your head left the clouds and you remembered my reputation. But it was also because I love you too and I wasn't prepared to admit that!"

He stared at her with his dark eyes, wide with shock, and ran his hands through his black hair, as if coming to terms with what he'd heard. "You do?"

"Yes." She took a deep breath. "I'm sorry I said such hurtful words to you."

Nathaniel's jaw tightened for a moment, but then he stepped forward, gently placed his hands on her face, and kissed her with madness.

She wrapped her arms back around his neck and returned his kiss, so utterly beyond happy to be in his arms again. She didn't care that the kiss lingered, or that anyone still present could see what they were doing. And she didn't think much of it when she heard a carriage approaching. All she knew was that Nathaniel loved her, and she loved him, and despite their success after this long day, they still had a huge problem to deal with. Which meant dinner, which her hollow stomach told her should have been approaching, would have to be delayed further.

But it did catch her attention when she heard a woman shout out, "Oh, blast, we're too late!"

Immediately recognizing the voice as her sister, Helen, Julia broke the kiss, felt the blood drain from her face, and turned to find her family climbing out of a hired hack. Because her trip up here had taken so long, it took a moment for her to remember a train could get her letters to them and bring them here in a twenty-four-hour period, not a week.

"Helen!" Julia tried to sound excited. She was happy to see her family, of course, but they really couldn't have arrived at a worse time. They didn't like him. So much for cautiously bringing up Nathaniel and what was going on between them.

For a moment, the Honeyfields stood beside the hired hack, eyes darting back and forth between Julia and the Duke of Rivenhall as if they were sure they were seeing incorrectly. Mama wrung her hands and frowned. Papa's face held no expression, which always terrified Julia more than anything else. Helen, meanwhile, rushed up to Julia and grabbed her hands. "I got your letter this morning and I told Papa we had to fetch you immediately because you had gone mad." Helen looked at Nathaniel. "But it appears I'm too late."

"You are a few days too late, I fear," Nathaniel replied, but he didn't sound too sorry about it, either.

Helen pressed her lips tightly together and then she studied their surroundings. "This is the mill, then, is it?"

"This is the mill," Julia replied.

"Fascinating place," Helen added.

Julia and Nathaniel exchanged a glance. That was not how Julia would have expected her sister to describe the mill. Personally, Julia thought it looked a bit frightening.

But that thought was interrupted by Papa and Mama as they finally approached from the hack. Mama's bottom lip shook and then she pulled Julia tightly to her ample bosom, nearly squeezing the life out of her. "Oh, my precious girl. I have been in such a fit without you near, and then to find you compromised by the Duke of Rivenhall, of all people!" She then turned to Papa and lightly hit his arm. "This is all your fault!"

He rubbed the spot as if it hurt, but Julia knew he was simply pretending in order to appease his wife. "Now, now. Julia is old enough to be kissing a gentleman, though I will say I'm surprised she was so public about it. She is our daughter, though, after all."

Mama sniffed. "I suppose."

Papa glanced over at the last few workers waiting in line for their pay. They had, along with Mr. Fitzhugh, stopped what they'd been doing to watch the unruly Honeyfields with interest. Vera stood off to the side, her arms crossed, studying Papa with guarded curiosity.

Papa turned to Nathaniel and crossed his arms, his brow furrowed. "You and I need to speak. First, though, Julia, please update us all on what had happened during your trip. Highwaymen? Collapsed bridges? Hypothermia? Is that all true?"

Julia nodded and took her time explaining everything that had happened on their trip in more detail, as her letter to them hadn't gotten nearly into it all. As she told the sprawling tale, Mama gasped quite loudly a number of times at the right moments to make Julia feel loved and important. Helen kept darting glances at Nathaniel through narrowed eyes. Papa, however, was much harder to read. Julia couldn't tell what his thoughts were on any of this, but surely, he was not pleased.

Finally, she reached the part about the mill. "When we arrived, the women here were protesting against Mr. Fitzhugh. He had been stealing their wages from them and also harassing them horribly." She told her family all about that and how she'd fired him on the spot—and had been successful. "Papa, I hope you're not cross with me for doing that without your permission. But I simply couldn't let him stay! We had heard about him on our travels. He is infamous in the area for being horrific to work for, and someone before had tried to fire him, but he refused to leave. I was able to threaten him with prison and Nathaniel scared him with his muscle, and that convinced him enough!"

Papa pursed his lips and studied her quite intently now, his eyes sharp and observant. Her heart sunk. He was furious with her.

But then his face eased and he smiled. "Frankly, I'm a bit surprised you managed to do all that you did. It appears I severely underestimated you." He looped his hands behind him and bobbed on his feet. "You know, I did send you out here with a purpose, but it wasn't to figure out the mill business. I had been doing that during your absence, actually."

Julia raised her eyebrows quite high. What was he talking about? What did that mean?

"Lord Odstone." Nathaniel took a step forward, his face tense. "What are you saying?"

"Yes, what *are* you saying?" Mama frowned at Papa, evidently unaware of what he had been doing and obviously not happy about being left out, either. "Were you sneaking around behind my back?"

Papa took her hand and kissed the top of it. "I had to, dear. You wouldn't have kept it secret."

"'Secret'?" Julia and Helen said at the same time. Helen added, "What were you doing?"

Papa opened his mouth, looking around the family. "I was looking for a buyer."

"'A buyer'?" everyone echoed back in unison in various levels of surprise.

Papa cleared his throat. "Yes. And I found one, too."

"I couldn't find a buyer." Nathaniel crossed his arms. "How did you manage to do that?"

Papa chuckled. "Oh, it took some mental games is all. Wealthy industry men are all over the place these days. It took some searching, but I was able to find a few who were willing to help me."

How strange. "Help you how?" Julia asked. She wondered if there would be some way to convince the new owner to take on the changes for the workers she had promised. How she would go about that, she wasn't sure, but she would be sure she did.

"There are a few who have previously expressed interest in becoming members at White's and Brooks's, but, of course, they were turned down. Not the right family line, you see. Anyway, there were two fellows who took this more to heart than the others and I approached them about this idea I had concocted. I couldn't offer them anything like a membership—I was happy to recommend them, of course, but new members need two recommendations and they couldn't manage to get a second one, much less snag the vote that follows—but I *could* give them humorous revenge."

Julia tilted her head, interested. Everyone else stayed quiet, evidently hanging on to his every word as well.

"They spread the news that they heard about me winning a textile mill in a wager and were also quite interested in buying it. They shouted about it everywhere they could. *It's a great investment!* they told people. *That Lord Odstone is a lucky fellow!* Naturally, this got people talking. I still wasn't wholly convinced it would work, though, so imagine my surprise when people began asking me how much I would take for it."

Julia was shocked beyond belief; she'd had no idea her father was this shrewd. All this time, the trip *had* been to get her out of the way.

Papa waved his hand dismissively, unaware of her thoughts. "Anyway, I ended up getting an offer and accepted it." He made a motion of sweeping his hands together as if removing dirt.

"Why did I come out here, then?" she asked, her throat tight. Emotion roiled within her. "You didn't want me around?" It hurt that her father had felt he'd had to get her out of the way to this level in order to take care of the issue himself. He had seemed as if he hadn't cared about the mill fiasco at all, but now she was embarrassed to discover he had simply been tricking her. This entire time, she'd thought she was helping, doing something important, but she hadn't been doing anything. And now there was the promise she'd made the workers. She had only made everything worse, then.

It made her feel awful.

Papa's face fell upon sensing her distress. "Oh, my child, that is not why I sent you! You were so interested in the mill, so eager to come out here, how could I say *no*? And you did solve the impossible task of firing the foreman. But"—he held up one finger—"I did have a purpose for your trip, and it wasn't to *get rid of you*."

She frowned. "What was the purpose?"

Papa threw his hands out wide and bellowed, "For the duke to fall in love with you!"

Julia's eyes became enormous as she inhaled through her nose. Fury coursed through her. "I beg your pardon?"

Papa went over to Nathaniel, who had gone pale, and clapped him on his shoulder with a chuckle. "I wagered one of my daughter's hands with the duke the night I lost and became stuck with the mill. The next day, I asked him whom he would have chosen, and he said he would have chosen you, Julia!"

Nathaniel cleared his throat and shifted on his feet. "That's not—you're really not making this any better," the duke said in a dangerous tone.

But Papa only laughed. "Son. I know people don't take me seriously. I know they think I'm a fool. I don't mind because that means I can strike when I need to!" He shot a finger up in the air, causing everyone to jump. "When you came to our house the day after the wager, I saw the way you watched Julia and I saw the way Julia watched you. You had so far never spoken to her at the many events we have both attended at the same time. But I also knew that if you spent time together, you would see how wonderful, and kind, and smart, and overall amazing my daughter is. And then if that didn't work, I could resort to blackmail because you were traveling alone with her."

"Papa!" Julia shouted at him, but her eyes were starting to well. She had almost ruined everything with Nathaniel partly because she hadn't thought her father liked him and so he would deny a marriage request. Only to learn this had all been a ruse to get them married off together.

Shrewd, indeed!

Papa merely chuckled at her shout. "I was only jesting. Sort of. But did it work?" he asked Nathaniel. "Did you fall in love with my daughter?"

Nathaniel met Julia's eyes right as the tears started falling. She wiped them away, embarrassed. Nathaniel was so quiet, though, so serious, as if struggling with how to answer the question. Maybe, with being forced to answer it, he had realized that he didn't love her. That his feelings for her were easy to forget.

Papa didn't mean to, of course, but he was turning this into a mockery and she was just waiting for Nathaniel to get embarrassed by the situation, by her father's brazenness, and run off like always.

But to her pleasant surprise, not only did he not get embarrassed and not run off, but he came right up to Julia and took one of her hands in his.

"Run while you can," Helen jested to Julia, causing her to chuckle.

Nathaniel looked down at Julia, his eyes almost glittering. He rubbed his thumb over her hand. "No, there will be no running. Lord Odstone, I'm not quite sure how you could have predicted it so correctly, but yes, I have fallen hopelessly, deeply, impossibly in love with Julia. My pretty Julia, before your family and everyone else here, will you answer: do you love me, too?"

She wiped at her eyes as her heart seemed to glow as bright as the sun. "Yes, I do. I do love you, Nathaniel."

"I don't know what the blazes we're going to do about the land the mill sits on, but at least the mill will be taken care of. Will you accept that for the time being?"

She swallowed and nodded her *yes*.

"After spending all this time with you," Nathaniel continued, "I cannot be apart from you. I wish you to sleep at my side every night and wake up with me every morning. I want to go on this adventure of life with you. I had always thought I wanted to be alone, but I can't do that now. I need you, Julia. Will you do that? Will you be my wife, be with me for the rest of our lives?"

Julia covered her mouth as she let out a sob. "Yes, Nathaniel!"

Nathaniel cradled the back of her head and leaned down to give her a soft and gentle kiss. And when they'd grudgingly pulled apart, Mama and Helen cried and hugged Julia. Papa and Nathaniel shook hands. They may never quite become the best of friends, but their love for Julia bonded them.

As Julia, her mother, and sister began giddily speaking about weddings, Julia overheard Papa speaking with Nathaniel.

"By the way, the buyer is interested in the land, too," Papa said, clasping his hands behind his back. "I immediately suspected you still owned it when I had asked if anything else was included in the business transfer." He tapped at his head in a knowing way.

Nathaniel let out a long breath and rushed a hand through his hair. Perhaps he had underestimated Lord Odstone. Regardless, the relief was overwhelming. "Oh, that is excellent news. Who is the poor sod you tricked into buying it all?"

"Your friend, the Earl of Fenwick."

Epilogue

London
August 1875

T HE FIRST RIVENHALL ball since the duke had married his duchess was in full force. Julia had planned both their wedding and this ball at nearly the same time, which had made for a wild summer. Countless times, Nathaniel had asked what he could help with, but every single time, she'd waved him away, as she apparently had *not* needed his input at all, whatsoever. Thankfully, with the sale of the mill and the land it sat upon to the Earl of Fenwick, their finances were in much better shape. Thus, Nathaniel told Julia to do whatever she wished to with the two events, no expense need be spared for the special occasions.

The wedding, to his male eyes and sensibilities, was beautiful. His bride had worn a pretty lace dress with a long train and veil. Nearly in shock the entire time that his wedding day had finally arrived, he didn't remember much about the ceremony except *her*. Her walking down the aisle, her looking up at him with those doe eyes as he'd lifted her veil. Her small hand as he'd put the wedding ring on her finger. Their first kiss as husband and wife. The way his heart had raced the entire day.

It was the wedding of the century, the gossip papers said. A duke raised in working-class America. A baron's daughter who'd escaped the shackles of her reputation. A match made in heaven.

They actually had admirers, which he still couldn't understand. People wrote about them in the gossip papers all the time; there was even a baby watch. Of course, no one knew Nathaniel and Julia were simply enjoying being married for the time being. Though with the way they could hardly be apart for long, he was half-expecting a baby to surprise them despite their efforts to wait.

Their marriage was nothing but a bright spot in his life. His mother and Adrian had sent them a gift, a pretty vase from Tiffany & Co. in New York City, as his mother was not quite ready yet to return to the country that had brought her so much strife. They also broke the news that they would be marrying, too, now that she was widowed. Nathaniel never would have expected the raw emotion this lifted in him. He was happy for them, so utterly thrilled! His mother, Adrian—they both deserved happiness together.

There was a blip of darkness when it came to his wedding day, though. He knew Julia had been secretly hoping Evander would show up for the wedding. That, surely, it would somehow reach his ears, wherever he was. Surely, her brother would reappear for such an important day in the family. Nathaniel saw her sneaking glances over the guests as her father walked her down the aisle, but alas, the baron's heir wasn't there and no word came about him, either. But Julia, the strong woman she was, pushed through it and arrived at Nathaniel's side at the altar with a genuine smile of happiness and love. One day, he knew they would hear news about her brother.

But in the present, Nathaniel smiled to himself as he watched Julia flit around their large, opulent ballroom like an erratic butterfly. Tonight's ball was silver- and blue-themed and she was stunning in her head-to-toe silver gown. The food and drinks were blueberry-themed. Champagne glasses had blueberries muddled in them, and blueberry cakes and tarts abounded. Even the lamb served for dinner had a blueberry-based sauce. Everyone thought the blueberries were simply to keep with the color scheme, but in truth, it was a private joke between Julia and Nathaniel.

Admittedly, he did laugh heartily when he realized what she had planned under his nose.

He sighed with love and admiration as she stopped to speak with a group of people who hung on to her every word now that she was a duchess. As he watched her, though, she glanced in his direction and her face flushed as their eyes met. A moment later, she departed the group and came to his side.

Nathaniel leaned down to her ear. "I find myself unable to join the party, as I prefer to simply watch you the entire time instead."

Julia lifted an eyebrow at him and bit her bottom lip. "Is the evening becoming too much for you? Would you like to take a quiet moment with me?"

It wasn't even a question. He took her hand and led her out of the ballroom.

NATHANIEL LED HIS wife into the closest room with a modicum of privacy—the library—then picked her up and set her upon the desk. They kissed with mad desperation as he pulled her to the edge of the desk.

Nathaniel kissed her neck. "I love you," he whispered. Pressed another soft kiss on her earlobe. "I love you." Then he repeated the movements on the other side. "I love you, I love you, my pretty duchess."

Julia couldn't help but smile. She'd known being married to Nathaniel would be a dream, but she never would have imagined how wonderful it truly would be. What had she done to deserve such a perfect life?

Her own brave knight like the fairy tales?

She never would have thought they would be an ideal match

for the other. She had worried about how much she enjoyed parties versus how much he disliked them. Her sociability with his preference for being alone, it all promised to clash.

Once again, though, she found even here they complemented each other seamlessly.

When they were socializing and he needed to step away from it, she happily filled in for the both of them and, in fact, people hardly noticed his departure because she commanded so much attention.

"You know," Nathaniel nuzzled into her hair, "I'm surprised you're enjoying the ball."

"Why?"

"Because so many of these people have been unkind to you or your family."

While he peppered light kisses over her, she considered this. "That's very true, though I have been able to befriend a few people I didn't know well before. But may I confess something to you?"

He stopped placing kisses all over her. Briefly. "What might that be?"

"I'll happily host balls now to remind them *all the time* that I'm a duchess now. They have to be nice to me. I don't mind spending the next several decades flaunting my happy life before them."

Nathaniel chuckled, but the humor died away for both of them as their kissing became a bit more heated. Julia knew her dress would be intensely wrinkled when she returned to her party. It couldn't be helped. But she was in love, and she didn't care who knew it.

The princess and her brave fairytale knight who would live happily ever after.

⹊

About the Author

Born and raised in Chicago to an artist family, Arden Conroy grew up attending museums and played piano and cello for fifteen years. When she isn't writing or reading, Arden enjoys historical fashion, art history, and historical dramas and comedies. She has lived all over the United States from the Hudson Valley, NY to Tulsa, OK. Currently, she resides between Chicago and Pennsylvania with her husband and two children.

Website – www.ardenconroy.com
Facebook – facebook.com/profile.php?id=100083677291622